FLAME AND FORTUNE

A Miss Fortune Mystery

NO SMOKE WITHOUT FIRE

NEW YORK TIMES BESTSELLING AUTHOR
JANA DELEON

MISS FORTUNE SERIES INFORMATION

If you've never read a Miss Fortune mystery, you can start with LOUISIANA LONGSHOT, the first book in the series. If you prefer to start with this book, here are a few things you need to know.

Fortune Redding – a CIA assassin with a price on her head from one of the world's most deadly arms dealers. Because her boss suspects that a leak at the CIA blew her cover, he sends her to hide out in Sinful, Louisiana, posing as his niece, a librarian and ex–beauty queen named Sandy-Sue Morrow. The situation was resolved in Change of Fortune and Fortune is now a full-time resident of Sinful and has opened her own detective agency.

Ida Belle and Gertie – served in the military in Vietnam as spies, but no one in the town is aware of that fact except Fortune and Deputy LeBlanc.

Sinful Ladies Society – local group founded by Ida Belle, Gertie, and deceased member Marge. In order to gain membership, women must never have married or if widowed, their husband must have been deceased for at least ten years.

Sinful Ladies Cough Syrup – sold as an herbal medicine in Sinful, which is dry, but it's actually moonshine manufactured by the Sinful Ladies Society.

CHAPTER ONE

I stood in my living room and stared at Ida Belle and Gertie, certain that they'd both been sniffing that glue Ida Belle used to fix cracks in her boat and splits in tires, and once —according to rumor—to patch a leaky roof.

"It's official," I said. "You've both gone senile. I knew with our age difference, it was something I'd eventually have to deal with, but I really thought I had a few more years of sanity. At least with Ida Belle."

Ida Belle had the good grace to look at least moderately embarrassed.

"We wouldn't ask if we had a better option," Ida Belle said.

"Of course you have a better option—anyone but me," I said.

Carter looked over from his very comfortable spot in my recliner and grinned. "Come on, Fortune. Take one for the team."

"There are things beyond my limits for the team," I said.

"So you'll shoot someone for the team, but you won't wear a sequined dress?" Carter asked.

I nodded. "Exactly."

1

But it wasn't just any sequined dress. It was a formfitting, boobs-up-high, where-the-heck-did-the-back-go, and is-my-butt-crack-showing sort of dress. And it came with a crown and a sash and of all things, a scepter.

"I refuse to be the queen of anything, even New Year's," I said. "Ask Ronald. That outfit sounds right up his alley."

"He'll say the scepter should be titanium, the fake diamonds in the tiara aren't shiny enough, and the sash is knockoff satin," Gertie said.

I raised one eyebrow.

"I didn't say he'd be wrong," Gertie groused.

"Why don't one of you do it?" I asked.

"I volunteered, but Ida Belle won't let me," Gertie said and scratched her chest.

"Because I want to win," Ida Belle said.

"Win?" I was confused. "I thought you just propped some victim on a tacky float and drove it through downtown. I've never heard anything about a contest."

Carter laughed and picked up a gun magazine when I shot him a dirty look.

"There's an, uh, *unofficial* contest," Ida Belle said.

I reached over from my spot on the couch and grabbed the magazine out of Carter's hands. "Okay, out with it. What is she not telling me?"

"There's a standing bet down at the Swamp Bar on who has the hottest queen," he said. "Everyone at the bar votes that night. The team who puts up the winner gets the biggest cut of the entry money. Everyone who picks the right queen gets their name in a pot for the rest of it."

I stared at all of them in dismay. "You want me to be the subject of a Swamp Bar betting pool?"

"No," Gertie said. "We want you to be the *winner* of a Swamp Bar betting pool."

"But the queens are representing the two churches," I said. "What about vanity? What about gambling?"

"What about gluttony?" Carter suggested. "You *do* race for banana pudding on Sundays."

"Banana pudding is serious business," I said. "I'm pretty sure the reason Jesus walked on water was because Francine's banana pudding was on the other bank."

"Preach," Gertie said and scratched again.

Carter shook his head and grabbed another magazine.

"Will you stop scratching your boob?" Ida Belle said to Gertie. "It's distracting me from the very serious conversation we're having here."

"I can't help if it itches," Gertie said.

Since she refused to meet Ida Belle's gaze when she said it and then shoved both hands under her armpits, I was suspicious.

"What's wrong with your boob?" I asked.

"Good God!" Ida Belle said. "Do we have to have this conversation?"

"Agreed," Carter said.

"There's a recliner at your house," I said to him and turned back to Gertie. "Out with it. What injury do you have that's causing the itch?"

"I might have burned myself a little," Gertie said.

"Are you baking naked and on the sauce again?" Ida Belle asked.

"That's a thing?" I asked.

"You should try it," Carter said to me and grinned.

"I don't bake—naked or otherwise," I said.

"We put a 'no baking while consuming' warning on all bottles of Sinful Ladies Cough Syrup for a reason," Ida Belle said. "People kept burning their fingers. Then there's Gertie, who tried to make ten dozen sugar cookies while running a fever. She had bandages on parts that shouldn't have been anywhere near an oven."

"I was hot," Gertie said.

Carter's expression went from grinning to slightly pained. I didn't feel remotely sorry for him. He could opt out of the conversation by going home. Since I was already *at* home, I was stuck with finishing the burning boob conversation or shooting everyone. As shooting everyone would require cleaning, I opted to hear more about the boob.

"So?" I asked Gertie.

"I wasn't baking," Gertie said with a sly grin. "But I was definitely heating things up."

Ida Belle looked slightly afraid. "This isn't a sexy-time story, is it?"

"Fortune asked," Gertie said. "The rules state that I can't bring up the details voluntarily, but since she asked, you're going to hear about it. So I had a special Christmas outfit for Jeb and things went a little wrong."

"Please don't tell me you were wearing tinsel," Ida Belle said.

"Of course not," Gertie said. "I've learned my lesson on that one. I thought I'd never get rid of that rash. Couldn't wear underwear for a month. But I found some old Christmas tree lights in my attic and figured I'd make use of them."

Carter jumped up from the recliner and practically ran out the front door.

Ida Belle stared at her in horror. "*Old* lights? The kind that burn so brightly you can get a tan standing next to them? You put *old* lights on your boobs?"

"It did look really sexy," Gertie said. "And I think I would have been okay if there hadn't been that power surge. Jeb was just about to hang some ornaments on me when they flashed so bright they blinded him and he went sprawling over an ottoman. My boobs felt like Satan was touching them and I was jumping around, trying to get the lights off. Took out two lamps, a painting, and his mother's urn."

"Good God," Ida Belle said. "It's a wonder you haven't been banned from the entire state."

"Urn?" I was still cringing.

"That wasn't even the interesting part," Gertie said. "So while Jeb was struggling to get up from the floor, given his bad back and all, and I was still flinging lights everywhere, his coonhound decided to start digging in the pile of her ashes and flung them all over the rug."

Ida Belle and I were both apparently out of words. We just stared.

"It was okay though," Gertie said. "Jeb said she wasn't a pleasant woman anyway, so we vacuumed the rug and deposited her in the flower bed out front."

"I was beginning to question why we're friends when you told us about the lights," I said. "But you sort of redeemed the whole thing with the efficient flower bed disposal part of the story."

"I'm guessing Jeb's mother might feel differently," Ida Belle said.

Gertie shrugged. "The best part about dead people is that they can't complain."

I nodded. "A blessing considering my former line of work."

Ida Belle shook her head. "Well, at least put some aloe vera on it so you stop scratching like a hound dog with fleas."

"I already did," Gertie said. "But it dries so quickly, I'd have to be putting it on every ten minutes to keep the itching down. At least the left one isn't bothering me anymore. Just give the right one another day and it will probably be okay. I have my secret salve that I got from Nora, but I can only use it at night."

I looked over at Ida Belle, who was studying Gertie with a somewhat concerned expression. I'd met Nora when we set her up to alibi us with Carter when we'd been inserting ourselves into police business. Nora had a hot tub and a ton of recreational drug stories. The drug stories almost always led to her male conquest stories.

"Would your boobs set off a drug-sniffing dog?" I asked.

Gertie laughed. "Definitely. Nora made this salve from her own stash and it's supposed to be really low in THC, but that must mean at Nora's tolerance levels. I rubbed some on last night, and me and my boobs were high as a kite for a good two hours—not in the literal physical sense, unfortunately. Gravity is still winning on that one."

"It's a good thing Carter left before all this came out," Ida Belle said. "Hearing this would have given him hives, and then he'd need Nora's salve."

I laughed. "I'm pretty sure Carter is an automatic 'no' to anything Nora is offering."

"That's because she'd be offering Carter more than salve," Ida Belle said.

We all grimaced.

"So enough about my boobs," Gertie said, breaking the uncomfortable silence.

"Thank the Lord," Ida Belle said. "Back to the matter at hand—"

"I'm still not going to be Miss New Year's Hoochie to be put up for a Swamp Bar vote," I said. "What I can't figure is why the two of you thought I'd go along. You know me. Sequins? A dress that barely covers the important parts—and wouldn't if I bent or, God forbid, sneezed. I'd love to hear where you think I'd put my pistol. And don't tell me you expect me to leave it at home, because then I'll assume you don't even know me."

"Lord no!"

"That's just crazy talk!"

They both responded at once.

"We just figured that since you're so fit, you'd be perfect to wear one of those thigh straps so you can stick it on the inside of your thigh," Gertie said. "I think they're sexy as hell but when your thighs already rub, you don't go putting ridged metal in between them."

I stared at her in dismay. "The two of you were discussing my thighs?"

"Would it sway you any to know that the betting pool is projected to pay out 5K to the winning team?" Ida Belle asked.

"Holy crap!" I said. "And that's just a cut? I didn't even know there was that much loose change in Sinful."

"People pony up for the important stuff," Ida Belle said.

I frowned. "If this is such a big deal then why didn't I hear about it last year? I went to that parade. I don't remember a queen and certainly nothing about a bet."

"This will be the first time we've had it since the Big Horrible ten years ago," Gertie said.

"What was the Big Horrible?" I asked. "A hurricane?"

"No, but it *was* catastrophic," Gertie said. "At least for Millie Turner."

I looked at Ida Belle because clearly, I wasn't going to get a straight answer from Gertie.

"She died, all right?" Ida Belle said. "Wrong place at the wrong time. There was this freak accident with a flock of geese, a diesel fuel trucker, and a fire-breather. That one is not on us. The Catholics' queen was the fire-breather."

"Which was sort of appropriate given that she was one of Celia's friends," Gertie said. "But you know how fire is with old party decor."

It was official. I'd set up house in Crazy Town.

"No," I said. "I don't know about flammable party decor because I haven't gone sitting on a float surrounded by it, and it doesn't sound like I'm ever going to. Definitely not in Sinful—home of deranged geese and poorly placed diesel fuel truckers."

"Oh, it's different now," Gertie said. "We have a fire truck positioned downtown, all of the floats have extinguishers, and there's volunteers all along the route, just in case."

"You say 'just in case' like that's not the expected outcome," I said. "This is Sinful. 'Just in case' is everyday business around here. If it's so safe now, then why haven't you had a queen since the night of the fire-breather horror show?"

"We weren't allowed," Ida Belle said. "The mayor banned queens from the New Year's festivities for ten years. He never liked the Sinful Ladies or God's Wives."

"I'm pretty sure he thought most of us would be dead by the time that decade of undue punishment rolled around," Gertie groused. "But we showed him. The only one from back then who won't be attending the parade is the mayor. May he rest in discomfort."

"That's not very Christian," Ida Belle said.

"Neither is lying about how I feel," Gertie said. "I went with the lesser offense."

"So what do you say?" Ida Belle asked. "We can split it three ways?"

I thought for a moment, then narrowed my eyes at them. "These floats aren't pulled by horses, are they?"

"No," Gertie said. "We decided horses were too risky, so we opted for regular pickup trucks. The floats will have a big throne on them so that everyone can see the queens over the cabs as they approach."

"I'm surprised you didn't opt for tractors for a more Southern flair," I said.

"It was suggested, but the noise level is too high," Ida Belle said. "And then there's the exhaust. We didn't want you guys covered in soot by the end of the route."

"Is it really a good idea to collect a bunch of drunk Sinful residents around moving vehicles?" I asked. "We've been that route before, and I'm figuring New Year's is when even people who don't normally drink have a few. Sounds like a recipe for disaster."

Gertie nodded. "Marie thought so, too, so she approved the parade for Thursday night. With New Year's Eve being Friday and with some people still having to work that day, she figures that will keep the worst offenders from living it up too much at the parade. That and they'll want their reserves for the parties Friday night."

I blew out a breath. I could tell it was important to them, and I really wanted to help, but I didn't want to provide the kind of help they needed.

"I don't need the money," I said. "And for that matter, neither do you, Ida Belle. Gertie, however, needs it for LED lights and a skin graft."

Gertie waved a hand in dismissal. "I've got the special cream, and after that incredible first round with it, I was thinking about bringing it to Jeb's and have him try—"

"Nope!" Ida Belle threw up a hand.

"It's not really about the money," Gertie said, giving Ida Belle the side-eye. "Sure I can always find something to spend it on, but it's really about gloating rights over Celia's crew."

"So ask Ally," I said. "She's gorgeous, and being Celia's niece would make winning even sweeter."

"We already asked," Gertie said. "She said she'd rather eat cinnamon rolls from a can."

I stared. "That's a pretty serious statement. So what are you not telling me? Why is Ally so adamant against doing it?

She was the something-or-other queen before. Why not this one?"

"I think she wants to avoid any comparison with the competition," Ida Belle said.

I narrowed my eyes. "Who is Celia's crew putting up?"

Gertie rolled her eyes. "Riley-James Rogers."

"Why does she have three last names?" I asked.

"It's a Southern thing," Ida Belle said. "They're all family surnames."

"There isn't some weird requirement in Sinful that you have to name the fifth baby born in the year of the Octopus using three surnames, is there?" I asked.

Ida Belle shook her head. "That was free will."

"Fascinating," I said. "I've never heard of her. And I definitely would have remembered if I had, especially with the name thing."

"You've never met her," Ida Belle said. "She shot out of Sinful like she was on fire seven years ago and hasn't been back since," Ida Belle said.

"Until now," Gertie said.

"I'll bite," I said. "Why is she back now? Why does Ally hate her? And why would she want to be the New Year's Queen if she hates Sinful so much she fled?"

"I wouldn't say that Ally hates her," Gertie said.

"Cinnamon rolls from a can," I reminded her.

"True," Gertie said. "Well, the long and short of it is RJ—as she was referred to as a teen—"

"Well, thank the Lord someone had the common sense to shorten that down," I said.

"RJ left town to become a country-and-western singer," Gertie continued. "She swore she was destined to be the next Faith Hill."

"I'm going to guess that didn't happen," I said.

"One-hit wonder," Ida Belle said. "She and Brock Benoit, a local boy, were thick as thieves and took out of here together right after high school, swearing they were going to make it big. She sang and he played guitar. They managed to get a song they wrote on one of those collaboration albums not long after they got to Nashville. It made the country charts for a couple weeks, but they were never able to duplicate the success."

Gertie nodded. "Rumor mill said after that they took up the bar circuit and doing some party gigs—birthdays, weddings, that sort of thing—but worked day jobs like regular people to make rent."

"The actual fact mill says Brock's girlfriend was pregnant when he took off with RJ," Ida Belle said.

I whistled. "So again, why is she back now? Sounds like she'd have a target on her back, and I can't imagine she could pay the bills singing at the Swamp Bar. There's certainly not enough locals who'd be interested in hiring her. Easier to crank up the stereo and spend the money on more beer."

"Agreed," Ida Belle said. "And jury's out on why she's back. I'm going to guess trouble, and since her return was a solo act, I'm going to go further out on that limb and say trouble with Brock. That's assuming they're even still a pair."

"Maybe Brock's afraid to come back as his ex-girlfriend's father might fill him with hot lead," I said.

"Also a possibility," Gertie agreed.

"So were RJ and Brock ever a couple?" I asked.

"Maybe," Gertie said.

"More like probably," Ida Belle said.

"I guess someone forgot to tell the girlfriend," I said.

Gertie nodded. "But that was high school. Lots of things can change."

"Well, apparently not Ally's dislike of her," I said. "So what's the story there?"

"RJ was part of the mean girl crew," Gertie said. "She hung around with Pansy a lot."

I frowned. Pansy was Celia's daughter and Ally's cousin. She'd bullied Ally her whole childhood and tortured her in high school by going after every guy Ally dated. Pansy had made a return trip to Sinful herself shortly after I arrived, and she'd gotten murdered due to involvement in all kinds of shady behavior.

"If this RJ has the same standards Pansy did, then Sinful wives better gird their loins," I said.

Gertie nodded. "I would say I'm praying that she doesn't bring trouble with her, but RJ and trouble are pretty much attached at the hip."

"Great," I said. "So why is Celia pushing for RJ to be the queen?"

"Because of the record thing and she kinda looks like young Sofia Vergara with green eyes," Gertie said. "Tall, curvy, long dark hair, perfect skin...your basic nightmare."

"You want me to run against Sofia Vergara?" I asked, completely dismayed. "I could fit a whole butt cheek in one cup of her bra. I don't have curves or long sexy hair. And I've caused trouble in Sinful a lot more recently than her. I don't think I'm the shoo-in you guys are looking for."

"You've also got a lot of supporters in Sinful," Ida Belle said. "You've helped a lot of people."

"And there's also the fear factor," Gertie said. "It could get you some votes."

"Besides," Ida Belle said, "high school might have been a while back for RJ, but people in Sinful hold a grudge like they do a rare two-for-one beer coupon to the mini-mart up the highway. And RJ definitely racked up detractors."

They both looked at me, all earnest and hopeful, and I felt myself crack just a little. It *was* always nice to get one over on Celia, but that still wasn't enough for me to wear sequins and a push-up bra. It was the fact that RJ had been so mean to Ally that she still held a grudge that had me wavering. I hated mean. Deadly, I could appreciate, but mean was just cowardly.

"I'm not getting extensions again," I said. "And I'm not wearing one of those bras with wire."

"Butt cheek in bra," Gertie reminded me.

"Gel pads is as far as I'm willing to go," I said.

"Sold!" Ida Belle yelled, causing Gertie and I to jump.

I gave Ida Belle the side-eye. "You are overly happy about this, and it can't be about the money."

"It's because RJ's mother—Sawyer-James Rogers—has been hitting on Walter for a decade," Gertie said.

"Wait," I said. "RJ is Ally's age, but her mother is after Walter? Not to be ageist or anything, but isn't that a bit of a gap?"

"RJ was a late baby," Ida Belle said. "*Very* late and very indulged. Sawyer had her when she was forty-two. Yes, there's still some age difference, but I think that just makes her want him more. After Sawyer's third husband took off, she started looking for security."

"This woman flirted with Walter?" I asked, just making sure to clarify.

"Unmercifully. Tactlessly. And obnoxiously," Gertie said.

"And she's still alive?" I asked.

Ida Belle shrugged. "Since it bothers Walter more than anyone else, I didn't see the point in wasting a bullet."

"I guess you marrying him ended the hassle," I said.

"Oh, she's still at it," Gertie said. "She's counting on Ida Belle dying before her and still getting her man."

I laughed. "If she only knew that Ida Belle will outlive her just out of spite."

"Got that right," Ida Belle said. "So we can count on you for this? For real?"

"I can't believe I'm saying this, but yes," I said. "You know you guys owe me huge. Really. Huge. Because I'm never going to hear the end of this from Carter."

"Name your price," Gertie said.

"A housekeeper," I said. "For a year. Every two weeks should be good."

"That will take up all our winnings," Gertie complained.

"But it won't take up any of the bragging rights," I said. "Fine. I'll have pity on you and say for two months. At least that'll get this place back in shape. And I want a case of beer. Carter's always over here drinking mine."

"Men can get expensive," Gertie said. "But there's all those side benefits."

"We are not going to talk about benefits," Ida Belle said. "Side or otherwise. What we need to talk about is your dress."

"I get it," I said. "I have to wear a dress and shove my boobs almost out of the top. Where is it? Might as well get this part over with."

"We haven't exactly bought it yet," Ida Belle said.

I stared at her in dismay. "You expect me to shop, too? Good God. Is the apocalypse happening and I missed the Rider of Death?"

"The dress needs to be formfitting," Gertie said. "And the only way to make sure that happens is for us to see your form in it."

I sighed. "*Two* cases of beer."

CHAPTER TWO

"GOOD LORD, WOMAN!" RONALD YELLED FROM THE BACK seat of Ida Belle's SUV. "You drive like a lunatic. Are you trying to get us killed?"

"She's trying to make us younger," I said, although his outrage wasn't a good sign as we'd barely made it a block from my house.

Slightly mollified, Ronald lessened his death clutch on the door handle by five percent. Ida Belle looked over at me and raised one eyebrow. That eyebrow said everything.

Why did we have to bring him?

Ronald was my neighbor, and the word *eccentric* did a substandard job of describing him. In the time I'd been in Sinful, he'd gone from hating me to imitating me to trying to better my social and wardrobe standing, with an uncomfortable recent focus on my undergarments that I'd been trying to avoid an actual conversation about. We'd finally settled our relationship some place in the midst of frustration, fear, and tentative friendship.

When I'd pitched the idea of bringing Ronald for the dress shopping, Ida Belle had instantly thrown her hand on my forehead, and Gertie, who had been watching entirely too many of those body-snatching-alien movies, had started easing her Mace out of her purse. Clearly, they were solidly against the idea. But when I pointed out that Ronald had the best wardrobe—man or woman—in Sinful, and he knew every designer and what they had for breakfast yesterday, they finally agreed that someone more in tune with the fashion industry couldn't hurt.

So all four of us were in Ida Belle's SUV, headed to NOLA to find me a dress that would give me the official title of Swamp Bar Bet Winner. I wasn't sure who would be more excited about the outing—Ronald or Gertie—but when Ronald showed up wearing a black tuxedo, sans shirt, silver high heels, and a sash that declared him Emperor of the Universe, I figured Ronald had it in the bag.

Every time I glanced back at him, I questioned my sanity.

As we drove through downtown, Carter stepped out of the sheriff's department and waved us over. Ida Belle pulled into a parking space as Carter sauntered over to my open window. He took one look in the back seat and some of the color left his face.

"Ronald," he said and gave the man a nod. "You know you're known by the company you keep. Some people can be trouble."

Ronald's eyes widened. "I am *not* trouble."

Carter smiled. "Wasn't referring to you."

"Yes, well," I said. "If you're done having your bit of fun, then we need to get to the business at hand."

"Dress shopping?" he asked.

"You're such a good detective," I said. "Anyway, I don't know how long this will take since these three won't let me leave with the first thing I grab off the rack. So I'm canceling official dinner in case we run long. If I get the urge to shoot them, they'll feed me in jail."

"No worries," Carter said. "I'll pick up dinner from the café. If you're not back by then, I'll leave you something in your microwave."

He gave us a wave as he continued down the sidewalk toward the General Store.

"That man is a fine wine," Ronald said. "Fifty bucks says he's going to be a killer even when he's old and gray."

He looked at me. "You know I hate you sometimes, right? Not quite as much as that sod married to Margot Robbie, but you're pulling dangerously close."

I blinked. "Margot Robbie?"

Ronald nodded enthusiastically. "Yes! The most beautiful woman in the world, in my opinion. There is no one worthy of her love. Not even me."

"But I thought..." I trailed off. "Never mind."

"So where am I headed to first?" Ida Belle said, probably worried that continuing down this conversation with Ronald might result in sexy-time talk. Or even worse, *fantasy* sexy-time talk.

"Enchanted Evening," Ronald said. "They just got in next year's gowns, so this year's will be on sale. Sinful residents won't know if you're wearing this year's Prada or last year's Walmart, so a bargain can possibly be had."

"A sale sounds good," Ida Belle said.

"That's because you and Gertie have to spring for the dress," I said. "I should punish you and demand that fancy French-sounding designer that Ronald always talks about."

"Haute couture is not a brand, honey," Ronald said and reached through the seats to pat my arm. "It's okay. I've got this."

I was glad someone did, because my knowledge of evening

wear was so limited it wasn't even measurable. And I wasn't anticipating it getting any better. I simply wanted to find a dress that everyone was thrilled with, stuff my boobs up for a couple hours, then spend at least a week recovering from the abject embarrassment in my very clean house with plenty of beer to console me.

Enchanted Evening was in the French Quarter, the name painted in fancy lettering on the window. Beautiful planters of real flowers stood on each side of the door. Stick-thin mannequins stood in the display, glittering dresses shining brightly against their white finish. Ronald paused reverently and closed his eyes a couple seconds before he opened the door and went in.

A woman with bright red lips and a pile of platinum hair hurried over when she spotted Ronald, and they exchanged air kisses then launched into compliments on clothes, shoes, and skin.

Forty-five but probably lies and says she's thirty-nine even though she can't pull it off. Five foot five without the heels. Five foot ten with them. A hundred forty pounds—something else she probably lies about —and very little of it muscle. Except for her calves. They had either developed due to her uncomfortable choice in footwear or atrophied while swollen. Despite all that, I sensed she was a huge threat. Especially to my boobs, butt, and feet.

Ida Belle cleared her throat when the conversation appeared to be moving on to face creams, and Ronald waved his hands.

"I'm so sorry," he said. "Daphne, this is Fortune, Ida Belle, and Gertie, friends from Sinful. And this lovely lady is the New Year's Queen. She needs a fabulous gown."

Given that I'd elected to dress a bit down from Ronald's attire for our trip, I didn't expect Daphne to be impressed. Okay, maybe so far down it would take a backhoe to get there, but last season's Walmart was going to have to do. She gave me a once-over, and I waited for the *Pretty Woman* brush-off I was certain was coming, but instead, she narrowed her eyes and walked around me like a wolf stalking prey. Since I'd had six pancakes for breakfast, I considered sucking in my stomach, but that felt like more effort than the entire situation warranted.

"She's got great lines." Daphne gave Ronald a nod. "The long, toned legs and arms, that delicate neck, and the bone structure. I can work with this."

"Well, 'this' would just like to find a dress as quickly as possible and get home to a beer and her recliner," I said, somewhat offended that any part of me could be considered 'delicate.'

"She's more attractive when she's not talking," Ronald said and pushed me toward a private sitting area with velvet chairs. "Sit, and Daphne and I will take care of everything."

"The first thing we have to do is get her out of that sports bra," Daphne said. "We need to fill up the top of the dress."

"You're going to need some help with that," Ronald said. "The rest of her is as lean as her legs and arms."

As both of them were staring at my chest and frowning, I felt more than a little uncomfortable.

Ronald raised one finger. "I don't suppose you would consider—"

"I am not getting implants!" I said.

Ronald waved a hand in dismissal. "Maybe for your wedding. Think about it."

"She doesn't do wire either," Gertie said.

Daphne sighed. "Pads will have to do. You don't have to do yoga or do any kind of aerobic activity for this queen gig, do you? Because I'm going down on the bra size to squeeze everything out of there that we can get."

Ronald frowned. "She has a bad habit of running off to shoot people, but I'm really hoping that this event goes down without a crime."

Daphne's mouth opened a bit and stayed there. "She shoots people?"

"Former CIA," I said. "And I try not to shoot people now that I'm a regular civilian."

"Civilian, yes," Ida Belle said. "Regular, no."

"Anyway, we've already discussed that I can put my gun on a strap between my thighs," I said. "Just make the dress short enough to run in—maybe with one of those slit things up the side—and we're good."

Daphne stared at us as though she was waiting for the punch line. When none was forthcoming, she turned around and motioned to someone across the store. I heard fingers snapping behind me and then a younger woman appeared with a bucket of wine and a tray of finger foods. A second woman followed to pour the drinks and provide linens. I sighed and leaned back in my chair. They were serving food. There was no chance of getting out of there anytime soon.

And so it began.

Daphne stuffed my chest into a bra so tight I had to breathe shallowly, as if I were giving birth. I drew the line at her placing the gel pads in there, but it took ten minutes of very specific instruction and adjustment before she was satisfied with my work. She declared my underwear a travesty against all women. But since I refused to let her or anyone else discuss that part of my wardrobe—and I was holding my gun at the time—she decided that offense didn't need to be addressed. At least not by her, but she left no doubt that it was a huge character flaw. It didn't help that Ronald yelled 'I told you so' over the dressing room door when Daphne commented on them. The only plus was I was out of embarrassment before the dress part started.

So I thought.

I sucked in and squeezed and held my breath longer than a Navy SEAL as Daphne put me through the wringer. Then I had to parade out into the sitting room and turn around so that everyone could critique. When I finally wrangled a break—with instruction to not jostle my chest, as if that were possible—I retrieved my phone from my pile of discarded clothes and hid in the bathroom.

I had a text from Carter asking how it was going. I didn't bother to answer because I knew he didn't really care. He was just ribbing me over dress shopping. I had another text from Ally and when I read it, I shrugged. What the heck? Couldn't hurt.

I headed back into the sitting room and announced, "My friend Ally said to get something that matches my eyes. That way they look like tinted ice."

Daphne and Ronald froze and stared at me. I was just about to suggest someone check their pulses when they both whirled and ran from the room.

"I saw it first!" Ronald yelled.

"It's my store!" Daphne argued.

A couple seconds later, they were back with a turquoise sequined dress. It had tiny straps, a plunging neckline and a pretty much nonexistent back. It had cutouts on each side of the waist and a hemline that would settle over my knees when standing but with a split on both sides that would have men drooling, women fuming, and Pastor Don praying.

I grabbed the dress and headed into the room to give it another go.

And darn if it didn't look good.

I still would have preferred to be in the crowd wearing blue jeans and a sweatshirt, but since I had agreed to this charade, there was no point in doing it halfway. This definitely wasn't halfway.

I stepped out and the entire room went silent, then Gertie let out a single woot.

Ronald pulled a silk hankie out of his pocket and started crying. "Oh my God. It's beautiful. You're beautiful. You are *so* going to win this bet."

"Incredible," Daphne said. "I don't know why I didn't think of it, but it's perfection."

Ida Belle gave me an approving nod and a thumbs-up. Gertie took a picture with her phone. She hadn't stopped grinning since she'd issued the battle cry.

"I can already smell the money," Gertie said.

"And the gloating," Ida Belle said. "Nothing smells better than gloating."

"You'll need shoes and earrings," Daphne said. "I'm thinking silver, strappy, and shiny for the shoes, subtle for the earrings, no necklace. We don't want to distract from that neck. I don't have anything on the shoe end that works, but Ronald knows the best shoe shops in New Orleans. You'll find something. I have the perfect earrings, though."

She motioned to the dressing room. "Now get out of that dress before something happens to it. There's no way we could find anything better."

The earrings were a slam dunk, so ten minutes later, we stood at the counter while Daphne rang up a dress that was sure to make Ida Belle's credit card cry and that would grace my body exactly one more time—something I didn't feel remotely guilty about. As far as I was concerned, Ida Belle was getting her money's worth.

Daphne was packaging up the spoils in those expensive bags with tissue paper that you only get when you pay way over the production cost for things, when the door opened and I heard a big huff behind me. I knew that huff. Everyone in Sinful knew that huff. We all turned around and stared at Celia and another woman, who looked enough like a worn-out Sofia Vergara for me to assume this was RJ.

Five foot six, a hundred thirty pounds, curves as advertised and—darn it—in all the right places. Thin build otherwise, but very little body tone. No threat at all in a fight but could be a problem if she shook those boobs at the Swamp Bar voters.

Celia huffed again, then gave Ronald a derisive look before glaring at Ida Belle and Gertie. RJ gave me a once-over, apparently cluing in that I was her competition. Based on the resulting smirk, I had to assume she wasn't impressed.

"She's built like a boy," RJ said and leaned against the doorframe, clearly bored.

"Since brains aren't stored in your chest, I'm good," I said.

Ronald sniffed and pointed to the rear of the store. "There's a discount rack in the back for your discount queen."

RJ straightened and gave Ronald a dirty look. "Only full price for the real deal, honey."

Ronald snorted. "*Honey*, you could make Gucci look cheap. What did you use for those highlights—paint stripper? It looks like we need to bale hay on your head."

"Bet she wears cheap underwear," I said, stoking the flames.

"Please," Ronald said. "This one doesn't even *own* underwear."

Ida Belle grinned. "Hear that, Daphne? Don't let *this one* try anything on unless you want cheap butt rubbing on your fine fabrics."

"I cannot believe you're putting that...that disreputable thing up as queen," Celia said to Ida Belle. "She's been a blight on Sinful since the day she arrived. But then, I shouldn't expect a show of class from the likes of you."

Gertie opened her mouth to speak, but Ronald held up a hand.

"I've got this," he said.

He stared directly at Celia. "*You* have always held the vote for the worst taste in clothes and behavior in the entire town, and because we're a God-fearing community, everyone has put up with it. But now, you're showing us all exactly how petty and nasty you are."

Ronald waved a hand at me. "This *lady*—and it's a shame we don't have more of them left in this world—is the person who exposed your daughter's killer and saved you from the same fate. And you have the audacity to disparage her?"

Celia had the decency to blush, but she wasn't about to give up. "If she hadn't been distracting Carter with her antics, I'm sure he would have gotten the job done."

"Nothing distracts Carter from his work," Gertie said, "which you always have a complaint about. So don't go using him as your defense now."

"I don't need a defense," Celia said and pointed at Ronald. "And drafting this plague on our community to help you in your pathetic attempt to upstage my group is a new low, even for you, Ida Belle."

Ronald just laughed, but Ida Belle's face turned red. She took two steps toward Celia, who had the good sense to take one back.

"You have the nerve to call Ronald a plague?" Ida Belle asked. "The man who single-handedly funded the bulk of the new youth center? You know—the fundraiser that *you* insisted on ramrodding the show for but couldn't raise the money because no one likes you?"

Celia's eyes widened and I glanced over at Ronald, who

looked as surprised as the rest of us. As that particular six-figure donation had been anonymous, I guess he hadn't considered that someone might not only know but also let the cat out of the bag.

Ida Belle took two more steps forward and poked Celia in the chest. "I have had it with you and your nasty attitude. You contribute nothing to Sinful but darkness and despair. You're the Angel of Death right here on Earth. And I'm done putting up with your crap."

"Assault!" Celia cried and looked over at Daphne, clearly panicked. "Call the cops! She assaulted me."

"I didn't see anything," Daphne said as she checked her fingernails. "But I'm going to have to ask you to leave. I don't think our store has anything for you."

I laughed. "She totally *Pretty Woman*-ed you."

RJ glared at me. "Are you calling me a prostitute?"

Gertie shook her head. "Pretty sure pros charge."

"I never liked you, you hateful old hag!" RJ yelled and lifted the foam cup she was holding.

The foam cup filled with red liquid.

In a high-end dress shop.

CHAPTER THREE

I TOSSED MY SHOPPING BAG BEHIND THE COUNTER AND lunged for the cup just as RJ reached to take the lid off. Gertie had scrambled for the door and flung it open, so in one fluid motion, I grabbed the cup, shoved RJ outside, then tossed the contents onto her as she fell onto the sidewalk. Celia ran for the door, shoving Gertie as she rushed outside. Gertie fell backward into the window display and a shower of sequins and feathers rained down on her.

"Oh my God!" Daphne screamed. "Not the Valentino! Those feathers are a hundred dollars each!"

The distraught shop owner took one look at the collapsed display as a disheveled Gertie rose up, with what I presumed were some of the ridiculously expensive feathers sticking to her head, then sprinted out the door and tackled RJ right as she stood up.

"That was a Super Bowl Sunday kind of move," Ida Belle said as she leaned back against the counter and pulled a bag of peanuts out of her pocket.

Ronald took one look at Gertie in the destroyed display and Daphne rolling around in the street, ruining her Dior—

according to him—in what looked like strawberry daiquiri, and passed out.

While I was trying to decide which situation needed my attention the most, Celia waded into the grappling match out in the street and started swinging her purse at Daphne.

"Two against one," Ida Belle pointed out and popped another peanut in her mouth.

I sighed, more worried about the spectators and their phones. Celia would be yelling for the police in a matter of seconds, and Daphne didn't deserve to go to jail for helping us out. As I headed out the door, Celia gave the purse a home-run swing and hit Daphne's rear. The purse clasp broke and what looked like a shrimp pie spilled out. A dog at the corner, who'd been legs-up in a coffin with his fake priest owner giving last rites when we'd passed earlier, made a miraculous recovery and bolted out of the coffin and straight for the spoils.

I figured he'd grab the random pie and be on his way, but apparently the purse contained a bigger score than the sidewalk. The dog leaped up and grabbed the bag and got into a tug-of-war with Celia. Ida Belle strolled out of the dress shop with a wrench, loosened the valve on a fire hydrant, and stepped back to finish her peanuts as the water gushed out.

The stream was a direct hit on Celia and sent her sprawling into the street. The dog took that opportunity to bolt away with the purse, his owner running after him, waving his Bible in the air and yelling things that no priest would ever say. Celia had made an unfortunate sprawl with the hem of her skirt downstream of the blast. The bottom flew up and over her head while her big underwear proceeded to give her the king of all wedgies. Two teen hustlers who had been working the street doubled over laughing.

"Hey, lady," one of them said. "I can tell you where you got dem shoes and when."

Celia crawled out of the stream of water and glared up at them. "I can tell you where these shoes are going to be in about ten seconds."

The other hustler elbowed the first one. "We better bounce. Her butt's eating her clothes. Don't want to follow them big panties into the void."

They both ran off, still laughing.

Celia managed to pull herself up and her skirt down. She didn't even bother giving the panties a tug, but then that stream of water had probably lodged them somewhere near her tonsils, and the whole process might take more doing than was legal on a public street. Even New Orleans had limits. Outside of Mardi Gras.

RJ and Daphne were still rolling around in the daiquiri spill, both so covered with the bright red liquid that they looked like stabbing victims. Gertie had finally managed to crawl out of the display and came running out of the shop, feathers still clinging to her head. Ronald had pulled himself upright on the doorframe but as soon as he got another look at the Dior, he went straight down again, and I was pretty sure he was crying.

Celia waded into the daiquiri fray but only managed to fall on top of the fighting women. Gertie started cheering, and I reached over to pluck the super-expensive feathers off her head, figuring Daphne had already been through enough with us that day. I had just stuck the last one in my bra when an unmarked vehicle pulled up and Detective Casey—a cop we'd met during a previous investigation—stepped out, grinning.

"You're early," I said. "There's no homicide yet."

Ida Belle finished off her peanuts and motioned around. "This is below your pay grade, Detective."

"Couldn't help myself," Casey said. "A call went out about a zombie dog, old ladies, butt flashing, and a WWE smackdown, and I just had a feeling. Although I'm finding the location a bit confusing." She motioned to the storefront of the dress shop.

"Yeah, there's a thing," I said.

Casey raised one eyebrow. "There's *always* a thing, but women who look like you don't need an evening gown to get it."

"God, isn't that the truth," Ronald said as he sidled up and clutched my arm for support. "Life is humongously unfair."

"It's more of a Sinful women's group rivalry thing that has a betting pool attached," I said.

Casey laughed. "So a *gang* thing. Walking on the wild side there, Redding. What's the rivalry—who can find the most sequins?"

"I've been coerced into wearing an evening gown and being Queen of the New Year representing the Baptists," I said. "My competition is put up by the Catholics. Hottest queen wins."

Casey stopped laughing and her jaw dropped. "Come back?"

"I get the biggest cut of the betting pool, a couple cases of beer, and housekeeping for two months," I said and motioned to Celia. "That, along with making sure the scourge on Sinful loses, has spurred me into participating in the madness."

"So there's still a chance of a homicide," Casey said.

"I'd give it better than a chance," Ida Belle said.

"I have to push my boobs up," I explained.

Casey shook her head. "Just don't go for stilettos. The last thing you need under those circumstances is a weapon."

Ronald rolled his eyes. "That whole killing-with-the-stiletto thing is so retro Hollywood. People don't actually kill with their footwear."

Since killing a terrorist with a stiletto was exactly how I'd wound up in Sinful in the first place, Ida Belle, Gertie, and I just maintained silence. Ronald looked at the three of us, his expression shifting from aggrieved to horrified.

"Please tell me they weren't designer," he said.

"Prada," I said.

The blood rushed from Ronald's face and he fanned his face with his hand.

Casey laughed again. "On that note, I think I'll get back to work."

Celia, who'd finally managed to get up from the fray and start stomping again, huffed up to Casey and pointed a finger at me. "You're a cop, right? You have that look. Aren't you going to arrest her?"

Casey smirked. "I'm a homicide detective, lady. You don't need my services...yet."

She climbed back into her car and drove away with a wave.

"I like her," Ronald said.

RJ and Daphne had finally separated and were staring at each other like lions in the wild. Celia pulled out her phone.

"I'm calling the cops," she said.

"There's a shocker," Gertie mumbled.

"No," RJ said and grabbed her arm. "They'll just say we started it and I might end up in jail. Then I can't do the float thing."

"Gee, I wonder why you might end up in jail?" Ida Belle said. "Got a warrant out by any chance?"

The hard line of RJ's jaw told me Ida Belle had hit the nail on the head. Interesting. Celia stared at RJ for a couple seconds before finally cluing in on the issues at hand. She whirled around to face Ida Belle and pointed her finger.

"This isn't over," she said.

"This has been over since the day you were born," Ida Belle said. "You just won't admit it."

RJ glanced around, probably worried that regular cops were

going to materialize, and tugged on Celia's sleeve. Celia shot us all one last dirty look and stomped off after RJ, who'd already given us the finger, then fled down the sidewalk.

"She's lovely," I said, gesturing toward RJ.

Ronald laughed. "She's no better than she's ever been—a spoiled, narcissistic bully. The shell was pretty before it got so worn out, but everything beneath the skin has always been as ugly as that troll Celia."

I nodded. "Well, she made a mistake bullying Ally. I'm going to wipe the road with her."

Ronald threw his arm around me and squeezed. "Of course you are."

He gave Ida Belle a stern look. "But *you* are in trouble for telling my secrets."

Ida Belle sighed. "I didn't mean to let the cat out of the bag, but that woman puts me into the red zone sometimes."

"It was a really nice thing, funding the youth center," Gertie said. "And it would have eventually gotten around."

"I suppose you're right," Ronald said. "Well, at least it put Celia in her place for the moment. Sort of a bonus. But Ida Belle is still buying lunch, and I refuse to eat a sandwich. *And* I want to sit down with actual linens, no paper."

I grinned. "We're in the right place for eating."

"Then let's get our things and head out," Ida Belle said and headed back inside with the wrench.

"Where the heck did you get the wrench anyway?" I asked as I followed her.

"Working girl display," Ida Belle said and pointed to a mannequin wearing a sequined suit and sitting on a set of pipes. The wrench was now leaned against them.

Daphne stumbled in, clutching one shoe with a broken heel and looking as though she'd starred in *Carrie*. Ronald relapsed, beside himself over her clothes, shoes, hair, and pretty much everything.

"I'm really sorry about all this," I said. "Is there some way we can make it right?"

Daphne shook her head. "Just promise me you'll beat that cow. I don't care if you have to shove your boobs up under your chin. Just do it."

I nodded and pulled the feathers out of my bra. "I snagged these before they could blow away."

"Oh my God!" She grabbed the feathers and petted them like a prize dog. "I have a seamstress who can put them back. Thank you! That dress will cover six months' rent on this space."

A salesgirl, who'd hidden behind the counter during the fray, handed me my bags. I figured the best thing we could do for Daphne was clear out of her shop.

"Thanks for everything," I said to Daphne. "When this is over, I'm happy to bring the dress back. Maybe you can sell it at a discount and recoup some of the damage."

Daphne smiled. "That's very kind of you. Hopefully, the parade will go better than shopping did."

Famous last words.

CHAPTER FOUR

EVEN THOUGH I WAS PRESENT AND COMPLETELY SOBER FOR the entire thing, I'm still not sure how I managed to be stuffed into a dress, my pistol strapped between my thighs, more gel under my boobs than in the entire state of California, and slightly less in my hair—obviously not in the same format. Ronald and Ally had fussed over my hair and makeup for longer than it took some people to build a house, but when I'd said as much, Ronald had stated that we were starting at the same place—my foundation was good but everything on top of it needed to be remodeled.

Every time I'd wanted to jump out of the chair and declare myself done no matter where they were in the process, I'd remembered that smug look and flipped finger of RJ's, then laid eyes on Ally's sweet face, and I'd kept my butt planted in the chair. Revenge was really a strong emotion. One even I couldn't conquer, apparently. And since karma was flaky, you couldn't really count on it. Or at least, you couldn't count on it happening when you preferred *and* in front of you.

So now I stood at the far end of downtown, ready to climb up on a flatbed trailer that had been decorated to look like an ice castle, which I had to admit, looked pretty darn good. They'd used glass blocks to create glaciers and had inserted white and turquoise LED lights inside them. Turquoise and silver poinsettias and ribbon adorned the display, and they'd even constructed a throne from the glass blocks, complete with a shiny turquoise cushion.

Gertie had confided that Ida Belle had already spent her share of the winnings and a hunk of her quarterly investing profit on me and the float. Apparently, RJ's mother had sprained her ankle and was shopping in town more, so she'd used that excuse to ratchet up the flirting with Walter. And in another ridiculous and hopeless move, had sicced RJ on Carter.

Carter had been far more disturbed and less amused than Walter, who'd been putting up with it for years. Myrtle, one of the sheriff's department dispatchers and our inside source, had reported that RJ showed up daily the entire week with baked goods for Carter—baked goods she'd bought from Ally, then transferred onto her mother's dishes to try to pass them off as her own. Like a detective wouldn't know the goodies he ate practically every day.

Myrtle had also commented that RJ's cleavage was showing more dough than the baked goods, to the point that Deputy Breaux had taken to running out the back door every time she walked in, claiming her look wasn't fit for a strip club, much less the sheriff's department. I found his sense of propriety in this day and age both unusual and charming but told him he still had to make a jaunt down to the Swamp Bar and vote for me, regardless of how much of me was coming out of my parade dress.

RJ had also made a few trips to the Swamp Bar in tight jeans and even tighter shirts. Rumor had it she wasn't wearing a bra, then the rumor was confirmed when she 'accidentally' spilled a glass of beer on her top every night. Ida Belle was calling dirty pool as the queens weren't supposed to act like they were politicians on the campaign tour and the Swamp Bar was technically off-limits, but no one was surprised by RJ's shenanigans.

Ida Belle had tried to convince Carter to run RJ and arrest her for the warrants Ida Belle was certain she had outstanding. But Carter said that unless RJ broke the law, he had no reason to run her and he wasn't about to put up with her all day long in jail over some unpaid tickets or whatever other nonsense she hadn't gotten around to handling. I could see his point, but had to admit I was disappointed. If RJ had been in jail, then I might have gotten out of this whole thing.

"You look incredible," Ally said as she walked up. "I know I was there for the hair and makeup and saw the dress, but when it's all put together, it's...wow! Just wow!"

"It's also itchy," I said. "The sequins pinch under my arms, and I'm not even going to talk about what my pistol is doing. I'm pretty sure I've strained muscles in my chest, and I'm certain that hair gel is seeping through my scalp and lowering my IQ. Why do women do this?"

"Mostly to get one over on other women," Ally said.

"It's a heck of a lot easier to shoot them," I said. "And way more comfortable."

Ally laughed. "But you won't go to jail this way."

"You say that like jail's the worse thing that could happen here," I said. "And besides, this is a Sinful celebration and Gertie's here. Jail is not off the table."

"And on that note, I've got to go get in my spot so I'll have a front-row view for that possibility," Ally said.

"Is someone saving you a space?" I asked.

She blushed and looked down. "Mannie said he'd get us a good one."

"Things must be heating up if he's coming to a Sinful parade."

"Oh, that's not because of me. When I told him you were going to be wearing a dress with a crown and riding on a float, he said nothing short of death would keep him away. Besides, I'm pretty sure Big made it part of his job duties."

I sighed. "This is going to be on YouTube, isn't it?"

"Probably about two seconds after the end of the parade and livestreaming everywhere else."

"And to think, for years, the entire world was unaware of my existence."

Ally smiled. "Well, I, for one, am happy you came out of the shadows. You've changed Sinful for the better and given me a whole new lease on life. Before, I was just plodding along, day to day. I honestly don't think I would have ever had the courage to pursue my bakery without you pushing me."

"You're stronger than you think," I said. "But I'm glad I came out of the shadows too. I just hope I don't come out of my dress."

She grinned as she hurried off.

I suddenly found myself in the very rare position of being alone. I was pretty sure that except for showering, that hadn't been the case for at least a week. I glanced at the float in front of me—RJ's ride. It looked like a Disney princess had visited. Lots of pink sashes and glitter. My ice castle looked so much cooler. Given the dirty look RJ had given it when she'd huffed past, I assumed she thought so too.

At least the weather had cooperated. It was a cool but manageable fifty-five degrees and there was only a light breeze. That was a huge plus, given that I was downwind. I didn't have to worry about all the sashes and glitter blowing off RJ's float and onto mine. Pink might go with turquoise on unicorns and in kids' rooms, but it would definitely clash with my scene.

And the last thing I needed was Ronald rushing out to vacuum as we went.

I had to give RJ credit, though—the white dress she had on did everything to show off her curvy figure. Her hair was piled on top of her head in one of those fancy swirly-looking buns, leaving more skin showing below the neck, which was the intent. Her makeup was thick and up close, I could still see the dark circles under her eyes and wrinkles around her mouth. But from a distance, no one would be able to tell she'd lived hard and looked years older than she was.

Despite it almost being time to load up, RJ was nowhere in sight. I glanced around and caught a flicker of white by the fire truck posted at the end of the street. It was RJ, but I didn't recognize the man she was talking to. He definitely didn't look happy and based on her stiff body and hand in the air, I gathered the conversation wasn't a polite one. I squinted a bit, trying to make out what he was saying as her back was to me, but could only get a piece of the conversation.

One way or another...money...or else...

She whirled around, her jaw set, and stomped back my direction. As Celia approached her, she plastered on a fake smile, but her rigid body gave away her anger. The man lit a cigarette and took a puff as she walked away, studying her for a couple seconds, then turned around and disappeared behind the fire truck.

It didn't take a wordsmith to fill in the blanks.

It looked as though RJ's homecoming wasn't about paying a long-overdue visit as much as it was hiding from her obligations, but then, Ida Belle and Gertie had suspected her motives weren't family related. That guy arguing with her probably wasn't family and definitely wasn't a legitimate debt collector. They harassed you by phone and mail. They didn't show up at parades in small towns, issuing threats. The long and short of it was that whatever RJ thought she was hiding from had followed her to Sinful. I just hoped she left before things got ugly. Sinful had enough issues. We didn't need to import more.

"You ready?" Ida Belle's voice sounded behind me and I turned around, plastering on my fake smile.

She gave me a critical eye. "That smile is actually not bad. I didn't think Ronald could do it, but he's managed to pull off miracles in all areas."

"He told me to think about baked goods," I said.

She snorted. "I would have thought he'd go for Carter wearing nothing but a towel."

I shook my head. "My relationship with Carter can be problematic, so a smile isn't the default result as it depends on where my thoughts go. My relationship with baked goods is solid."

"I feel the same way about my SUV and guns," Ida Belle said.

RJ chose that moment to hurry by, with a nasty side glance our way, before stopping to talk to two women next to her float, who I took to be mother and daughter given the similarities and age difference.

Mother midfifties based on body movement but face looked older. Five foot four. A hundred twenty five pounds, with her clothes and enormous handbag. Zero threat unless she packed her purse like Gertie.

Daughter midtwenties. Also five foot four. A hundred ten pounds. Low muscle tone for her age. Completely vacant expression until she saw RJ, then it shifted to a frown. Zero threat that I could discern, although vacant expressions usually made me raise an eyebrow.

The mother smiled as RJ hugged her, then RJ indicated to her daughter to climb up on the float. The daughter had kept the blank expression during the entire exchange but when she looked up at the float, a slow smile appeared. Still, something about her seemed off.

"Who's that?" I asked.

Ida Belle looked over and frowned. "Christina and Marigold Forrester. Marigold ran around with RJ in high school."

"She was a mean girl?" I was a bit surprised as she didn't exactly look the type. She was the average-looking girl who most people would pass on the street without noticing, while RJ was the type who insisted everyone notice.

"Not a mean girl," Ida Belle said. "More like she was the girl with plenty of spending money who was desperate to be popular, so RJ and Brock took advantage of that. Unfortunately, she paid a huge price for her popularity ride. Got into a car wreck driving them home from a party and sustained a brain injury. She's been nonverbal ever since."

"No seat belt?"

"None of them were wearing one," Ida Belle said. "But Brock and RJ were drunk—you know how that usually goes."

"They walked away unscathed," I said. "That sucks, especially to happen to someone so young."

Ida Belle nodded. "Her father left about a year after. He couldn't deal, so it's just been Christina and Marigold making things work for a while now."

"It's nice of RJ to put her up on the float."

Ida Belle snorted. "To the best of my knowledge, RJ didn't visit that girl once after the accident. More likely, she's putting her up there hoping for the sympathy vote, but then lots of people say I'm cynical."

"Also highly accurate." I sighed. "So she's using her again. Well, hopefully, Marigold doesn't realize and can get a bit of enjoyment out of the deal."

"She's overdue, that's for sure."

I saw RJ head to the rear of her float for a bit, then return with a box spray-painted pink that she shoved at one of Celia's crew. One of the volunteers helped her onto her float and stuck the box next to her throne. I assumed they were her crowd goodies, and it was almost showtime. Mine were already cleverly entrenched in a set of glass blocks next to my throne, so all I had to do was climb up and put on my happy face.

Ida Belle pulled her phone out of her pocket and checked a text. "That's Marie. We're ready to start, so get up on that float with your high boobs and your visions of baked goods dancing in your head. This thing is about to kick off."

"I'm not sure I'd use the words *kick off* in relation to a public event in Sinful."

"Hmm. Probably true. Remember to wave. And I don't want to see a single strand of beads remaining in that container. Those muffin coupons on the end of them are worth their weight in gold."

I grinned. "Ally really upped our voting game. The Swamp Bar crowd loves beer, but they also love food."

Normally, I would have vaulted up onto the float, but given the dress, I had to go the route of the makeshift stairs that had been built for my climb. I headed up, got positioned on my throne with the container of beads nearby, then gave my chest one last push-up, crossed my legs so that people weren't getting more of a view than I intended, then gave Ida Belle a nod.

She gave me a thumbs-up and headed off to meet Gertie, who was already working the crowd like a campaign manager. I shook my head. If someone would have told me back in the CIA that I'd be stuffed in a dress on a throne for any other reason than completing a mission, I would have laughed them out of DC. Yet here I sat—flashing my goods not to rid the world of its most dangerous criminals but to gain some beer and a clean house.

If my father were really dead, he'd be rolling over in his grave.

My mother would be smiling.

Chocolate cookies with peanut butter chips. Maybe even Carter eating them wearing a towel.

I broke out in a smile as the float started moving.

Sinful had really turned out for the parade. But then the combination of the aforementioned good weather, the Swamp Bar betting rivalry, and the rumor of discount muffin coupons was enough to entice people to turn on their DVRs and catch their favorite shows later. Especially given that Sinful events were often way better than anything that showed up on TV. I just hoped we had more of a Hallmark movie moment than a *Forensic Files* one.

The parade started at the south end of downtown and went the length of Main Street, officially ending when the neighborhood started. At that point, the floats would circle around to the park, where there was plenty of space to unload the queens and remove anything from the trailers that could become litter in the winds of the storm due later that night. The sheriff's department sponsored a hot chocolate stand for everyone helping with teardown, and the Sinful Ladies were on hand to doctor up their wares with Sinful Ladies Cough Syrup, just in case anyone had a throat tickle that needed attention.

Downtown was still decorated for Christmas, and I had to admit it was pretty. Louisiana didn't have snow, but every business had painted its windows frosted white. Light poles were wrapped with ribbons and lights with giant bows on top. All down the sidewalk were huge red, white, and silver planters stuffed full of poinsettias, and in the open lot where one of the docks stood was a huge Christmas tree. It was covered with ornaments and so much light I could see the glow from it at my house.

As the float inched forward, I waved and threw beads and laughed at the scramble for them and was suddenly surprised that I was actually enjoying myself. The excitement and joy from the crowd were infectious. The muffin coupons were a big hit, but honestly, I knew enough about Louisiana to know that residents would fight over most anything as long as it was flung during a parade. Fortunately, it was just chilly enough that no one flashed me their boobs for my wares.

Near the end of the parade route, the floats stopped so we could do a final wave for the parade-goers and ditch any remaining goodies to the ever-hopeful crowd. As I was flinging a clump of beads, I caught sight of the guy I'd seen talking to RJ before the parade. He was standing at the edge of the street and looked straight up at her when her float stopped next to him. RJ's head whipped to the opposite side of the street, and I felt my spidey sense tingle again.

I saw Gertie standing nearby and motioned for her to come over, hoping I could get her to either identify or take a quick pic of the guy. I had a feeling something was poised to go down between those two and wanted to have all the documentation I could get up front. Gertie pushed through the front row and hurried up. I hopped off my throne and leaned over to speak, but the crowd rushed around her, still vying for beads.

I couldn't exactly yell out what I needed and no way this group was going to back off when I was still clutching the goods, so I flung the beads behind them, then reached down and pulled Gertie onto the float. I explained what I needed, and she glanced over at the man, who was still staring up at RJ, and nodded. The float offered the best chance of getting a clean shot, so I told her to stay put and take some pics of me and the crowd so that he wouldn't suspect anything.

The float started moving again, so I hopped back on my throne and Gertie took up post at the front on a block of fake ice and started taking pics. The man was standing at the back of the float now, but instead of looking up at RJ, he was staring across the street. A flicker of fear rushed through his otherwise angry expression. I looked on the other side of the street and saw someone standing on the sidewalk, just out of reach of the light from the lamppost. He was wearing a trench coat and had a ball cap pulled down over his forehead, but I could tell he was looking across the street. He lifted a single gloved finger and pointed, then slipped around the corner of the building and was gone.

I turned my attention back to the float and saw Gertie aim toward the man who'd been arguing with RJ. But as soon as she directed her phone toward him, he whirled around and disappeared in the crowd. Darn it! I hoped she'd gotten a good shot before he got away. Something about him and his interactions with RJ bothered me, and now there was the stranger on the sidewalk. I'd had this feeling before and it always ended with a corpse. I didn't like RJ one bit, but I didn't want her to get murdered. And if someone was going to pop her, I'd prefer they do it back in Nashville. Carter didn't need more problems.

As my float moved toward the end of the route and stopped again, I spotted Ally in the crowd, Mannie beside her grinning and pointing a phone in my direction. I gave him one of those queen waves and he and Ally started laughing, then he gave me a thumbs-up. If I could run him down after the parade, I was going to tell him to drop by the Swamp Bar and vote. It was the least he could do since I'd provided entertainment for him and his bosses.

All of a sudden, a gust of wind rushed past me and blew my sash up in my face. A second later, I felt a tingle on my arms and looked down to see pink glitter. Crap. I stood up and looked at the floats, hoping we could wrap this up before another gust started taking the ribbons and other decor off the floats.

Then my bloodhound nose caught a whiff of smoke.

CHAPTER FIVE

I ZEROED IN ON RJ'S FLOAT AND SAW FLAMES UNDER THE platform that housed her seat. I yelled, but no one could hear me over the cheers of the crowd, and the guy pulling my float was busy flirting with one of the parade-goers. I knew the fire extinguisher was behind my throne, so I vaulted off and ran around to grab it. Gertie had clued in that something was wrong and was trying to figure out what and where.

I didn't have time to explain because as soon as the fire hit all those paper flowers glued to that throne, RJ was going to be the Queen of the Damned instead of New Year's. I yelled, "Fire!," and did a running leap off the ice block Gertie had vacated as she saw me barreling her way, then landed in the bed of my tow truck. I didn't even pause before scrambling up the top of the truck and dashing across the hood and making one last leap onto RJ's float.

By this time, the flames had become visible to the crowd, and they were frantically motioning for everyone to get off the float. I directed the extinguisher at the throne just as it went up in flames. When the smoke and white haze cleared, I looked over the collapsed throne at RJ, who was standing on the front of the float, covered in foam.

"I've got it!" Gertie yelled from the side of the float, fire extinguisher in hand.

It was then that I realized her glasses were covered in foam.

"No!" I yelled as I bailed off the float, but it was too late.

She squeezed the trigger but had her hand way down on the wand. The thing waved around like a snake, spraying foam all over the fleeing crowd as Gertie whirled around in a circle, trying to gain control. When she finally let go of the trigger, she swung her head from side to side, still unable to see anything.

"Is the fire out?" she asked.

"My dress is ruined!" RJ shouted.

"It's off the rack and not designer!" Ronald yelled as he rushed toward me and stared at my foam-covered dress in dismay.

"You could have been killed, you idiot!" Gertie yelled in RJ's general direction. "'Thank you' wouldn't be out of line, but that would require manners."

"Ma'am, I need you to get off the float," a fireman said to RJ. "We have to make sure the fire is contained."

"Stop calling me ma'am!" RJ yelled and climbed over the side of the float, flashing the crowd most of her wares. Fortunately, Ronald had been wrong about the underwear. RJ adjusted her dress down once she hit the sidewalk, then huffed off, the crowd parting like the Red Sea as she went.

Ronald's gaze had never left my dress. He was standing there staring, tears filling his eyes, hand over his mouth, and I was afraid he was going to call for Pastor Don to pray.

"Why don't you go home and have a drink," I told him. "We can worry about this tomorrow."

"My daughter! I need a paramedic!"

I looked over and saw Christina and Ida Belle hunched over Marigold, who was sitting on the sidewalk, gasping for breath. A paramedic rushed over and strapped an oxygen mask to Marigold, then motioned for a gurney. Christina hurried after the paramedics as they carried Marigold to the ambulance, shooting a final glare at the float as she went.

Gertie wiped the foam off her glasses, and we met up with Ida Belle on the sidewalk.

"Is she okay?" I asked.

Ida Belle nodded. "I think she's having a panic attack. Christina was smart enough to Marigold off before they inhaled smoke or foam. Only that idiot RJ insisted on standing there like a statue."

"A dangerous situation, fireman, sirens, and lights," Gertie said. "For years, Christina had to give her a sedative to get her into a car. All this probably brought the night of the car wreck back."

"That sucks," I said. "Hopefully they can get her calmed down."

"How did the fire start?" Ida Belle asked.

"That's a good question," I said. "It started under the back of the platform in the rear of the float."

"So under the throne?" Gertie asked.

"Or somewhat behind it," I said. "I couldn't tell from my angle, but I'm sure the firemen will be able to discern the starting point."

"And what started it." Ida Belle stared at the torched float, a grim look on her face.

I caught her expression and stared at her.

"You think this was arson?" I asked.

She shook her head. "Or something worse."

———

Because the crowd was blocking downtown, Carter ordered everyone but the necessary personnel to disperse. My float was towed around the smoldering one and we headed to the park to disassemble it, but even the hot chocolate stand couldn't make up for the dismal end to the evening. Because I wasn't dressed for a teardown and was dripping foam everywhere, I only stayed for a couple minutes. Then I hitched a ride in the bed of a local fisherman's truck and headed home for a much-needed shower. I figured it was going to take every bit of hot water I had and probably an entire bottle of shampoo to get that gel out of my hair.

Two hours later, I was reclined in my living room, drinking a beer and enjoying potato chips when Carter knocked on my front door, then unlocked it and stuck his head in. He looked tired as he made his way in and flopped onto the couch with a sigh.

"Long night," I said.

He nodded. "And I didn't even have to wear gel in my hair *or* my bra."

"Ha. Hard to believe I got the good end of the deal, but there you go. Did they figure out how the fire started?"

"Yeah. A cigarette under the platform for the throne."

My mind flashed back to the man RJ had been arguing with—the man smoking a cigarette—and I sat up, sloshing my beer.

"I saw a guy arguing with RJ before the parade started. He was smoking a cigarette. And I saw him again at the end of the parade route, next to the float."

"Right before it caught on fire?"

I nodded. "But he wasn't smoking then. Not that I could see, anyway. What caught, exactly? Because that platform was heavy plywood. It would have taken some time for it to flame that way."

"Some genius decided to store some spare tissue flowers under the platform—you know, the ones they had all over the float. But, of course, no one is admitting to it."

"Figures."

"Could the guy you saw have tossed a cigarette underneath the float without anyone seeing?"

I considered this. "I'm not sure because I didn't have him in sight the whole time. But I suppose he could have flicked it in there while everyone was scrambling for goodies. I managed to move a whole crowd of people just by flinging beads. And people were crowded right up around the floats at the end of the parade route."

He sighed. "So now I just have to figure out who this mystery guy is, find him, and see if I can pin an arson rap on him."

"Gertie took pictures of him, or at least I hope she got him. I forgot all about it when the fire broke out."

He raised one eyebrow. "Why did Gertie take pictures?"

"Because I asked her to. There was something about the guy...I don't know. I just had a bad feeling."

He nodded. "Tell her to send them over. I'll see if anyone can identify him."

I grabbed my phone and sent Gertie a text. A couple seconds later, photos showed up on mine and Carter's phones.

"That's him," I said. "The guy in the dirty denim jacket."

Carter narrowed his eyes at his phone and zoomed in on the guy. He frowned, then looked at the next two pics, zooming in again.

"Do you know him?" I asked.

"I'm not sure," he said. "He sort of looks like Brock Benoit, but Brock was an athlete. This guy looks worn all to heck and at least ten years older than Brock would be."

"Wasn't Brock the guy RJ left town with?"

Carter nodded.

"RJ looks pretty rough herself close up. Maybe they've been living in the musician fast lane."

I sent a text to Gertie.

Could that guy be Brock Benoit?

A couple seconds later, the reply came.

Now that you mention it, yes. I should have realized, but he looks so old.

I showed Carter the text and he laughed.

"Says the woman who used to burp Jesus," he said. "But she's not wrong. Well, hell. I guess first thing tomorrow, I've got to find Brock."

"He doesn't have family here anymore?"

"No. His mother ran off when he was in junior high. His father was an abusive piece of crap. Last I heard, he was doing a dime in Angola for armed robbery. As soon as Brock aged out of the benefits system, his dad took off. Nobody was sorry to see him go—not even Brock. The house was a rental and they were about to be evicted. No other family that I know of."

"What did Brock do after his father left?"

"Lived with a friend on the football team. There was only a couple months left in the school year. He took off with RJ after that and I haven't seen him since."

"What about RJ? Have you seen her visit since she left?"

"Once or twice, but not a lot considering her mother is still here. Sinful was never really RJ's scene, though."

"How do you mean?"

"She needs constant adoration, and she wants it from a lot of people. A small town was never going to do it for her. She wants the entire world to worship her and along with it, fame, fortune...the whole nine."

I laughed. "Tell me what you really think."

"I think she's a spoiled brat who thought she was better than she was and was intentionally unkind. I could forgive the first part. The second is what I have a problem with, especially as I've seen no evidence that she's changed."

"But I thought she *loved* you. After all, she's been slaving over all those baked goodies to bring to you every day."

He snorted. "The only person RJ has ever loved is herself. But she hates losing, and by hitting on me, she thinks she's getting a dig in on you."

"If she only knew I'm not the jealous type."

He raised one eyebrow. "A man might consider that a slight."

"A regular man might, but you wouldn't. You'd consider it a compliment that I trust you enough to be amused by her pathetic attempts to distract you."

"I wouldn't call them completely pathetic. She *is* buying those cookies from Ally, so at least she's springing for the good stuff."

I narrowed my eyes. "You've been nice to her, haven't you? Just to continue the bakery freebies."

He shrugged. "I didn't start the game, but I saw no reason for myself and my staff not to reap the rewards, especially as they wouldn't last beyond the parade."

"You have more patience than me. I'd rather pay for my own cookies."

He laughed as he rose. "That kind of goes without saying. Anyway, I'm going to head out. I need a shower and Tiny hasn't had dinner yet. And I've got to get at least six hours of sleep in as I'm predicting a very, very long night tomorrow with all the parties. Plus, I have to call in my vote to the Swamp Bar."

"I didn't know you could vote by phone."

"You can't. I can. Whiskey gives law enforcement special allowance."

"Because he'd prefer not to have you in the bar."

"Exactly."

"So who are you voting for?"

He leaned over and kissed me so soundly, it made my chest clench.

"Wouldn't you like to know."

CHAPTER SIX

I WAS UP EARLY THE NEXT MORNING. NOT BECAUSE I wanted to be, but because Ronald was banging on my front door, insisting that he collect my dress for cleaning. He'd declared it a miracle that I didn't rip it while 'playing fireman' and said that God had spoken to him in a dream and told him the dress could be restored with a hand cleaning.

I stopped listening when he started in on Q-tips. Clearly, the man was nuts, but if he wanted to spend the next fifty years hand cleaning each individual sequin on that dress, he was welcome to it. It wasn't as if I'd be wearing it again. I still had bruises on my chest from that ridiculously tight bra, which had gone straight into my fireplace when I'd gotten home the night before. Immediately after I'd cut it off me.

I wandered into the kitchen and set a pot of coffee on after Ronald left with the dress. Since Merlin had been startled awake along with me, I indulged him with some tuna for his trouble. He scarfed it down then headed off to the living room —probably to take up residence in my recliner and bathe for the next two hours.

I poured a cup of coffee and sat at the kitchen table,

wondering what I should do that day. It was Friday, which was technically a workday by US standards, but I didn't have a case at the moment. My laundry was up-to-date for a change, and since I was hoping for free housekeeping in the very near future, I couldn't see spending what I'd mentally declared an official day off slinging a mop around.

I also wondered when we'd hear about the Swamp Bar vote. My understanding was that Whiskey gave people until closing on parade night to get their votes in, then tallied them the next day. As the Swamp Bar didn't have regular hours and it was the pre-New Year's party after the parade, I assumed that meant they'd closed in the wee hours of the morning and Whiskey wouldn't be up and around until noon, at best.

My phone signaled an incoming text from Ida Belle. *You up?*

Me: Yep. Ronald was here to collect the dress for cleaning.

Ida Belle: That man is obsessed.

Me: Apparently, God told him to do it.

Ida Belle: Well, why didn't you say so? That makes all the difference.

I grinned. I could see the sarcasm dripping off my phone.

Ida Belle: I've got news.

Me: Good. I'm bored.

Ida Belle: Great. Be there in a few. Stopping for muffins at Ally's.

Me: Get cranberry if she has them.

My mouth was watering in anticipation when Ida Belle and Gertie tromped into my kitchen ten minutes later and Gertie held up a box.

"They had cranberry," she said. "You want this heated?"

I nodded and she popped some muffins in the microwave while Ida Belle poured them some coffee.

"You're trending on YouTube," Gertie said. "Someone got video of your big fire rescue. When you made those jumps, that dress came up so high it was close to being against terms of service."

I sighed. This was not the way I'd planned on ringing in the new year.

Gertie grabbed the muffins from the microwave and when we'd all stuffed at least one bite in our mouths, I changed the subject.

"So what news do you have?" I asked Ida Belle. "Is the vote in already?"

"No," Ida Belle said. "I don't expect that until this afternoon, but we might have a mystery to work on."

Gertie perked up. "Who died?"

"Does someone have to die before we get involved?" Ida Belle asked.

Gertie shrugged. "Before or after...it's usually on the agenda."

"Well, it so happens you're right this time," Ida Belle said.

"At least it's not someone we like," Gertie said, and popped another bite of muffin in her mouth.

"How do you know that?" I asked.

"Because she would have said we have a problem, not we have a mystery," Gertie mumbled, crumbs falling out as she spoke.

"Great!" I said. "Then I don't have to feel bad about enjoying this muffin so much while someone is dead. So who is it?"

"Brock Benoit," Ida Belle said.

"What?"

"You're kidding!"

Gertie and I both spoke at once.

"So it *was* Brock Benoit at the parade," I said.

Ida Belle nodded. "Appears so."

"How do you know he's dead?" I asked.

"Myrtle called me as soon as she got off shift," Ida Belle said. "Deputy Breaux took the call and found Brock at our favorite motel with a needle in his arm. Heroin is the current call."

"That explains why he's aged an additional ten years," Gertie said.

"But not why you think we have a mystery to solve," I said.

"Deputy Breaux found a pack of cigarettes matching the one that started the fire on RJ's float," Ida Belle said. "So he called for the forensics team to see if they came up with anything."

"So the mystery is, did Brock set the float on fire and if so, why?" I asked.

Gertie shook her head. "That one is going to be easier than a Nancy Drew story. Fortune saw him fighting with RJ right before the parade started, and then she had me take pictures of him standing right up by her float just before it went up in flames. The only thing we don't know is what they were fighting about."

I frowned. "Money. At least, that's what I got out of the tiny bit of conversation I understood."

Ida Belle nodded. "Since when does it make sense to kill the person you're trying to get money out of?"

"You're right," I said. "Sometimes people get killed for not paying out, but that's usually only after they've been given some time to cough up the dough and the guy collecting figures he's never going to see it. Even then..."

"Maybe he just wanted to scare her," Gertie said. "He had to figure she wouldn't die on the float, but also that she'd know it was him that did it. Maybe then, she'd take him seriously."

I shrugged. "Maybe so, but if that's the case, then I still don't see where we have anything to investigate. If Brock had been *murdered*, then the whole thing flops around and RJ becomes the potential perp, but otherwise..."

Ida Belle smiled. "Brock had a knot on the back of his head—like he'd been struck with something."

"Now, that *is* interesting," I said. "Was that cause of death then, and not the heroin?"

"Won't know for sure until the ME makes the call," Ida Belle said.

"*We* won't ever know," Gertie said. "It's not like they advertise their findings. Besides, he could have been drunk or high or whatever and fallen and hit his own head. Even if that's what caused his death, it doesn't mean it wasn't self-inflicted."

"We really need a mole down at the ME's office," Ida Belle said.

"Not necessarily," I said. "If Carter starts investigating, then we'll know it was ruled suspicious at least."

Suddenly, I remembered the guy who had been in the shadows across the street from Brock at the end of the parade. I hadn't even mentioned him the night before because he hadn't been anywhere near the float, and the mystery of the moment had been how the fire had started and by whom.

I told Ida Belle and Gertie what I'd seen.

"Did you get a good look at him?" Ida Belle asked.

I shook my head. "Aside from height and frame, I couldn't tell you anything. He was back too far in the shadows and wearing a trench coat, gloves, and a ball cap pulled down low."

"The trench coat alone is odd," Gertie said. "I know they said on one of those fashion shows that they're supposed to trend again, but they were never popular with men around Sinful."

"They weren't with me either," Ida Belle said. "Too much restriction on movement."

"Well, assuming the guy was pointing at Brock, maybe he

wasn't from around here," I said. "I didn't think to gauge his height in relation to the building, so I'm just guessing based on memory, but I'd say six foot or so and broad shoulders."

"Which describes a ton of people," Gertie said.

"So do we assume Brock and RJ brought trouble to Sinful or that it's been waiting here for them all this time?" I asked. "Or did Brock follow RJ and cause her enough trouble that she snapped, and the man I saw in the crowd was just coincidence and wasn't pointing at Brock at all?"

Ida Belle blew out a breath. "That's a tough one. Seems like RJ was mad enough based on what you saw, and if Brock followed her here to squeeze her for money, that might send her over the edge enough to throw something at him, which would explain a blow to the back of his head. The girl always had a temper, and she likes throwing things, as you saw the other day at the dress shop."

Gertie nodded. "And Lord knows, there's no shortage of people in Sinful with a grudge against Brock. Cecil Tassin comes to mind for sure."

"The father of the pregnant girl Brock skipped out on?" I guessed.

"That's the one." Gertie nodded. "That girl should have never been mixed up with Brock—her dad had already warned her off, but you know that only makes them want the boy more. She wasn't even Brock's type, which is probably why he had her around."

"Let me guess, not really popular and average-looking but with some spending money," I said.

"You got it," Ida Belle said.

"Like Marigold," I said. "You know, the more I learn about those two, the more I dislike them."

"Get in line," Gertie said. "I'm afraid this is one of those cases where there's no shortage of people who wanted a piece of Brock. Before he dashed out of Sinful, he stole the cash stash from the family who let him move in and finish high school."

"Wow. That's some serious character flaw," I said. "But how many of those people he wronged would actually commit a murder? You know them."

Ida Belle shrugged. "Potentially all of them if the circumstances fell just the right way."

"That is a very dark and cynical opinion of our fellow citizens," Gertie said.

"But likely accurate," Ida Belle said. "Anyone's capable. They just have to be pushed in the right way. Or the wrong way. However you want to look at it."

"Does Cecil still live here?" I asked.

"Yes, and Gina," Ida Belle said. "Her mother died shortly after Gina had the baby—massive heart failure. It ran in her family, but Gina's situation probably didn't help matters. Gina finished high school but didn't do anything after. She still lives with her dad and he helps her with her son. She keeps a couple of other people's kids at her home for some money. As far as I know, Brock has never even seen the boy."

"So he's probably not paying support," I said.

"In order to pay support, you'd have to have money," Gertie said. "I know for a fact Cecil made Gina get a child support order, but if Brock's been playing bars and other off-the-books work, she probably hasn't seen much of anything."

"Interesting," I said. "Still, it's been years since Brock left, and if Cecil is helping support his daughter, would he risk trouble with the law over a run-in with Brock now?"

"I'd like to think he's smarter than that, but it *is* his daughter we're talking about," Ida Belle said. "And then with his wife dying right after all that went down... Let's just say I could see where the man might still be holding a big grudge."

"For sure," Gertie agreed. "But it looks like RJ is going to be in the hot seat if it's deemed suspicious. Especially given what Fortune saw Brock say and with it looking like he was the one to set the fire to her float."

"I assume she's staying with her mother?"

"Of course," Ida Belle said. "So they can plot their takeover of the two best men in Sinful."

I nodded and stared out the window. "I wonder why RJ came home. Carter said he couldn't remember her doing so but a couple times. So why now?"

"To get away from Brock?" Gertie suggested.

"But this is the first place Brock would look, and it appears that's just what he did," I pointed out. "Would RJ's mother give her money if she asked?"

"Sure," Ida Belle said. "And being broke and in trouble is probably the reason RJ's here. But there's money and there's *money*. Sawyer-James isn't exactly Sinful's richest citizen. She's not even average."

Gertie nodded. "Marie told her she'd be fined if she didn't fix her front porch. It's about to fall in, along with several other things at her house."

Ida Belle snorted. "She tried to get Walter to fix stuff for free...well, not free, but 'in exchange.' Anyway, he wasn't interested. Felicia, down at the bank, told me Sawyer put in for a draw on her line of credit and was pitching a fit because it wouldn't be approved until next week. Apparently, she had a line on some cheap contractor only in town for the holidays."

"More likely she'd have paid up front and been taken for a ride," Gertie said. "She was never good with finances. Her last husband complained about her spending all the time. Most think that's why he left her."

"Or she was trying to get the money for RJ," Ida Belle said. "She's foolish enough to think RJ would pay it back."

I shook my head. "Well, at the moment, RJ looks like the number one suspect if this turns out to be foul play. So unless she's got an ironclad alibi, this isn't much of a mystery. Most likely, she knew it was him that started the fire and if her mother couldn't cough up whatever Brock was asking for, then maybe she decided to confront him."

"And tossed an ashtray or something else fairly heavy at him," Ida Belle said. "I could totally see that happening, but if that's the way it played out and if the head injury was the real cause of death and not the drugs, the DA would likely call it manslaughter rather than homicide."

Gertie nodded. "Either would put RJ in prison. It's just a matter of time allotted."

I turned up my hands. "Well, until we know for sure that Carter is investigating, there's no crime except the arson and that's pretty much solved as far as I'm concerned. And if it *does* turn out to be suspicious, we still don't have a related client and aren't likely to get one given the victim. So I can't see a reason to shove ourselves into an investigation."

"What about dying of boredom?" Gertie asked. "Is that a good enough reason to get involved?"

I had to admit, I was beyond bored. And catching a murderer would be a great way to kick off the new year, but I had to weigh my abundant free time against the flak I'd get from Carter if I jumped into his investigation with no stake. It wasn't as though Brock was a friend or that a friend had been accused of killing him.

But the boredom was so very real. Unfortunately, so was the solution to the mystery.

"I suppose it wouldn't hurt to ask some questions," I said. "Assuming Carter takes it on. If he doesn't, then we have to assume Brock was clumsy and the drugs killed him. But I have to tell you, I think this one is going to be a slam dunk."

"Good enough," Ida Belle agreed.

"Any word on Marigold?" Gertie asked.

"She's going to be released this morning," Ida Belle said. "No lung damage. Just an anxiety attack, although in Marigold's case there's not really a 'just.'"

I nodded. "They probably drugged her up to calm her down. Is she in therapy?"

"She was for a while after the accident happened," Ida Belle said. "Not sure if she still is, although she probably needs to be, given the way she reacted to the fire."

"A lot of soldiers stay in therapy the rest of their lives," I said. "Keeps them balanced out enough to function. Kinda like taking a pill for high blood pressure. You can't really go off it unless you find another way to manage the issue."

"Well, hopefully she'll be able to put it behind her," Ida Belle said. "Christina's had enough to deal with all these years. She doesn't need things going from bad to worse."

"We should drop by later with a casserole," Gertie said. "At least dinner would be one thing off her plate."

Ida Belle sighed. "Great. That gives us all of one thing to do today while we're waiting on Whiskey to crawl out of bed and count those votes."

"I know," I agreed. "I was just trying to figure out something to occupy time when you texted."

"At least we have Nora's New Year's party tonight," Gertie said, shifting the tone from serious to cheerful. "I can't wait!"

I looked over at Ida Belle, who shook her head.

"I don't think Carter shares your enthusiasm," I said.

Given Nora's recreational drug habit and large bank account, she took a couple trips every year just to sample new and different drugs or the same drugs but in a different way. She spent her time in Sinful regaling the locals with tales of her adventures and attempting to share contraband with people who visited her. How she managed to get stuff into the country without getting arrested, I have no idea. Carter tended to walk away as soon as her name came up in conversation. Given that she was harmless and donated a lot of money locally, he didn't want to have to arrest her. So it was a case of not knowing meaning not having to do something about it.

"At least we know the booze will be good," Ida Belle allowed. "Nora's a professional drinker, and her taste doesn't run to the cheap stuff."

"I know for a fact she hired Molly to cater it," Gertie said.

"Really?" I perked up. Molly was a caterer I'd met during a case, and although she looked like the Hulk and spent her spare time cage-fighting, she cooked like an angel.

Gertie nodded, looking excited. "I saw her at the boat store when I was getting some aluminum weld, and she told me she had a bunch of trays to drop off and that we'd better get in line fast because she expects everything to go quickly."

Ida Belle narrowed her eyes at Gertie. "Why were you getting aluminum weld?"

Gertie waved a hand in dismissal. "I just need to make a small boat repair."

"What's wrong with your boat?" I asked.

"I had an accident with a pier," Gertie said.

"What kind of accident?" I asked. "And whose pier?"

"The bigger issue here is that Gertie plans on fixing her boat herself," Ida Belle said. "Propane, welding..."

"Ah," I said, now on board with Ida Belle's train of thought. "Yeah, you and fire are not a good look. Why don't you ask Scooter to do it?"

"I'll think about it," Gertie said, but I was willing to bet she was already done thinking and had no intention of hiring out for the job. I just hoped she didn't burn her house down.

"Is Molly going to stay for the party?" I asked, turning the conversation away from another potential fire event.

"Nora invited her, of course," Gertie said, "but Molly has a date, so she passed."

"A date?" I asked.

"Must be with a superhero," Ida Belle said. "I can't see her respecting anyone she could take in a fight."

"Fortune respects Carter," Gertie pointed out. "And she can outshoot him."

"Yes, but I don't think she could take him hand-to-hand," Ida Belle said.

"Maybe not, but he'd have to catch her first," Gertie said, and we all laughed.

"So, anyone got any ideas what to do today?" I asked. "Anything that doesn't involve shopping or watching television. I am maxed out on both."

Gertie gave us a sly look. "We could take a look at RJ's float, maybe see if we spot something the arson investigator didn't."

"I thought it was torn down last night," I said.

"Nope," Gertie said. "The arson investigator said they had to hold it until he got the official okay to close the case."

"And now that a death might be linked to it," I said, "that means it might have to sit for longer."

"Sure," Ida Belle agreed. "But where is it being stored? Because none of Celia's crew is going to let us stroll over and inspect it."

"Beatrice Paulson's house," Gertie said.

I perked up. "Really?"

Beatrice was a member of Celia's crew, but Ida Belle had brought her over to the dark side years ago after her husband had been dead for the required number of years to be a Sinful Lady. They'd kept the entire thing between Ida Belle, Beatrice, and Gertie with Beatrice serving as Ida Belle's spy in Celia's organization. Given that Beatrice hadn't been in the know on much lately, we suspected that Celia was onto her, but no one was letting the cat out of the bag just yet.

"Remember, in the backyard, her husband built that eyesore of a storage building for that eyesore of an RV," Gertie said.

"That's right," Ida Belle said. "The mayor made him plant the biggest trees he could find around it to try to block the view from the street."

Gertie nodded. "Well, Beatrice sold the RV before her husband's body was even cold—she always hated the thing— but she never got around to tearing the building down. The float fits inside, and it's enclosed so it can't be damaged by the weather."

"And since the float was the purview of Celia's crew, the investigator figured it would be safe there," Ida Belle said.

"Well, given that the only other options were to convince someone to spend the night cleaning out space in a barn or store it at Big and Little's place, Beatrice was his best option," Gertie said. "Except for the part where the investigator—and Carter for that matter—don't know that Beatrice is really on our side. So what do you say?"

"Give her a call," I said. "It can't hurt to take a look, and it's not like we have anything better to do. Besides, I've spent entirely too much time doing girlie things this week. I'd like to finish on a different note."

Gertie clapped her hands and pulled her phone out of her purse.

CHAPTER SEVEN

BEATRICE WAS HAPPY TO INDULGE US BUT SAID WE NEEDED to get over there quickly as the arson investigator had just left and told her he was hoping to release the trailer that afternoon. I figured they'd either decided to pin it on Brock or chalk it up to blatant stupidity. But with no one injured and no expectation of it happening again, given that the main suspect was dead and the parade was over, it seemed a reasonable decision.

Of course, Carter still wouldn't be pleased if he found out what we were up to, so we needed to make this happen quickly and with as little fanfare as possible.

Beatrice was waiting outside when we arrived. Ida Belle had parked at the end of the block in front of one of the Sinful Ladies' homes and we'd hiked it up the sidewalk, hoping no one was paying close attention. Beatrice ran down her front porch steps as soon as we arrived and motioned us to the side gate. She was practically huffing as she rushed us to a large metal building partially hidden by trees.

"That arson investigator called," she said as we hurried

behind her. "He's releasing the float soon. Celia will have her people over here to get it right away, I'm sure. The decorations and the wood to build the platforms were donated but the trailer belongs to one of the local farmers. Celia rented it and he's raising hell that it wasn't back today for him to use to haul hay. He's charging her a full day's rent again and she's fit to be tied, especially after what she spent on dressing that floozy up for the parade."

"I'm sure it won't take us long," I said, which wasn't a lie because I didn't expect to find anything of merit. "We'll just get a look and some pictures and be long gone before any of Celia's crew shows up to collect the float."

Beatrice punched in a code on a keypad near the huge garage door and it slid noisily up. "Needs oiling—but then everything around here creaks." She laughed.

"Why not come in using the side entry door?" Gertie asked.

"One, because it sticks," Beatrice said. "Two, because the lights don't work. This place has had electrical problems since it was built. Of course, that would be because my cheap husband insisted on doing the wiring himself. Anyway, if that garage door weren't open, you wouldn't be able to see a thing given there's no windows."

"What about the neighbors?" Gertie asked.

"You're okay," Beatrice said. "The fence prevents anyone ground level from seeing inside when the door's open and that big oak up front blocks anyone upstairs in the house across the street from getting a view."

Ida Belle nodded. "Then get back to your house and play lookout. If anyone shows up, text me and we'll clear out."

"I'll close the blinds on the back of the house," Beatrice said. "In the event of an emergency, just leave the garage door open and head across to the other side of the yard and exit through that gate. Don't risk going over the fence and into someone else's yard. I'm surrounded by people with big dogs with bad attitudes."

"Got it," I said, hoping that no emergencies cropped up. Running across a backyard to exit through a fence gate didn't sound like a big deal, but then, a whole lot of things that happened during our investigations hadn't seemed like a big deal going in and had turned out to be disasters. Fortunately, not all of them were on YouTube. Especially fortunate as most of the disasters included things that weren't exactly legal.

Beatrice hurried off and I started walking around the float, checking it out. The platform that held the throne was the most scorched, although the trailer itself was fine since the bottom was metal. It just had a black spot that hopefully wouldn't affect the integrity since the fire hadn't burned for too long.

"Looks like the fire didn't get farther than the platform," Ida Belle said. "There's some charring on the outside of the bottom and up around the throne where it crept up."

"Probably ran up those tissue flowers," I said. "I thought you had rules about flammable stuff."

"It's not possible to be entirely nonflammable," Gertie said. "Even people are flammable."

"There's a pleasant thought," Ida Belle said.

"Just saying," Gertie said. "But all the paper wasn't the best call. Still, there's only so many things to decorate with, and with the fire extinguishers and volunteers on hand, we figured it would be all right."

"Technically, it was," I said. "No one died."

Gertie laughed. "The advantage of setting the bar really, really low."

"I'm not so sure that 'no one died' is a low bar in Sinful," I said.

I pulled out my phone and took some shots of the float from the rear. I could see where the fire had started underneath the platform. The ash from the paper flowers was long gone—likely during transport to this building as the cold front had started to move in right at the end of the parade. I could see the scorch lines up the outside of the platform that Ida Belle had identified and made sure I captured several shots with them in it. I had no idea if the pictures would be useful, but what I did know was that soon, it wouldn't be possible to get any.

I took a couple steps back and got a shot of the entire float from the rear, so that I could put things into perspective later, if needed. Then I asked Gertie for a glove and a baggie, since she always had supplies in her giant and questionable handbag. Once gloved, I tugged on one of the flowers next to a bare spot on the back of the trailer until it came loose, then popped it in the bag.

"What are you going to do with that?" Gertie asked.

"I don't know," I said. "Just thought I'd snag one before they all go in the trash. Looks like the forensics team did it, so I figured we should too."

"I wish we had our own lab, like James Bond," Gertie said.

"Bond is a government spy," I said. "Their budget is a little better than ours."

Ida Belle started to say something, then stopped and pulled her phone out of her pocket.

"Crap!" she said. "Celia and RJ are here and demanding to see the float. Beatrice won't physically restrain them, and you know Celia's not going to just leave."

"What the heck does she want with the float?" I asked as I ran for the door.

"Who knows?" Ida Belle said as she ran past me.

"Help! I'm caught on something!"

I whirled around and saw Gertie, trying to run, but held in place by her handbag, whose strap was lodged in a crack in the trailer frame. I ran back and tugged on the strap as Gertie slipped out from under it, but it was stuck in there good. Leaving the handbag wasn't an option because Celia would know right away who it belonged to. Gertie and I yanked on the strap with everything I had but it didn't budge even a millimeter.

"Please tell me you have something in there that will help besides dynamite," I said to Gertie.

As I opened the purse, Ida Belle, who'd apparently circled back to see why we weren't coming, reached around me and cut the purse strap on both sides of the rail with the knife she always carried. As I whirled around with the bag, I heard voices outside the fence.

Crap!

As predicted, Celia had ignored Beatrice and was about to come into the backyard. It was too late to make a dash for the other side of the yard and with the garage door wide open, we were sitting ducks. I ran for the garage door opener and hit it before sprinting for the rear of the garage. There had to be someplace to hide.

But the rear of the building was completely void of anything. Apparently, Beatrice *really* didn't use it. There wasn't even a trash can to hide behind and with no windows at all and no rear door, we were out of options. I looked up, hoping for an answer, and something about the roof bothered me. I scanned the length of the building, then looked along the floor on the back wall and my pulse shot up.

There was a gap between the metal wall and the concrete that was too big to not be intentional, but I couldn't see daylight under it. I scanned the walls and found a spot where the metal didn't quite align and pushed on it. A secret door popped open and we hurried inside, barely getting the door closed before the garage door started going up again.

The room was pitch black except for the tiny strip of light coming in under the metal wall that hid the room from the rest of the structure. I turned on the flashlight on my phone and shone it in the dark, just in case there was a secret exit on the outside of the building. Directly behind us was a huge gun safe. Large enough to fit people inside, but the door was standing wide open and it was empty.

I turned to the other side and saw that the room was about five feet deep and ran the whole width of the garage. On the opposite side from the safe, I saw familiar metal tanks with tubes and elbowed Ida Belle. She looked over and I felt her body tense. It was a moonshine still. Good Lord Almighty! No wonder Beatrice didn't want law enforcement at her house. She was making moonshine in her backyard.

Not only was it illegal—it was dangerous as hell. One clogged line or a thin vapor leak and any form of spark would blow the still right through the walls, which was why Sinful residents hid their stills in the bayous. Ida Belle grabbed Gertie's arm and motioned to the still, then pointed at her purse. Good call. There was probably no end to the additional trauma Gertie's purse could add if things went up in smoke.

I heard footsteps and we all leaned against the wall to hear what was happening.

"Who's in here?" Celia said.

"No one," Beatrice said.

"Then why did that door close?" Celia asked.

"Electrical problems," Beatrice said.

"You're sure no one else has been inside?" Celia asked.

"I already told you that arson investigator said no one

could be in here," Beatrice said. "That includes you, incidentally."

"I paid for the contents on that float," Celia said. "And besides, you said he's going to release it. What difference does it make if I'm here now or later?"

"Apparently, it makes a difference to you, since you wouldn't accept 'later' as an answer," Beatrice said.

"I've a very busy woman," Celia said. "And RJ needs to find her bracelet."

"You know, it's probably melted to the bottom of the trailer," Beatrice said. "But knock yourself out. I'm going back inside so that if arson investigator shows up, I'm not the one in trouble."

"I don't get why we're here," RJ said a bit later. "I wasn't even wearing a bracelet."

"We're here to figure out how that fire started," Celia said.

"I already told you it was that psycho Brock," RJ said. "I left Nashville to get away from him and he followed me here. He was standing right next to the float before that fire broke out."

"But how could he do it without someone seeing?" Celia said. "And that arson investigator was downright insulting—accusing me of storing paper flowers under the platform. He made it sound like I was to blame for this. And with Marigold Forrester going to the hospital over it. I don't need the kind of trouble that could bring."

I could practically feel Ida Belle and Gertie's disgust at Celia's statement. Marigold might not have been physically injured, but her mental state was precarious enough to start with and no one knew how this would affect her long term. But Celia was making herself the victim, as usual.

"Marigold will be fine, I'm sure," RJ said. "I was closest to the fire and I'm breathing fine. She's always been a sensitive sort, but there's nothing wrong with her."

"Well, I don't care what that man says," Celia said. "I did not leave paper back here."

"Maybe it was one of the others," RJ said. "There were lots of people helping. Or maybe something blew under the platform when the wind picked up. Brock might have seen it happen and taken advantage of the situation. Maybe the cops can get it out of him as soon as they run him down."

"You think he's still hanging around?" Celia asked.

"Doubt it," RJ said. "I'm sure he hightailed it back to Nashville before the cops could go looking for him. Anyway, if you're done, I really want to get out of here. I was hoping to drop by the Swamp Bar and see if I could butter up Whiskey, maybe swing that vote counting in my favor."

"I don't like the idea of you hanging out with that disreputable man," Celia said.

"It's money for me and a chance for you to lord over Ida Belle and Gertie," RJ said.

"Well, I suppose it wouldn't hurt for you to talk with him—maybe offer to sing at the bar for free?"

Even though no one could see, I couldn't help rolling my eyes. I had no doubt about RJ's intent to offer up freebies, but I didn't think for a minute it was going to be about her singing.

"I'm just trying to see—" Celia said. "What the hell is wrong with the lights in this place? Beatrice should keep this maintained properly."

I could hear Celia flip the light switch over and over and then the light inside the secret room came on, blinked on and off, and I heard a familiar sizzle. Panicked, I whirled around and shoved Ida Belle and Gertie into the safe, then crammed in with them and pulled the door.

Just as the still exploded.

I heard screaming outside the safe. One was Celia—I'd recognize her voice anywhere. I assumed the other was RJ. Then footsteps running away from the garage. I leaned against the safe door to peer out, but it didn't budge.

Holy crap! We were locked inside.

CHAPTER EIGHT

"Open the door," Gertie said. "I'm getting claustrophobic."

"Something must have hit the handle in the blast," I said.

"We're locked in here?" Gertie asked.

"Don't panic," I said. "Beatrice will be out here soon and can open the safe."

"How much air do we have?" Gertie asked.

"Less if you keep breathing like you're in labor," Ida Belle said.

"Beatrice won't even know we're in here," Gertie said.

A wave of panic washed over me. Gertie was right. Beatrice would assume we'd hightailed it out of the building before Celia arrived. I pulled out my phone and looked at the display, but I already knew the score. A cell signal wasn't going to penetrate that much metal.

I did a quick assessment of the size of the safe and three people's oxygen needs, and it didn't come up favorable. The blast would certainly send the fire department running, but the question was, would they make it in time?

"Oh my God!" Beatrice's voice sounded outside. "Nora, what have you done?"

Nora? I shook my head. The still was now starting to make sense.

"Beatrice!" I yelled. "We're in the safe! Help!"

A couple seconds later, I heard the sound of metal scratching against the door.

"Fortune?" Beatrice asked.

"Yes. We're trapped. Open the door?"

"Oh my God!" Beatrice said. "What's the combination?"

"It's your safe!" I yelled, trying not to panic. Or panic more.

"I know," she said. "Let me think. I opened it to sell the guns after my husband died."

Okay. Full-on panic. I didn't know exactly when Beatrice's husband died, but I knew it had to be ten years at least before she was eligible to be a member of the Sinful Ladies.

"I might have it written down somewhere in my kitchen," Beatrice said. "Or maybe it's in my safe-deposit box."

"We don't have that kind of time," Ida Belle said. "Think! It had to be something easy or he wouldn't have remembered it either."

"Your birthday?" I suggested.

Gertie snorted. "Men don't remember birthdays."

"I guess their anniversary is out then," I said.

"*His* birthday."

"1-2-3."

"His lucky number three times."

Gertie and I started throwing out ideas, but there was no sound of movement coming from the other side of the safe door.

"The day he won the state fishing rodeo!" Ida Belle yelled.

"That's it!" Beatrice said and I heard the clicking of the dial.

"It's not working!" she yelled seconds later. "I can't remember if I spin it twice past or three times, then twice. I only opened it once."

"Just stay calm, Beatrice," I said. "Things can't get any worse."

"Sure they can."

Carter's voice sounded outside the safe.

Busted.

———

WE SAT ON THE BACK PORCH WITH A CLEAR VIEW OF THE building, which now sported a huge hole in the roof and back wall, as Carter stood above us, frowning. The blast had sent sparks of fire in every direction and the already-damaged float was now a smoldering mess. The entire floor of the building was covered with ash and water from the firemen's handiwork.

Beatrice ran around us, trying to ply us with water and aspirin and begging us to breathe, even though we were clearly all right. Physically, anyway. Criminally, we were way over the line.

Carter had managed to get the safe open with the fishing championship date, and we'd sprinted right past him and across the yard just as the firemen pulled in the driveway. We'd stayed in Ida Belle's SUV until the fire was out, then headed back to face the music. We couldn't leave Beatrice hanging out to dry, even though she'd been the one harboring an illegal still and Celia had been the one who caused it to blow with all that light-switch flipping.

Of course, Celia and RJ had taken off right after the explosion, I'm sure with zero intention of admitting they were anywhere near the mess, much less part of the reason for it.

"I don't even know where to start," Carter said.

"You could start by letting us get the heck out of here before the arson investigator shows up," Ida Belle said.

"And why would I do that?" Carter asked.

"Because we don't want him to get the wrong idea," I said.

"Ha," Carter said. "And what would be the right idea?"

"That I was here to look at the gun safe?" Ida Belle suggested. "I might want to buy it."

"Uh-huh. And you just failed to notice the still in the room?" he asked.

"Yeah, that won't work," Ida Belle agreed. "Okay, how about Beatrice never knew about the secret room or the still and we were never here."

"I can work with that," Beatrice said.

"Why is there a secret room in your garage?" Carter asked.

"My husband did it, the old fool," Beatrice said. "Toward the end, he was convinced someone was coming for his guns, so he built the room and hid all his guns and ammunition in there."

"And he ran that still out here?" Carter asked.

"Lord no!" Beatrice said. "I was, um, storing it for a friend. But I swear, it wasn't running when it was put in here. I don't know why it exploded."

"What friend?" Carter asked.

"I'd rather not say," Beatrice said.

"I don't care what you'd rather not do," Carter said. "That still has been running, and recently, or it wouldn't have had a vapor leak. Someone better tell me what the heck is going on here. Did it belong to the Sinful Ladies?"

Ida Belle glared at him. "I would *never*."

"Then who?" He stared at Beatrice.

"I was storing it for Nora," Beatrice said. "She was over here yesterday to check on it. But I didn't know she was...but I guess she..."

I swear Carter paled a bit. "Nora?"

"You see, there was this DEA agent who came sniffing around her camp," Beatrice said. "And she was afraid he'd find the still, so she asked me to hide it for her until things cooled off. But I swear, she wasn't supposed to run it until she got it back out in the bayou."

"That woman is going to bring the entire federal government down on us," Ida Belle said.

"I didn't even realize Nora was making her own brew," Gertie said. "I bet it's fantastic."

"I can vouch," Beatrice said. "But you only want to take one shot and you should probably be sitting down in your own home when you do it. She calls it Instant Coma. I only tried it once and slept for twenty-four hours. It also takes rust off metal pipes."

"I bet it's a real joy for the kidneys," I said. "Remind me not to drink anything at Nora's tonight that doesn't come out of a bottle—a bottle I personally opened."

"Assuming we're not in jail tonight," Gertie grumbled.

Beatrice's phone rang and it startled her so much she dropped it. "Good Lord, I need to get it together. I don't know how you three do all this sneaky stuff. Oh Lord, it's that arson guy."

She answered the phone and did a lot of nodding, which the arson guy couldn't see, but finally hung up, the panicked look returning.

"He said he'll be here in five minutes," she said.

"Now or never," Ida Belle said to Carter.

Gertie nodded. "Otherwise, you're going to have to arrest

all of us and then pay Nora a visit. Do you really want us taking up all your jail space on New Year's Eve?"

Carter looked at all of us, and I could see all the implications running through his mind as he weighed the benefits and costs against the homicide investigation he might have to launch. He must have decided, as I had, that the still explosion didn't have anything to do with Brock's death or the float fire and would only muddy the waters if he mingled the two, because finally he sighed and gestured to the street.

"Go," he said. "Before I change my mind."

We didn't need to be told twice.

We jumped up and headed across Beatrice's backyard for the second time that day.

"Not you, Beatrice," Carter called out, and I looked back to see a guilty-looking Beatrice, plodding behind us.

"Go with the story about not knowing the still was there," Ida Belle said. "The bad electricity could have set off that still, whether it was running or not. And since it's in pieces all over the backyard, no one will be able to prove it was on."

Beatrice perked up a little. "Really?"

Ida Belle nodded. "Just offer it up as soon as the arson investigator gets here, and that way Carter will have to roll with it."

"You think he will?" Beatrice asked.

"For Carter, skating past the truth about something illegal where no harm was done, except to a building, is a much better option than having to arrest Nora," I said. "Trust me on that one."

Gertie nodded. "Especially on the day when half the town is invited to her house for a party. He does not want her sitting in jail and all those people with nowhere to go. That's a recipe for disaster."

She didn't look completely convinced but turned around

and headed back to the driveway as we set off for the side gate, then down the sidewalk, half running. We were all huffing a little when we got into Ida Belle's SUV—partly from the half running, partly from the stress, and mostly because we'd recently had limited air and breathing a lot right now just felt good.

"Well, that was interesting," I said as Ida Belle pulled away.

"Right?" Gertie agreed. "I had no idea Nora had a still."

I looked back at her. "Everything that just happened, and Nora's still is the first thing that comes to mind?"

"The secret room was an attention grabber as well," she said. "And I'm a little surprised that Carter let us go. I know he doesn't want to tangle with Nora, but still...get it, *still*."

She started laughing and Ida Belle sighed.

"I think she's talking about Celia and RJ," Ida Belle said. "You know, the investigation?"

"Oh," Gertie said. "Well, Celia showing up to lord over Beatrice wasn't a surprise. Or her completely ignoring the arson investigator in favor of what she wanted right now. What Celia wants is her default."

"I know that," I said. "I was referring to her claim that there wasn't anything under the platform."

"She just doesn't want to be on the hook for anything wrong with Marigold," Gertie said.

"I'm sure that's part of it," Ida Belle said. "But as much as Celia hates being wrong, she also hates being ignored. If she told her people not to store anything under the platform and one of them did anyway, she'll be on a rampage."

"Especially if she thinks she's on the hook for it," I said.

"But she's not on the hook," Gertie said. "Unless she's the one who threw the cigarette on the float, and we already know that was Brock."

"*Probably* Brock," I said.

Gertie waved a hand in dismissal. "The fact is there's no law or rule against putting things under the platforms. It's just not good common sense."

"Well...Celia," I pointed out.

"I find it more interesting that RJ is going to try her wiles on Whiskey to swing the vote her way," Ida Belle said. "Along with her comment about the money and Brock."

"I'll bet she was hoping for the bet winnings to pay off Brock, and her backup was to skip town to somewhere he wouldn't come looking for her," I said.

"But she told Celia that Brock had probably hightailed it back to Nashville." Gertie's eyes widened. "Which means she doesn't know Brock is dead. Which means—"

"She didn't kill him," Ida Belle said.

I nodded. "Which makes the unknown guy I saw at the parade a whole lot more interesting."

———

ASIDE FROM CHECKING IN ON MARIGOLD AND CHRISTINA once they got home from the hospital, we didn't really have anything else to do. Or that we wanted to do, I should say. Domestic responsibilities tended to pale in comparison to a murder mystery, and as much as we were all itching to stick our noses into police business, we didn't have an avenue of investigation to pursue at the moment.

The motel would be crawling with cops, so it was off-limits until they cleared out. There was no point in questioning RJ. She'd fling whatever she was drinking on us when she opened the door. And her mother wasn't about to dish on her own daughter, so we had no way of knowing what had happened in Nashville that had caused the rift between her and Brock or sent her back to hide in Sinful. Gina Tassin would be neck-deep in toddlers, and no way was I going to attempt to work Brock into a conversation with her son there when he was the child's nonexistent father. And since she lived with her father, he wasn't a good option for questioning either.

I had a grocery order waiting for pickup at the General Store, so we decided to head there and maybe make a swing by Ally's just to see how business was going. At least Gertie would get a chance to pump her for information on her relationship with Mannie. So far, Ally had been really tight-lipped about spending time with the Heberts' right-hand man, much to Gertie's dismay. I knew Ally had seen Mannie a couple of times since her store opened, but the parade was the first time they'd been in public together.

Of course, given that everyone in Sinful knew Ally was my best friend and most knew I was 'in' with Big and Little Hebert, they probably didn't think much of seeing Mannie and Ally in the same public space. Besides, everyone knew they were friendly as Mannie had done the security installation for Ally's bakery. If anyone suspected they were more than just casual acquaintances, they weren't letting on.

Neither was Ally. But I knew better.

Walter had my groceries boxed and stacked behind the counter, so I stayed to pay while Ida Belle and Gertie headed out to load them up, then I would meet them at the bakery. The store had a steady stream of people picking up last-minute items for the night's celebrations. There probably wasn't anyone in Sinful who wouldn't be celebrating in some way, whether in groups or alone. Walter had stocked up on snacks in anticipation, but the shelves of chips, nuts, and cookies were still already half empty and it wasn't even noon yet.

"Looks like you could have handled more snacks," I said as the store emptied out and Walter was finally able to ring me up.

"Nah," Walter said. "Everyone gets out early because they're afraid I'll run out, so the big rush is over. This afternoon will be all the people hungover from partying at the Swamp Bar last night."

"Makes sense," I said.

The bell sounded and Walter smiled and waved. I turned around and saw Carter headed toward me, but he wasn't returning Walter's smile.

Uh-oh.

"Something wrong?" Walter asked Carter.

"We might have had some trouble this morning," I said.

Walter raised an eyebrow. "It's not even noon."

"We're overachievers," I said.

"Ha," Carter said. "That's leaving out a whole lot of description, but it's best if that particular achievement doesn't get around. Especially as Beatrice just finished lying to the arson investigator and I went along with it."

Walter held up his hands. "I don't even want to know. So is that what's bothering you?"

"Not exactly," Carter said. "But I can't talk about it."

Walter nodded. "You mean about Brock Benoit being dead?"

Carter looked over at me, I assumed waiting for the surprised look. When none was forthcoming, he sighed.

"So now I know the reason for your morning of over-achievement," he said. "How did you two find out?"

Walter raised one eyebrow. I just shrugged.

"Ida Belle," Carter said. "I should have known. She probably knew before I did. That woman has spies everywhere."

"She does," Walter said. "But by lunch, half the town will have heard about it if they haven't already, and that won't have come from Ida Belle. You know how things are."

"Is it a suspicious death?" I asked.

He frowned but remained silent.

"If you start investigating, I'm going to have my answer anyway," I said.

"As of now, it's suspicious," he said. "The official determination won't happen until the ME is done, but I'll start questioning people right away."

"You talked to RJ yet?" I asked.

Walter laughed. "Given that she was in the bakery this morning loading up on chocolate chip cookies, I'm going to guess that's a yes."

"It so happens, I haven't been to the sheriff's department this morning," Carter said. "I've been busy with a suspicious death and an even more suspicious explosion."

"What explosion?" Walter asked. "Is that what I heard earlier?"

"That would be the overachieving thing," I said. "You might want to check stock for a minute."

Walter clued in and fled to the storeroom.

"Celia and RJ were in Beatrice's garage looking at the float this morning," I said.

Carter cursed. "You've got to be kidding me. What for?"

I told him what we'd heard, including RJ's plan to go tempt Whiskey for votes.

He frowned as I spoke, and I knew he was processing the information and arriving at the same conclusion I had.

When I was finished, he blew out a breath and ran one hand through his hair. "I'm going to need you and Gertie to come in sometime today and give an official statement about the parade fire."

"Okay," I said. "We were about to check in with Ally, then I'll get my groceries home. We can come back after. Does that work?"

He nodded. "Anytime this afternoon is fine. Deputy Breaux can record it and get it typed up. I'm going to be out..."

"There is one other thing," I said.

He stared at me and sighed. "I'm afraid to ask."

"At the end of the parade, there was this guy standing on the sidewalk on the other side of the street from Brock."

I told him what I'd seen.

"I didn't mention it last night because I didn't think it was relevant," I said. "He wasn't close enough to be involved with the fire, but now that Brock's dead, and it doesn't look like RJ knows that yet..."

Carter nodded. "You can't tell me anything else about him?"

"Sorry, no. Cecil Tassin might be a good one to talk to," I said.

Carter grimaced. "Yeah. That thought had already run through my mind."

He didn't look thrilled with the prospect, and I couldn't say that I blamed him, even though I planned on talking to the man myself as soon as he was available.

Walter poked his head out of the storeroom, and Carter waved him over.

"You're good," Carter said. "And I best get going. I'm already behind and with New Year's tonight, my day isn't going to get any better."

He gave me a hard look. "I know it goes without saying—"

"Don't get involved in police business," I said. "Don't worry. I think one explosion is enough for today."

Walter put his hands over his ears. "Not listening again."

"Probably a good idea," Carter said.

"The sheriff needs to retire," Walter said as he removed his hands. "*That* would be a good idea. Then you could take his seat and hire someone else to help. You've been pulling double weight for far too long while the sheriff rides around on his horse, causing more problems than he solves."

"Some more help would be nice," Carter said, "but you know as well as I do that the sheriff is going to die on that horse, wearing that badge. I'll see you later."

He headed out and Walter watched him go, shaking his head. "That boy is having to work entirely too hard. This town is changing—has been for a while now. One man, a deputy with minimal experience, and an old coot who can't remember what day it is most times aren't enough to keep this place in line anymore."

I nodded. "Maybe he should talk to Marie—see if there's funds in the budget to add a new deputy even if the sheriff is still on the payroll."

"He should, but he won't. You know how stubborn he is, especially about admitting he might need help."

"I get it, but it's not a matter of if he can handle things—he has been. It's a matter of whether or not he *should* be handling everything, and I agree with you that Sinful is ready for a bigger police presence. Tell you what, I'll pass the idea by Marie myself. If I'm suggesting something on behalf of Carter's well-being, she'll take it seriously."

Walter nodded. "And I'll keep the fact that you're going to do so a secret because neither one of us needs the grief we'd get."

"Isn't that the truth. You going to the party tonight?"

Walter grimaced. "Since I haven't figured out a decent way to get out of it, I suppose I have to. I would say I'm hoping Nora doesn't cause a scene, but the woman was pretty much born into the role."

"Could be worse. You could be going to a party at Celia's."

"Everyone has that line in the sand for what they'll do for love."

"Good thing for you that Ida Belle likes Celia even less than you do. I'll see you tonight."

"Uh-huh. Don't you three go 'overachieving' again in the meantime. Carter needs help, but he won't be liking any from your direction."

I turned in the doorway and grinned at him. "We can't always get what we want."

CHAPTER NINE

I CROSSED THE STREET AND HEADED OVER TO THE BAKERY. Ally was doing a brisk business and had a line of people at the counter. A young woman I'd never seen before was behind the counter with her. Since she was wearing a T-shirt with the bakery logo on it and currently stuffing muffins in a bag for a customer, I assumed Ally had hired some help.

Twenty-ish. Five foot five. A hundred fifteen pounds. Good muscle tone. Threat level lower than the blood sugar spike those muffins would give me.

Ida Belle and Gertie had taken up residence at a table in the back corner and were sipping lattes. There was a plate of some kind of Danish-looking thing in my spot, along with a latte, and I sank into the chair with a smile.

"I guess you haven't had a chance to harass Ally about Mannie," I said, pointing at the counter.

"Not even a millisecond," Gertie said. "That line hasn't stopped since we walked in."

"It's great for Ally, though," Ida Belle said. "And besides, if she doesn't want to talk about her and Mannie, she doesn't have to. Some people prefer to keep their romantic entanglements from public consumption."

"Says the queen of the down-low," Gertie said. "Just how long were you and Walter on the sly before you agreed to marry him?"

Ida Belle grinned. "I'll never tell."

"Who's the new girl?" I asked.

They both shook their heads.

"Never seen her before," Gertie said. "If things ever clear in here, we'll find out."

Ally saw me sit down and gave me a hurried wave. She looked both tired and energized at the same time, but that made sense. She'd worried about opening her bakery in such a small town, thinking there might not be enough business to support it. But if the past weeks were any indication of future performance, I'd say Ally had a very busy year ahead of her.

She'd already gotten standing orders from a couple of office buildings and the 'good' hotel up the highway, and the churches had both placed orders every week for one type of meeting or another. Even Francine had become a customer, thrilled to give up the super-early-morning baking that had been her routine for decades. It was no wonder Ally had hired someone. She'd been living on a couple hours' sleep for weeks now.

I took a bite of whatever it was in front of me and groaned. "Maybe we should pool our money and open a seamstress shop," I said. "This bakery is going to increase waistlines."

"That's the benefit of age and the acceptability of elastic-waist pants," Gertie said.

"My yoga pants are elastic waist," I said.

"They're formfitting so that doesn't count," Gertie said.

We continued eating the decadence on a plate and after about ten minutes, the line finally cleared out and Ally came over and sank into the chair next to me and motioned for the new girl to come over as well.

"Ladies, this is Lillie Mae Wilson," Allie said. "She's Francine's cousin from north Louisiana and my new employee. Thank God."

"Ask Him for a miracle and He'll drop a hard worker in your bakery," Gertie said.

Ally nodded and gave our names. "These ladies are my best friends in Sinful."

We all exchanged greetings and then Ida Belle and Gertie started with the required inquisition.

"Why did you move to Sinful?" Gertie asked.

"My dad got a job transfer," she said. "They'd been wanting to move but he'd been putting it off so I could finish high school."

"You didn't want to go with them?" Ida Belle asked.

"To Singapore?" She laughed. "Figuring out the rest of my life is hard enough in the States. I didn't want to add a whole other language and culture to the mix. Not now, anyway. But they've always wanted to go, and I'll be happy to visit."

"So you're staying with Francine?" I asked.

She nodded. "Francine has always been that cousin I looked up to. She's talented and accomplished. Her café is awesome."

"But you're working here," I pointed out.

"I didn't figure it was a grand idea to work with someone all day and live with them all night," she said. "Neither did Francine, which is why she asked Ally about needing help."

Ally nodded. "Since I took over the majority of the baking for the café, Francine is part of the reason I need that help. And Lillie Mae has a great career ahead of her as a cake decorator. She is very talented."

Lillie Mae blushed. "Ally is exaggerating. I still have so

much to learn, but working here is going to be great for that. I'm a decent artist, but if the cake tastes like crap, it doesn't matter how pretty it is."

"Everything that comes out of Ally's kitchen tastes like angels made it," Gertie said.

"I know!" Lillie Mae said. "I start classes at a culinary school twice a week in a couple months. Between the classes and working with Ally, I'll learn everything I need to know about baking. But the sampling is killing me."

"I have the same problem," I said.

Lillie Mae looked confused. "You're in great shape."

"She runs more than an entire Olympic marathon team," Gertie said.

I nodded. "Because I'm friends with Ally. Well, and beer."

Everyone laughed and then a timer went off in the kitchen. Lillie Mae jumped up.

"I'll get it," she said. "I love the smell of banana nut muffins just out of the oven."

Ally smiled as she walked off to the kitchen.

"She's been a lifesaver," Ally said. "Pays attention to everything and remembers it all the first time. She's friendly with the customers—even the difficult ones—and it's not an act. She's even cheerful when doing tedious and dirty jobs."

"She's a Stepford Baker," Gertie said.

"Just young and ambitious and had some good raising," Ida Belle said. "Like another baker we know."

Ally blushed at the compliment.

"This is the first time the place has been empty since I opened today," Ally said. "There was actually a line of people waiting when I flipped the blinds. Startled the heck out of me. It wasn't even daylight yet."

"A good problem to have," Ida Belle said.

"Definitely better than the alternative," I said.

"No new cases, I guess?" Ally asked.

I shook my head. "I'm all done with my insurance work. I think some more is coming in next week, but they never take long. People are so stupid. I rarely need more than two outings to catch them doing things they're not supposed to."

"Well, I suppose you could always wander into uncharted territory," she said. "I heard Brock Benoit was found dead at the motel."

There was an intake of breath and we looked over to see a young woman standing in the doorway of the bakery.

Midtwenties. Five foot four. A hundred forty pounds. Decent muscle tone in arms but offset by her clearly lacking cardiovascular fitness. Zero threat unless she was holding one of the toddlers she babysat, because I was guessing this was Gina Tassin.

Ally jumped up from her seat and rushed over. "Gina, I'm so sorry. I didn't see you come in. Please sit down. I'll get you some water."

Ally guided Gina to a seat at our table and hurried off for the water. Gina took in a deep breath and slowly blew it out before looking over at Gertie.

"Is it true, Ms. Hebert?" she asked.

"I'm afraid so," Gertie said. "There hasn't been an official announcement, but we have it on good authority."

"And you're sure it's Brock?" she asked as Ally put a glass of water in front of her, then sat down. "He hasn't...he never comes..."

Gertie nodded. "I saw him myself last night at the parade and the police identified him. I'm sorry you had to hear about his death like this. It must be a blow."

A flush began to creep up her neck, replacing the earlier pallor, and she shook her head. "Honestly, I'm more shocked that he had the nerve to step foot in Sinful than I am that he's dead. I've been expecting to hear that for years."

"What do you mean?" Gertie asked.

She shrugged. "Just the way he did things. He drank like crazy in high school and I know he tried some of the hard stuff when he had the opportunity. It was his personality. He and RJ were alike that way. So when they took off together, I figured sooner or later we'd be reading an obituary for one of them. I'm only surprised it took this long."

"Did you have any contact with him after he left?" I asked.

"I haven't heard one word from that coward," she said, clearly angry. "I hunted him down after I had the baby—sent him texts and emails and left messages. He never answered."

"Were you getting some financial support at least?" Ida Belle asked.

"Ha! My daddy hauled me to a lawyer, and he filed all the stuff to get child support, but Brock didn't have what you'd call a regular job. My guess is no one would keep him on long enough for the child support documents to catch up with him anyway, or he was working side jobs for cash. Either way, you can't collect when there's no money."

"What about the music?" I asked. "Did he make some money off that one song?"

"If he did, I didn't see any of it," she said and narrowed her eyes at me. "You're that CIA lady, right?"

"Fortune Redding," I said and nodded. "Sorry we're not meeting under better circumstances."

"Oh, the circumstances are fine by me," she said. "Probably gonna be even finer by my daddy."

I cringed a bit. "Um, you might want to give him fair warning when you lay the good news on him."

She frowned. "What do you mean?"

"Brock's death is being treated as suspicious," I said.

Ally sucked in a breath and Gina's expression changed to confused, then shocked.

"You're saying Brock was murdered?" Gina asked.

"Not exactly," I said. "When the police treat it as suspicious, they start the investigative process to provide evidence to help the ME make a decision. The ME has the final say, but suspicious means it wasn't obviously natural causes."

"Did you talk to Carter?" Ida Belle asked.

I nodded. "He came in the General Store after you guys left. He was off to start questioning people, so it's no secret at this point."

Gina straightened in her chair. "And you think he's going to question my father? Unbelievable! That sorry excuse for a human being has caused so much trouble for my family and he's managing to cause even more dead. This isn't right."

"I know it seems unfair," Gertie said, "but your father has a motive for wanting to harm Brock."

"He might have had a motive years ago," Gina said. "But he also knew that Brock leaving was the best thing that could have happened for me and my son. My father is the only man in my son's life, and he needs him. So do I. There's no way he'd risk our family to settle a score with Brock. It isn't worth it. *He* wasn't worth it."

"Don't worry," Ally said. "You know Carter and you know he's not going to railroad anyone. He'll find out who did it, but he has to question everyone. Trust me, I've been a suspect myself, so I know how crappy it feels."

Her eyes widened. "You were a suspect in a murder investigation?"

Ally nodded. "And...uh, you're probably going to be as well."

"Me!" Her jaw dropped. "I couldn't...oh my God. If you only knew how much I hate Brock right now. He changed the entire course of my life. And now that I've finally accepted that I'll never do the things I wanted to, like college and a career, and I've created something in Sinful for myself and my son, he's upended everything again."

"I wouldn't volunteer how much you hate him," Gertie said gently. "We all get it, of course, but the only thing that can help you right now is an alibi. Did you go to the parade?"

"No way I was going to watch that bi—fake cow RJ lord over the town," Gina said. "I spent my teen years watching her in all her perfection. Her mother lives right behind us, you know. Every weekend, RJ was out back in a lawn chair, tanning her perfect body with her perfect nails and perfect hair. Her mother paid a fortune for her salon visits. For a high school girl."

"The snooty vein always ran deep with Sawyer-James," Gertie said. "She raised RJ to be the same."

"Well, she did a great job instilling that snobbery," Gina said, "because RJ never grew out of it. When I was in the backyard playing with the kids the day of the parade, she was in her bedroom, strolling back and forth in front of that big picture window she has, all dolled up in her evening gown. She knew I could see her. She used to do the same thing every weekend when we were in high school. I'd be sitting in my backyard reading a book and she'd be ready for a date and just flaunting it because she knew I didn't have one."

"The more I hear about her, the lovelier she sounds," I said.

Gina gave my sarcasm an appreciative nod. "When the kids were distracted, I gave her the finger. It was childish, but it felt good."

"What did she do?" I asked.

"I don't know," Gina said. "I refused to look up again."

"Bet that killed her," Ida Belle said. "Getting in the last word is part of RJ's genetic makeup."

"So you stayed home with your son and your father on parade night?" I asked hopefully.

She shook her head. "Billy had a sleepover at a friend's house and my dad was playing poker with friends."

"And you?" I asked.

She sighed. "The parents of the kids I watch have today off, so I have a holiday as well. Since I didn't have to be up early today, and I'd spent part of the afternoon working up a humongous mad over RJ, I went to the store and bought way too many snacks and a bottle of wine. I went straight from my car to the back patio and sat right in my favorite lawn chair and consumed everything in that bag. Woke up some time after midnight with a raging headache and a crick in my neck. I've never been much of a drinker, so I went inside, got promptly sick, then went to bed."

"You didn't hear your dad come in?" I asked.

"I could have had a brass band next to me and I wouldn't have heard them," she said. "I forgot to turn off my alarm and didn't hear it for almost twenty minutes this morning. I've been sitting in my room in the dark since I got up. I finally came to the bakery for some croissants. It's the only thing I could think of eating without feeling sick again."

"Been there," Gertie said and patted her hand. "Try not to worry. It will just make things worse."

She shook her head and rose from the table. "That's what people have been telling me ever since I got pregnant. But the worry never stops. Even though I know I didn't do anything to Brock, I have to worry about people thinking I did. Or that my dad did. Then I have to worry about how they'll treat Billy because of the rumors that will fly, especially if Carter never catches the guy who did it. And worst of all, at some point, I have to explain to my son that his father—whom he still asks about—is dead."

She headed for the door and Ally jumped up. "Wait!"

Ally ran behind the counter and shoved some croissants in a bag and hurried them over to Gina. "I hope you feel better, and if you need to talk, you know where to find me."

Gina gave her a small smile. "You always were the nicest person in Sinful."

She headed out the door and Ally looked over at us, clearly upset.

"I know we told her not to worry, but this really isn't good, is it?" Ally asked.

"Hard to say," I said. "Assuming it *is* murder and if the ME can pin down time of death, maybe her father was still playing cards. That would give him an alibi, at least."

"But if it happened in the middle of the night, then it's more likely *everyone* was asleep in their homes except the person who killed Brock," Ally said. "So anyone sleeping alone has opportunity."

"But we don't all have motive," I said.

"But too many people who *do* have a motive and *didn't* do it won't have alibis either," Ally said. "Gina and her father, specifically, because there's no way she killed someone. She's had a rough enough time already. And she's right—if Carter doesn't pin Brock's murder on someone else—she or her father will be the default in everyone's mind, even if they're never charged."

Gertie nodded. "And living here won't be pleasant. Look at the grief Marie got for decades over her husband."

Marie had long been suspected of killing her husband, who'd disappeared from Sinful years before I set foot in Louisiana, and his disappearance ended up being the first homicide I was involved in. Marie hadn't killed him, of course, but that hadn't stopped people from giving her grief. If Gina and her father had to live under the same cloud of suspicion, it would make things really hard on them and even harder on Billy.

"Which is why you can't let it happen to Gina," Ally pleaded. Then she stared at me for a moment and laughed. "You're already doing it. That's why you asked her all those questions."

"Let's just say we're interested," I said. "Because technically, we don't have a client, so therefore no justifiable reason to be poking around."

"I get it," Ally said. "Well, Carter won't be hearing anything from me—except how there's no way Gina could kill anyone. You saw her. She practically passed out when she heard Brock was dead. She never expected to have him enter her world again."

I nodded. Yes, Gina had definitely been upset when she'd heard of Brock's passing. Which might mean she was shocked and dismayed to know that he had been in town and her son's father was deceased. Or it might mean she'd had a run-in with Brock the night before and he'd been alive when she'd left and died later from the blow.

So if she was the one who'd delivered the head injury, she might be the one who killed him.

CHAPTER TEN

AFTER WE LEFT THE BAKERY, WE TOOK CARE OF MY GROCERY unpacking, then headed back out for the sheriff's department. Ida Belle wasn't on hand for the fire extinguishing games but didn't have anything better to do, so she volunteered to chauffeur Gertie and me to do our duty with Deputy Breaux. She had some lures on back order with the boat shop up the highway and figured when we were done, we could head over there and kill some time. I knew we'd reached the height of boredom when a trip to the boat store was the best we could come up with. But then, we'd already had a potential murder, an explosion, and a near-death experience that morning, so the bar was set a little high.

It didn't take us long to give our statements to an exhausted Deputy Breaux, but despite his clear lack of sleep, neither of us managed to get more information out of him. Either Carter had put the fear of God into him, or he didn't know any more than we did.

We were halfway to the boat shop when I got a phone call from a number I didn't recognize. It was probably someone trying to sell me an extended warranty on my old Jeep or pitch me a refinance on my nonexistent mortgage, but as I didn't have anything better to do, I figured I'd answer.

"Hey, this is Shadow Chaser," a man said when I answered.

"Who?" I asked.

"The clerk at the Bayou Inn. You know, the one who needed therapy because of you?"

"Your name is Shadow Chaser?"

"It's a gamer thing. Anyway, I've been thinking about how you're always turning up here looking for criminals, because, let's face it, this place ain't the Ritz. And I decided that your job is kinda cool. You're doing stuff in real life that I'm only doing from my couch, you know?"

I didn't know but decided to roll with it.

"I guess so," I said. "So why are you calling?"

"Oh yeah. Okay, so a dude died here, right? And the cops came and even though I found the body and called them, they told me to go away when I tried to get in on the action. But then I remembered you and thought if you were coming by here to do your thing, maybe I could tag along and learn stuff."

"You want to be a PI?"

"Yeah...no, well, maybe. I want to try it out first. That's why I'm pulling a double shift—so I could get you out here to show me the ropes."

"Uh-huh, so what is it you think I can investigate if the cops have already been there, taken everything of merit away, and the guy's too dead to question?"

"The dude in the room next door complained about the dead guy fighting with someone last night. I called and told him to take it down a notch but a while later, the TV in the dead guy's room started blaring and dude called again. I called, then banged on the door, but the dead guy never answered."

"Amazing how that works."

"I know, right? Anyway, I finally let myself in and found the dead guy. I couldn't find the remote, and man, I just wanted to get out of there, so I had to unplug the TV because the buttons weren't working either and—"

"Did you take pictures after you found the dead guy?" I interrupted.

"Nah. I totally blew it on that one, but I was kinda freaked."

I sighed.

"Did the guy next door see who the dead guy was arguing with?" I asked.

"I don't think so, but I thought maybe you could talk to him and figure out something the cops didn't."

"And you could tag along?"

"That would be awesome."

"Okay. We'll be there in about ten minutes."

I disconnected and relayed the exchange to Ida Belle and Gertie.

"I'm not sure whether it's better to have him on our side or not," Gertie said.

"We have *you* on our side," Ida Belle pointed out. "How much worse can it be?"

"He calls himself Shadow Chaser," Gertie said.

"Given that he looks like he hasn't seen sunlight in a decade, that actually works," I said.

Ida Belle parked in front of the office at the motel and our newest recruit came hurrying out when he saw us. The second he stepped into the sunlight, he froze as if skin cancer were standing at the doorway ready to zap him. He ran back inside and emerged several seconds later wearing a hat, jacket, gloves, and sunglasses.

He was grinning as we stepped out of the SUV.

"I can't believe I'm going to be part of a murder investigation," he said. "It was murder, right? That's why all the cops were here?"

"At this point it's suspicious," I said. "Unless it's something obvious, like a bullet hole that he couldn't have made himself, the ME makes the call."

He nodded. "So it could go either way, but I'm betting it was murder. That guy looked shifty as heck when he checked in, and for me to say that in a place like this is saying a lot."

Given that outside of hunting season and fishing rodeos, the motel's clientele ran mostly to criminals, lowlifes, and cheaters, it was definitely saying something. I just wasn't sure what.

"How was he shifty?" I asked.

"He never looked me directly in the eyes and paid cash, but neither of those are unusual," he said. "But this guy was antsy. Couldn't stand still, you know? Kept jiggling his pockets and looking outside toward the parking lot entrance."

"Like he was expecting someone to be watching?" Gertie asked. "Or coming after him?"

He nodded. "Exactly. Which again, nothing unusual there with the number of married men we get coming here to step out on their wives, but this guy was different."

"Different how?" Ida Belle asked.

"He looked scared," Shadow said. "Really scared—not scared his wife would catch him scared, but something bigger."

I nodded. Maybe Shadow's enthusiasm for his new interest had him remembering things in an overly dramatic way. Or maybe he remembered it exactly as it happened, but Brock was also a drug user, which would explain the paranoia and the pocket jiggling.

"I assume the cops cleared the dead guy's room?"

He nodded. "They bagged up everything and told me to wait until they gave me the go-ahead to send in a cleaning crew."

"What about a vehicle?"

"He had an SUV. It's still parked behind the motel, but the cops cleaned it out as well. Said the bank was sending someone to repo it so they weren't going to bother towing it."

"So we're going to talk to the guy in the room next door, right?" I asked.

"Yeah, Jim Garmon," he said. "He's the guy who complained about the noise. But fair warning—he's an angry one. All that racket last night and then the cops putting him through the mill... He practically threw me out of his room when I tried to talk to him earlier."

Ah, the reason for Shadow's phone call to me became clearer. He'd already taken a shot at the investigation thing and hadn't gotten anywhere.

"Well, let's go see what he has to say," I said. "Assuming he's here."

"He's here," Shadow said. "I've been watching the entry. Can't see it well from the front desk so I have a crick in my neck from leaning over the counter, but I was on the job, so that's part of it, right?"

"Yeah, the ole crick in the neck is a real problem," Ida Belle said. "Almost had me retiring myself."

He nodded. "I know, right?"

"Lead the way," I said before Ida Belle's trigger finger got any itchier.

He practically skipped across the parking lot—for about twenty feet or so—then his aerobic conditioning was apparently spent, and he settled into a leisurely stroll. Gertie looked over at me and rolled her eyes. When someone over five decades older could outlast you in a footrace, maybe it was time to put the controller down and get on a treadmill.

We bypassed a door with police tape on it and stopped at the next one. Shadow knocked but we didn't hear any movement inside. He knocked again, this time announcing his presence but still, not a peep.

"I know he's here," Shadow said. "That's his car right there."

"Maybe he walked somewhere," Gertie suggested.

Shadow looked somewhat shocked. "The nearest place for food or anything is at least a quarter mile. No one walks a quarter mile for food. And this guy is big—I'm talking supersize. He'd probably drive to the vending machines and they're right next to the office."

"Then maybe he's finally sleeping," I said.

"So what do we do?" he asked. "Come back later? Leave a note? Go in with guns blazing?"

Ida Belle's eyebrows shot up. "Do you have a gun?"

"Well, no," he said. "Should I get one?"

"No!" We all responded at once.

He looked confused. "Don't all of you carry guns?"

"Yes," I said. "But we're prepared to shoot people. Can you shoot someone?"

His eyes widened. "God, no! I'm vegan."

"Eating them is optional," Gertie said.

"Oh, ha," he said nervously, clearly not certain she was joking. "I'll just stick to the information and observation side of things and leave the physical stuff to you guys. You seem to enjoy it."

"That's a good idea," I said. "Sooooo, Mr. Information and Observation, do you have a room key?"

"I have a master key," he said. "You mean we should just open the door and go in?"

"That's the idea," I said. "You *are* the acting manager. It's not like it's illegal."

"No," he agreed. "But it's sort of rude."

"What if he's dead, too?" I asked.

He sucked in a breath and jammed a key in the door. I figured he'd step back and let me do my thing, but apparently, he'd gotten his second wind. A normal person would have poked their head in and called out, but not video game guy. He shoved the door open and jumped inside like he was making an arrest—just as a very large man came out of the bathroom, wearing nothing but a towel.

Hanging around his neck.

Shadow Chaser yelled as though someone were killing him, whirled around, and got tangled in the drapes. He flailed around for a bit before the rod finally tore off the wall and the drapes came shooting off the freed end. Shadow took off out of the room, the drapes still wrapped around him. He made it five feet before he tripped in all the fabric and plowed face-first into a porch post.

He lay on the ground groaning until Ida Belle went over and tugged on the drapes, unrolling him into the parking lot. He grabbed hold of a truck bumper and pulled himself up, then stared at us in dismay.

"Is this what it's like for you—you walk in on naked people?" he asked. "The kind of people who you never, *ever* want to see naked in the first place?"

"It happens more often than you'd think," I said.

"No wonder you shoot people and blow up things," he said. "That is no way to live."

I nodded. "Maybe you should get back on your couch with your gaming controller."

"Definitely, but right now, I'm going back to the office to take a shot from the owner's whiskey stash and call my therapist. You can have this job."

"That went well," Gertie said.

"What do you people want?" Showering man sounded behind us and I eased my way around, hoping he'd located something larger than the towel to hang around the parts Shadow had complained about.

Six foot two. Mad as hell. Easily three hundred pounds, but at least he was wearing sweatpants now. Any muscle tone had been lost years ago and the tattoos on his arms were more the prison variety than the professional kind. At one point, they might have resembled something but now they just sort of clustered in a stretched, hanging bunch. As I'd gotten an unfortunate good look at the rest of him, I knew the legs weren't any better. No threat except to sensitive motel clerks and drapes.

"I'm sorry to bother you, Mr. Garmon," I said. "I'm a private investigator and was hoping you'd talk to me about what happened last night."

He snorted, his expression still angry. "You're telling me that A-hole had someone around who cared enough to pay for a PI? I don't buy it."

"Let's just say I represent someone who had reason to celebrate Mr. Benoit's demise and I don't want to see them railroaded by the cops."

"*That* I can buy," he said, looking somewhat mollified. "But I don't know what I can do to help. I didn't see anything—just heard that guy arguing with people."

"People? As in more than one?" I asked.

He nodded. "First one was a man. He was talking low at first, so I didn't even realize anyone was over there until the dead guy started yelling."

"How do you know it was the dead guy who was yelling?"

"Because I heard the same voice arguing with a woman after that."

"What time was the first argument?" I asked.

"Around midnight. I called that useless clerk when I heard something hit the wall. Things so cheaply made, that picture fell off." He pointed to a tacky painting of fruit in a basket with a crack across the glass.

"So they were fighting?"

"Maybe. That one thud on the wall is all I heard."

"Could you understand what they were fighting about?"

"Money maybe," he said. "I couldn't hear the other guy well enough to make out what he said, but the dead guy kept saying he needed more time. That he'd make everything right soon. Most of it was muffled. The woman said something about the dead guy not screwing her over again, so most likely money or personal."

"And what time did the woman show up?"

He shrugged. "Shortly after the man."

"And how long after that did the television fire up?"

"I don't know—right after? It's not like I had a timer on them and took notes."

"And you're sure you didn't look out the window or anything?" I asked. "Just out of curiosity?"

He shifted his weight from one leg to the other and finally nodded. "I might have looked out. But I didn't tell the cops and don't intend to, because then they'll be all over me even though I can't help them. My wife doesn't know I'm here, and I don't want them following up with me when I head home."

"Got a girlfriend?" I asked.

"What? No! I'm here duck hunting."

"Why would your wife care about you hunting?"

"She hates duck, and her mother is visiting. She hates her mother more than duck."

"So you skipped out on being the buffer," Gertie said.

"Smart man," Ida Belle said.

"Unless my wife finds out," he said.

"I won't share anything with the cops," I assured him. "They don't like PIs in their business. But if you saw anything that can help my client, I'd appreciate it."

"Didn't see much," he said. "The guy was normal size, I guess, and had on a ball cap and long coat. He walked off to the right and I lost sight of him. Didn't see him get into a vehicle. I didn't look out when the woman left. I was...ah, hell, I was occupied in the bathroom. Three-alarm chili after the hunt yesterday, which is why I didn't pay much attention to how long people were there or when they came and went. Anyway, when the TV broke the sound barrier, I called the clerk again."

"And everything went downhill from there," I concluded.

"Not really," he said. "The chili was rock bottom for me. After all, I didn't know the dead guy, so..."

"Well, thank you Mr. Garmon," I said and handed him my card. "If you think of anything else, give me a call. And I'd appreciate if you don't mention my visit if you talk to the cops again."

"As far as I'm concerned, we never met," he said.

We headed out and back toward the office.

"You think we ought to ask to see inside the room?" Gertie asked.

"To do what?" Ida Belle asked as we climbed into the SUV. "A forensics team would have taken everything out and it's not like we can dust for prints. Even if we could, we have no way to run them. Same with his vehicle."

"So what now?" Gertie asked. "The party starts in four hours. I know it only takes you two a pass through the shower to get ready, but I'd prefer a bit more lead time."

"We head back to Sinful," I said. "I have one more stop I want to make but it shouldn't take long."

"You want to question someone else," Ida Belle asked.

I nodded. "I need to talk to Whiskey."

Gertie clapped her hands. "Swamp Bar trip!"

CHAPTER ELEVEN

WE DISCUSSED THE CASE ON THE DRIVE TO THE SWAMP BAR. Gertie thought the man who threatened Brock at the hotel could be Cecil Tassin and the woman was RJ, figuring she lied to Celia about knowing where Brock was and had thrown something at him when they fought, but just didn't know he was dead when she and Celia were looking at the float. And it could have happened that way.

Ida Belle said the woman could have just as easily been Gina because if Brock had screwed anyone over, it was her. Since his late-night visitors were why I wanted to talk to Whiskey, I wasn't casting my vote yet. The reality was, it could have been Cecil, and Gina or RJ, or it could have been someone else completely. Like the mystery man at the parade.

"For all we know, someone could have followed Brock to Sinful, just like he followed RJ," Ida Belle said. "I doubt Brock offended fewer people in Tennessee than he did here."

"I'm sure you're right," I said. "I wish we knew someone, besides Sawyer, who knew what they were up to in Tennessee."

Ida Belle nodded. "It does seem like we're missing half the information if we don't know what's been going on since they left, but honestly, I can't imagine RJ shared the kind of things that would matter to the case with her mother. I'm pretty sure she started lying to her in the crib. Sawyer always thought RJ was a perfect angel."

"Ha!" Gertie said. "Sawyer's an idiot. But unfortunately, Ida Belle is right. The only person RJ would have spilled the dirt to was Pansy."

"I don't guess Christina Forrester would know anything," I said.

"Can't imagine she would," Ida Belle said. "RJ and Brock took off shortly after that car wreck, and with Marigold being nonverbal, it makes things hard. Not to mention, I can't see Christina caring enough to ask about them."

"What do you mean?" I asked.

"She never said anything, mind you, but Ida Belle and I always wondered if Christina blamed RJ and Brock for the accident," Gertie said. "Marigold was driving but the car belonged to Brock's father. I guess she figures that if RJ and Brock hadn't been drinking, then Marigold wouldn't have felt she had to drive. She never liked driving after dark unless it was in town. Bad night vision."

"Where were they?" I asked.

"They claimed they'd met up with some other teens in the woods—had a bonfire and all that mess," Ida Belle said. "The wreck was on the service road up the highway. They ran off into one of those big drainage ditches. Lucky it wasn't full of water at the time."

"A couple driving by on the highway pulled over when they saw the fire and called for help," Gertie said. "Brock and RJ had crawled out of the car, but Marigold was still inside when it caught fire. The couple got her out before the fire reached her but just barely."

"You think that's why RJ never visited Marigold after the accident?" I asked. "Guilt?"

"Please," Ida Belle said. "That girl has never felt guilty about anything her entire life. My guess is she stayed away because she didn't want to be blamed."

"There was still talk about the drinking, of course," Gertie said. "It's Sinful, after all."

"But then RJ and Brock cut out of town shortly after," I said.

"Leaving it conveniently all behind," Gertie said.

"You guys were planning on checking in on Christina and Marigold sometime today, right?" I asked.

Gertie nodded. "The least we could do is take them a casserole and some of Ally's cookies. I set one out to thaw last night, so all we have to do is pick it up and go."

"Good," I said. "After we pay Whiskey a visit, then we'll grab the casserole and that will be our last stop of the day. Before the party, I mean."

"You thinking Christina might talk after this latest crisis?" Ida Belle asked.

I nodded. "I think the parade fire brought back the car accident to Marigold. Some of that blame and anger you guys think Christina has might show itself."

We pulled into the Swamp Bar parking lot, which was basically a big space consisting of dirt, weeds, and gravel, and pulled up right to the front of the bar. There were only two other vehicles and I recognized one of them as Whiskey's. I didn't recognize the other, but it wasn't RJ's ancient Chevy, so that was good.

We headed inside, and I heard Whiskey's voice yell from the kitchen.

"We're not open until six!"

"Good thing we're not here to drink!" I yelled back.

A couple seconds later, Whiskey walked out and grinned when he caught sight of me. "I knew I recognized that voice," he said. "Are you here to collect your winnings?"

Gertie immediately broke into a celebration dance and Ida Belle gave Whiskey a high five.

"I won? Really?" I asked.

After seeing RJ in her dress and knowing she'd been pushing her wares at the Swamp Bar the last couple days, I was a little surprised.

"It was no contest," Whiskey said. "You pulled in eighty percent of the vote. That's the biggest margin ever. So congratulations."

"Thanks," I said.

Whiskey grinned again. "Quite frankly, I was surprised you agreed to do it, but you looked fantastic. Several of my regulars had video footage and I have to say, if you weren't already hooked up with Carter, I'd be getting a lien on my boat to take a run at you."

"That boat isn't worth a pair of movie tickets," Ida Belle said.

"Hey, it's worth the tickets," Whiskey said. "Just probably not popcorn. Anyway, I just finished the tally about ten minutes ago and hadn't gotten a chance to make the calls yet."

"Now you have one less to make," Gertie said and gave me a thumbs-up. "See, I told you that RJ flashing her goods over here wouldn't make a difference."

"Oh, it made a difference," Whiskey said. "If you mean that drink sales went up until the point where bar fights doubled."

"I'm surprised she didn't go right to the source and offer up a bribe in exchange for a count in her favor," Gertie said, shooting me a glance.

"She did," Whiskey said. "More than once and in fact, the last time was about an hour ago. But I don't want anything that girl is peddling. She always was trouble, and it doesn't appear anything has changed except she has a valid ID now."

"She used to come here in high school?" I asked.

"She tried," Whiskey said. "Made it in a couple times when someone new and stupid was running the door. All the bartenders knew better than to serve her, but it wasn't like she was buying her own anyway. She'd make out pretty good before an employee who knew better caught her."

"Or someone's wife or girlfriend," Gertie said.

"That too," Whiskey said.

"She wasn't here the night of that car wreck back in high school, was she?" I asked.

Whiskey frowned. "No. Thank God. I don't need that kind of trouble. Best I know, they never gave the actual location."

"It was one of those well-kept secrets," Ida Belle said. "And for Sinful, that's saying a lot."

"No one wanted to be on the hook for what happened," Whiskey said. "The kids were covering for someone. So somebody old enough either bought them the alcohol or brought it to the party."

"Or one or more of the kids lifted it from their parents' stash," Ida Belle said.

"And borrowed the keys to a parent's camp because no one is buying that bonfire story," Whiskey said, then shook his head. "Regardless, people weren't going to own up to being the source of the booze or the location that ultimately left a girl disabled. It's crap, but it doesn't surprise me. So don't tell me you drove all the way out here just to check on the vote count."

"No," I said. "Actually, I wanted to ask you about Brock Benoit."

"Yeah, I heard he was found dead at the motel and Carter was asking questions," Whiskey said.

"Had he been to the bar?" I asked.

"No way!" Whiskey said. "RJ stirred up enough mess with her flirting for votes, but letting Brock in here would have caused trouble even I couldn't have handled."

"What do you mean?" I asked.

"Several of my regulars hated the guy," Whiskey said.

"Why?" Ida Belle asked.

"All different reasons," Whiskey said. "He borrowed money from a couple of 'em and never paid it back. Borrowed girlfriends from more than a couple. Wrecked a guy's truck that he took without asking. Sank a guy's boat—same deal. Trust me, there is no shortage of people who will be not-so-silently toasting his passage tonight."

"He accomplished a lot considering he left here right after graduating from high school," I said. "You think people are still holding a grudge this many years later?"

"If you're asking would any of them have still taken a swipe at him if he was standing in front of them, then I'd say every one of them would have, which is exactly why I didn't want him in my bar," Whiskey said. "If you're asking if any of them were mad enough to kill him, then I'd have to go with no. Murder is an extreme solution to a high school grudge."

"But not unheard of," Gertie said.

"True," Whiskey agreed. "I've seen it on enough of those documentaries my dad loves so much."

He frowned.

"You thinking of someone in particular?" I asked.

He hesitated, then shook his head. "I don't want to speculate on someone. I know firsthand what that kind of talk does."

Not so long ago, Whiskey had been suspected of murder and had hired me to clear his name. I'd found the real killer, but during the investigation, Whiskey had to deal with plenty of negative talk, so I could see where he wouldn't be a fan of gossiping about something like this.

"I know how it goes," I said. "But your speculation wouldn't go any further than us, and you know that too. Our only interest in gossip and rumor is using it to figure out who needs help because someone else committed a crime. It's not sport for us."

"That's true," he agreed. "And God knows, you got me out of the hot seat. If I had to put someone at the top of the list, I'd say Cooper Guidry is the one I'd pick."

"Any relation to Floyd?" I asked.

Floyd Guidry had been Ally's next-door neighbor before he'd gotten himself murdered. He was an angry criminal with a bad gambling problem and generally disliked by everyone who'd ever met him.

"A cousin," Whiskey said. "But nothing like Floyd or he wouldn't be allowed in my bar."

"If he's nothing like Floyd, why is he your first pick?" I asked.

I'd only met Cooper once when he delivered some parts for my air conditioner. I knew he was a hotshot driver and lived just outside of town. He was young with a scrawny build and had stared at the ground the entire time I was signing for the delivery. I was having a hard time picturing him as a killer.

"He dated Gina Tassin after high school," Whiskey said. "Probably wanted to during, but she was tangled up with Brock. Cooper wanted the whole house-with-a-picket-fence thing, but she shot him down."

"Interesting," Ida Belle said. "Most men don't go around sharing that sort of thing."

"He didn't volunteer it so much as I hit on it accidentally," Whiskey said. "He came in here one night when things were slow, looking like someone had kicked his dog, and proceeded to blow through a couple drinks like they were water. He was never much of a drinker, so I started watering them down and figured if I couldn't find someone to take him home, I'd do it after I closed up."

I nodded, not even remotely surprised. Whiskey was a good guy. Just rough around the edges.

"Anyway, we were headed out about midnight, and he stumbled and this ring box fell out of his pocket. I picked it up and looked and it was an engagement ring. When I handed it back to him, the floodgates opened, and he didn't stop talking until I pulled into his driveway. He said he'd asked Gina to marry him, but she said she couldn't. He never told me why but said the whole thing was Brock Benoit's fault. That he'd ruined any chance they had of a future together."

"Was Gina still in love with Brock?" Gertie asked.

Whiskey shrugged. "I don't know. I can't see how she would be, especially after Brock ran off with her pregnant. And he never has supported the kid in any way. Cooper isn't going to set the world on fire, but he's a good guy and has steady work. Pays his bills, doesn't cause trouble. She could do a heck of a lot worse, but when I asked a few questions, he just got out of the car and went inside."

"Maybe she doesn't trust herself to have another relationship," Ida Belle said. "Brock totally took her for a ride and everyone knew it but her."

"Maybe," Whiskey said. "But Cooper wouldn't hurt a fly, and he really loves her and her boy. I could hear it in his voice. Anyway, that's why I'd pick him as the regular with the biggest grudge and the most recent."

"Was he here last night?" I asked.

"Yeah. I served him a couple times myself," Whiskey said.

"What time did he leave?" I asked.

"No idea," Whiskey said. "This place was shoulder to

shoulder until after midnight. But I can't even see Cooper confronting Brock, much less killing him. He just doesn't have it in him."

"What about a non-regular?" I asked.

"You got someone specific in mind?" Whiskey asked.

"Is your dad still playing poker when he's feeling up to it?" I asked.

Whiskey nodded, then his eyes widened. "You're thinking of Cecil."

"Did your dad play with Cecil last night?" I asked.

"Let me make a call," Whiskey said and pulled out his phone.

I gathered from Whiskey's end of the conversation that his father had already heard about Brock's death and the cops asking questions. I could hear his voice increasing in octave and volume as he talked, and when Whiskey disconnected, he was frowning.

"The game started around six," Whiskey said. "Cecil cut out around eleven. The rest of the guys stayed on until one or so."

"Did your dad say why Cecil left early?" I asked.

"Said he kept making stupid plays and went through his chips," Whiskey said. "That's not like Cecil. He's a conservative bettor and a first-rate player."

"He was distracted," Ida Belle said. "Everyone knew RJ was back in town, but I wonder if Cecil knew Brock was back as well."

Whiskey shook his head. "If he did, he didn't say so to my dad or I'd have gotten a warning call to look out for Brock at the bar. And RJ sure as heck didn't breathe a word about it. I didn't know until this morning when Carter called me asking if I'd seen or heard anything."

"Brock was at the parade," I said.

Whiskey's eyes widened. "Really? Then why didn't I hear about it sooner?"

"Because people would have had to take a hard look to recognize him," Gertie said and pulled out her phone. "I took this picture and didn't even realize it was him until I was asked if it could be."

Whiskey studied the picture and shook his head. "Wow. I see it because you said so, but I would have walked right by the guy without realizing it. Man, he looks like he's forty years old."

"Drugs will do that to you," Ida Belle said.

"Drugs?" Whiskey asked. "Well, can't say that surprises me. He was always one to try anything regardless of risk. Thrill seeker. But not in a good way."

"I know the type," I said.

Whiskey laughed. "You *are* the type."

"But in a good way," I said.

"I suppose," he said. "If chasing criminals and skirting the law while you're hooked up with the local deputy is a good way, then you're solid."

"Details," I said and grinned. "I know you've got to set up for the big throwdown tonight, so we'll get out of your way."

"But not before we collect our winnings," Gertie said.

"Oh yeah!" Whiskey headed for the kitchen. "Let me get it out of the safe and count out your share."

A couple minutes later, he came back with a thick envelope and handed it to Ida Belle. "There you go," he said. "Seven thousand four hundred thirty-six dollars. Best turnout we've ever had, and I chalk that up to Fortune being in the running against the returning prodigal daughter."

"Woot!" Gertie yelled.

"Thanks, Whiskey," Ida Belle said.

He gave us a nod and looked at me. "If you hear anything

on Brock, let me know. If you can. Man, I hate thinking that someone I know and like could have been involved in his death."

"Me too," I said. "Hey, I don't suppose you know anyone in the music scene in Nashville, do you?"

He narrowed his eyes at me. "You think maybe trouble followed him here?"

"Seems he was gifted at making enemies, so..."

He nodded. "I have to say, I like that solution, but I don't know anyone in that line of work. You know who probably does, though—Big Hebert. Years ago, rumor was he had some money in producing a country singer from New Orleans."

"Really?" I said, perking up some with this news. "That's great. I'll check with him. Thanks."

Whiskey laughed. "You're probably the only person in Sinful who looks happy when they hear they need to talk to the Heberts."

"We have a business arrangement," I said.

Whiskey shook his head. "Big Hebert doesn't do favors for people unless they're family. That man treats you like a daughter, which isn't a bad thing."

"Tell that to Carter," I said.

"Ha!" Whiskey said. "Yeah, well, I can appreciate his dilemma, but I wouldn't ever complain about someone like the Heberts having my woman's back. You ladies try to stay out of trouble tonight."

"We should be telling you that," I said. "This place will be a zoo."

"Nah," Whiskey said. "They'll be drunk, but they won't be any problem. Finale of *Yellowstone* is Sunday night, and no one will want to be in jail."

We headed out, Ida Belle still smiling.

"I can't believe it," she said and shook the envelope.

"Hey, where's your faith?" I groused.

"Sorry, but since you weren't in the goodies-flashing business and with men being men, I was a little worried," Ida Belle said.

"Well, apparently taste in Sinful isn't as bad as we thought," Gertie said.

"That YouTube push probably didn't hurt things," Ida Belle said.

"Don't remind me," I said.

I'd already gotten a text from my former partner at the CIA, and I could practically hear him laughing with every word. Granted, he'd seen me all dressed up before, but it was usually to go kill someone. Being a holiday queen—without a target attached—was something he never thought he'd see in a hundred lifetimes.

Gertie pulled out her cell phone. "I can't wait to start the bragging. Who do you want to text first?"

"Celia."

Ida Belle and I answered at the same time.

Gertie was practically giggling as she typed her message. "I'm thanking her for running a clean campaign and wishing her better luck next year."

"That's polite as heck," I said.

Gertie nodded. "It's really going to hack her off."

I pulled out my phone and sent a text to Carter.

Just talked to Whiskey. I am Sinful's Official New Year's Queen.

Of course you are. Do you still have that dress because I was thinking...

About cause of death?

That dress qualifies.

"You texting Carter?" Gertie asked.

I nodded and showed her my phone. She read the exchange

and rolled her eyes. "Men are so easy. How is it that they ran the world for so long?"

"They *thought* they were running the world," Ida Belle said. "I sent Christina a text. She and Marigold are at home. You want to head over there now?"

I nodded. Given Gertie and Ida Belle's suspicion that Christina might blame RJ and Brock for the car wreck, I wanted to see if this recent event would have her talking more freely. The more stories I heard about RJ and Brock, the more I formed a picture.

And those pictures helped solve crimes.

CHAPTER TWELVE

CHRISTINA AND MARIGOLD LIVED IN A SMALL HOUSE ON THE outskirts of town. The lawn was neat but the flowers in the beds were sparse and the exterior of the home had paint peeling. I could see some partially rotted boards on the end of the porch as we drove up, and two windows were missing screens.

"Looks like Christina could use some help," I said.

Gertie nodded. "But she's not the sort to ask."

"What about child support?" I asked. "How does that work in cases like this?"

"In Louisiana, you can be awarded child support indefinitely if a child is disabled prior to becoming an adult and is unable to care for themselves," Ida Belle said. "But being awarded something and collecting it are two different things. I don't know if she even pursued it, honestly."

"Marigold would be eligible for Social Security or disability or both, I think," Gertie said. "Not sure exactly how it works, but I'm sure it doesn't cover much."

"What about Christina?" I asked as we made our way to the front door. "Does she work?"

Gertie nodded. "She's a medical transcriptionist. Worked

in medical records at the hospital before the accident and took some courses so she could shift to working from home. It's a decent fit given that Marigold needs monitoring 24-7, but I don't think it pays a whole lot."

Ida Belle shook her head. "Two people to support—one with a lot of medical needs—and a mortgage to boot. It's not like it used to be. Everything's a lot more expensive, plus people don't do maintenance themselves the way they used to."

"Lack of skill or lack of time or both," Gertie agreed.

Gertie rang the doorbell and we waited. It was so quiet that I wondered if anyone was home. The garage was closed, so we couldn't check for a car, but after a minute or so, I heard footsteps inside. The door swung open and a harried-looking Christina peered out at us.

She relaxed a bit when she saw us standing there and forced a smile as she opened the door. "Gertie, Ida Belle...it's nice to see you. Please come in."

I introduced myself as we stepped into a pleasant but dated living room. Worn hardwood was covered by an even more worn rug. A couch and love seat with sagging cushions were placed around a brick fireplace. Two recliners sat facing a television over the mantel. An old upright piano stood against the side wall, magazines stacked on the bench.

Christina shook my hand and nodded. "You're the other queen. I just finished brewing some tea. Come back to the kitchen and I'll pour us up some."

"I brought you a chicken casserole," Gertie said.

"And a box of cookies from Ally's bakery," I said and held them up.

"We figured you'd be stressed and behind with everything that happened," Ida Belle said. "Thought we'd ease one task, at least for tonight."

Christina took the casserole from Gertie, and I sat the box of cookies on the counter. "I can't tell you how much I appreciate this," she said. "I was going to pick up some staples from the grocery store today and then this. Usually I take Marigold with me, but she can't handle it right now."

"Let me know what you need, and Walter will send someone with a delivery," Ida Belle said.

"Oh, I couldn't bother Walter with that," Christina said. "He's got a business to run and with tonight being New Year's Eve, he's probably running low on stock to begin with."

"Just snacks," Ida Belle said. "Eggs, milk, bread, and the like are fine. He could close the gap so you get through the weekend, anyway."

She put a tray of glasses filled with iced tea on the table and sank into one of the chairs. "Really? That would be a godsend, to be honest. Those items and some sliced cheese and butter would get us by fine. Especially since we have one of Gertie's incredible casseroles."

Ida Belle pulled out her phone and started texting.

"How is Marigold doing?" Gertie asked.

Christina sighed. "She's okay. She couldn't breathe and at first, I thought it was the smoke, but I didn't so much as cough, and I was right there with her and felt nothing. Anyway, it was a panic attack, I guess."

"PTSD?" I suggested. "Ida Belle and Gertie told me about the car wreck that caused her brain injury."

Christina nodded. "That's what the doctor said. I just... It seemed so severe a reaction, you know? She's had other episodes but never like this. They had to sedate her to get her in the ambulance. After the accident, it took a long time for me to get her to ride in a car again without anxiety meds, and even then, she always insisted on being in the front seat. I worry about how much this is going to set her back."

"I imagine it was upsetting for you as well," Gertie said. "But she's calmer now?"

"Almost too calm," Christina said.

"What do you mean?" I asked.

"She got out of the car when we got home, went straight to her room, and she's just been sitting there this whole time," Christina said. "I've offered her something to eat and drink, to turn on the television or read to her, but she just shakes her head and keeps staring out the window. I don't like it, but she doesn't seem to be in any distress, so I don't think the hospital is the right place for her either."

"Maybe she just needs some time to process things," I said. "You mentioned reading a book. Did her injury take away her ability to read?"

"Yes, and I think that might have been the biggest loss," Christina said. "Marigold loved to read. She was reading at a college level by the time she was six. Spent all her allowance on books after she blew through the Sinful Library in a single summer."

Christina reached for a napkin and dabbed at the tears collecting in the corner of her eyes. "I'm sorry. I should be past the emotions by now. I guess Marigold isn't the only one having a flashback."

Gertie reached over and patted her hand. "You've had a really rough go of it. I'd be more surprised if you weren't shaken up."

She nodded. "Thank you. I mostly take things one day at a time and try to be thankful for the things we do have. Aside from the brain injury, Marigold is otherwise healthy, which is a miracle given how that car looked. And she still understands people. She just doesn't talk herself."

"If she can't read, then she can't write either," I said.

"No. We tried teaching her sign language, but it didn't

make sense to her. Something about wires being crossed—layman's terms, of course. It was the same with the piano. She used to play but now, if you show her sheet music, she just shakes her head."

"I've seen some cases of unique inclusion and exclusion in functionality dealing with injured soldiers," I said.

She studied me for a moment. "That's right. You were CIA. I guess you know a little about PTSD then."

"Too much," I said. "Not personally, which I'm thankful for every day, but I've seen enough of the fallout to know it changes lives forever and never positively."

"It's definitely the most challenging thing I've ever faced," she said. "And I worry so much about what will happen to Marigold when I'm gone."

"You can't put that kind of pressure on yourself," Gertie said. "You've got plenty of time to figure things out and Marigold is still young. Scientists are discovering things every day. You don't know where Marigold will be in five years, much less fifty."

"Good Lord, I hope I'm not around another fifty years," Christina said. "I'm exhausted just thinking about it."

"Have you heard...I don't suppose anyone has told you about Brock Benoit?" Ida Belle asked.

"Brock?" Christina asked. "There's a name I haven't heard in forever. What about him?"

"He's dead," Ida Belle said. "The police are treating it as suspicious."

Christina shook her head. "I will admit I never liked the boy. I thought he was a bad one even back then and didn't want Marigold hanging around him, but you know what happens when you tell teenagers to not see a boy."

"You think Marigold had a romance with Brock?" Gertie asked.

"I think she had a crush on him," Christina said. "And Brock took advantage of that. Marigold wasn't the first or, I'm sure, the last person he took for a ride, mind you. Poor Gina Tassin proves that one up. I always figured he'd come to no good end living that way, so it comes as no surprise to hear someone might have killed him."

"You think he finally took advantage of the wrong person," Ida Belle said.

Christina nodded. "Sure, and from what I see on TV, the music industry is cutthroat. He probably met his match in Nashville."

"Oh, he didn't die in Nashville," I said. "He was here—at the Bayou Inn."

"Here!" She stared at me. "Why in the world would he be in Sinful? He's got no family and hasn't been back since he shot out of here like a bullet after high school."

"No one seems to know why he was back," Ida Belle said. "Our guess is it had something to do with RJ, but who knows."

"RJ...yes, I guess that could be, although I've never known him to come for a visit on the few occasions she has," Christina said. "You're dating Carter, right? What does he say?"

"Nothing," I said. "He doesn't like when I get into his professional business. All we know is that he's investigating it as a suspicious death."

I heard a noise in the doorway and looked over to see Marigold standing there, just staring at us and frowning. Christina jumped up and hurried over.

"Are you hungry?" she asked. "Do you want something to eat?"

Marigold shook her head and shuffled past us for the refrigerator. She pulled a bottle of water out and walked past us again, this time heading out the back door. Through the window, I saw her sit on the edge of the porch and flip open the notebook she'd been carrying.

"She's sitting on the end of the porch," I said as Christina couldn't see her from where she was standing.

Christina sank into her chair again, stress practically oozing out of her pores. "I wish I knew what to do. I've already called the therapist and she'll see her first thing Monday, but otherwise, I'm at a loss."

"Do you think something besides the fire is bothering her?" I asked.

"What do you mean?" Christina asked.

"I just wondered if seeing RJ seemed to cause her any distress," I said.

"I don't think so," Christina said. "I was surprised to hear from RJ. I haven't on any of the few occasions she's blown through town, but when she invited Marigold to ride on the float, I thought it might be a fun thing for her to do. And she was definitely excited about it. I haven't seen her smile that way in a long time."

I nodded and watched as Marigold used the pen on her notebook. I knew she couldn't be writing but wondered what she was drawing.

"Do you mind if I talk to her?" I asked.

Christina stared at me, surprised. "I don't know...I guess it's okay. But why?"

I shrugged. "Like I said, I've seen some things and just wondered if maybe I could recommend someone to help. The CIA doesn't just give you a gun and let you run around shooting people. We have to build cases and some of that building depended on witness testimony. Given our targets, the witnesses were often military and rarely in peak health, mentally or physically."

Christina's eyes widened. "I never thought of that, but

then I don't know much about the military or those government agencies. If you think you might be able to help, by all
means..."

I headed out the back door and walked over to where
Marigold was sitting. She never once looked back and didn't
even turn her head when I sat beside her on the porch. I
looked over at her notebook and saw what she'd been working
on, but it wasn't a picture. Not exactly. It was rows of stick
figures in different poses.

"Can I see what you're working on?" I asked.

She turned her head toward me, then stared directly at me,
not even blinking.

"My name is Fortune," I said. "We've never met but I'm a
friend of Ida Belle and Gertie's. You know them, right?"

She nodded.

"They're really nice," I said. "And lots of fun. We came by
today to see how you were feeling and to drop off a casserole.
Gertie makes the absolute best casseroles and we brought
cookies from Ally's bakery. Have you been to the bakery?"

She nodded again, this time smiling just a tiny bit. Score
another for Ally.

"Yeah," I said. "Ally makes the best cookies, pies, cakes,
and, well, anything with sugar that I've ever eaten. I had to
start running more after I met her because I was going to
outgrow all my clothes."

The smiled widened and she passed her notebook over to
me. I flipped back a page and this time, the rows were filled
with emojis of sorts. Hearts, stars, clouds—small, simple
objects that could be easily drawn. I riffled through the other
pages and saw the same things repeated.

"Your penmanship is excellent," I said when I handed the
notebook back to her. "Have you ever tried drawing anything
bigger? Like maybe the pier and the bayou? Or your house?"

She shook her head and pulled out a cell phone and accessed the images. Then she showed me pictures of the bayou and her house and pointed to the screen.

"Phones take good pictures, don't they?" I asked. "I especially like this one with the sunset over the water. Did you take it?"

She nodded and shoved the phone back in her pocket.

"I saw you at the parade last night," I said, watching her closely. "I was the queen on the other float. Do you remember?"

She nodded again but shifted her gaze to the grass.

"I'm sorry there was an accident with your float," I said. "Are you okay now?"

She nodded again but I could tell she was starting to get agitated.

"I'm glad you're fine," I said. "I better go back inside. Make sure you have some of those cookies."

She nodded but never looked up. I rose from the porch and headed back inside. Christina gave me an anxious look as I walked in.

"She responded to my questions," I said. "But she started to get agitated when I mentioned the parade. I didn't want to push it, so I left her alone. She was drawing stick figures in her notebook. The other pages have what looks like rows of emojis."

Christina nodded. "She started with the stick figures about a year after the accident. Then the emojis after I got her the phone and an iPad. I didn't see the point in the electronics at first as she couldn't read or write, but the therapist said she'd benefit from the mental engagement with the games and things like the apps for coloring. And I can play audiobooks for her. She loves the camera and is always taking pictures. I have to check it because she's been known to snap things she shouldn't. I wasn't aware until she showed one of me in the shower to a friend."

"Oh no!" Gertie said.

Christina smiled. "At least it was a lady friend. Could have been worse. The camera has come in handy though. I've taken pictures of different food and drinks and have a folder of them. That way, if she's wanting something in particular, she just has to find the picture and point."

"That's smart," I said.

"It definitely helps lower the frustration level with not being able to communicate," Christina said. "Were you... Did you see anything that gave you ideas?"

"Maybe," I said and pulled out my phone. "Let me have your phone number. I want to text you a lady's information. She's an expert on PTSD and works with some of the toughest cases that the military has."

"Oh, but she's got an important job and a full roster, I'm sure," Christina said. "She won't have time to help Marigold. Even if she did, I don't have the money to pay someone on that level."

"She'll talk to you because she's a friend of mine," I said. "And while she won't be able to treat Marigold, I'm sure she'll have some ideas and even some recommendations of people you can contact to implement the kinds of testing and training she suggests. She's got an enormous network as she has to find ongoing help for soldiers all over the country. Most of them work at discounted rates or even for free on the really difficult cases in exchange for permission to use the data for articles and books. No real names are included of course."

Christina put her hand over her mouth. "Oh my God! If someone with that kind of skill set could help, that would be a miracle. Thank you."

"All I'm doing is giving you a number," I said. "But hopefully, she'll have someone to pursue."

Christina jumped up and wrapped her arms around me. "It's more than just a number. It's your intention." She let go of me and wiped at the tears in her eyes. "There are times when I lose all hope—for Marigold, for myself, and quite frankly, for humanity. Then someone makes a gesture like this, and it restores my faith. I can't tell you how much I needed that restoration today."

I felt my chest constrict.

"I understand," I said. "As odd as it may sound, coming to Sinful is what restored my faith."

Christina raised one eyebrow. "If coming *here* restored your faith, then I don't ever want to dwell in the place you were before."

"No one does."

CHAPTER THIRTEEN

W<small>HEN WE FINISHED UP WITH</small> C<small>HRISTINA, IT WAS TIME FOR</small> all of us to head home and get ready for Nora's party. We'd double-checked with Beatrice, and so far, Nora wasn't on the hook for the still explosion so either the arson investigator had bought her story about not knowing her husband had one or he simply didn't want to deal with an old lady and her illegal-booze-making habits. I was voting on the latter.

I hadn't heard from Carter since I'd seen him at the General Store, but I hadn't figured I would. Between the fire, the explosion, Brock's suspicious death, and the upcoming run of parties planned, he had his hands full. Gertie had tried to talk him into making a stop by Nora's, at least to pick up some of Molly's food, but he'd even held out on that idea.

I took a long shower and pulled on jeans, T-shirt, and tennis shoes, happy to be back to regular clothes for my outing. Because I hadn't eaten since we stopped at the bakery that morning, I had a pre-party snack, then fed Merlin and made some notes on the case. I got a text from Ida Belle as I was shutting down my laptop and grabbed my cell phone and gun and headed out.

I could see Ida Belle's Lord-give-me-strength expression as I walked down the steps and figured I had a good idea what it was about. That was confirmed when I climbed into her SUV and took a look in the back seat at Gertie. She'd gone all out.

Her hair was streaked with pink highlights and spiked up in all directions. Her black tank top had lime green words on it that read *I'm with the Queen.* Her pants were turquoise and pink spotted, and she informed me gleefully that they glowed in the dark. Around her neck was a purple feather boa with flashing yellow lights. Her feet were clad in clear platforms with a huge bottom...with something moving inside.

"Are there goldfish in your shoes?" I asked.

She nodded. "Not real ones, of course. But they're in this gel and they flex so it looks like they're swimming. Aren't they cool?"

"Not the word I'd choose," Ida Belle said.

"I'm just glad I don't cover your medical insurance," I said. "Those shoes look like a minimum of a sprained ankle night."

Ida Belle nodded. "Twenty bucks and I'll put you down for ankle in the betting pool."

I passed her a twenty and Gertie shook her head.

"Oh ye of little faith," Gertie said. "It's a new year. That means another opportunity for a new me. You two could use a makeover, too, you know. Maybe approach this year in a different way than the past."

I stared at her. "It wasn't long ago that I left the CIA and DC, moved to Sinful, adopted a cat, quit my job, acquired a boyfriend, and for Christ's sake, I just wore a sequined dress and a tiara on a parade float. If there is any more change in my life, I might spontaneously combust."

"Well, Ida Belle could change something," Gertie said.

"I lowered my cholesterol," Ida Belle said.

"And got married," I reminded her. "Where's Walter, by the way?"

"He and Scooter ended up making some more grocery deliveries," she said. "He'll be there in an hour or so."

"And Jeb?" I asked Gertie.

"He and Wyatt had a doctor's appointment this afternoon, so they'll be a little late as well," she said. "Jeb told me he was going to ask for a B12 shot and some Viagra, so my new year is looking up already. Get it—up?"

"No!" Ida Belle said. "And we don't want to get it."

"If you did you might be in a better mood," Gertie said.

"I am *not* having this discussion with you," Ida Belle said.

I couldn't help grinning. After all, it was New Year's Eve, and instead of playing some fake role so that I could access and kill a target, I was just plain ole me and headed to a party with the best people I'd ever known to partake in incredible food and likely the most expensive booze collection in Sinful.

I was determined to take a night off and just have fun.

Famous last words.

Even though we were only ten minutes late from the actual starting time, we had to park a block over from Nora's house. We could hear the music blasting as soon as we climbed out of the SUV.

"I'm surprised no one has called the cops yet about the music," I said.

"Nora fixed that," Gertie said.

"Did she pay off the cops?" I joked.

"No," Gertie said. "She paid off the neighborhood. Those who aren't coming to the party got gift baskets with Ally's baked goods and expensive wine so they could have their own parties at home. And she set up child care at one of the parents' homes for the parents who want to party and don't have a sitter."

"Nora has some serious skills," I said.

"And a serious pocketbook," Ida Belle said. "But since we're all benefiting, I think I hear Molly's dip calling for me."

We made our way up the sidewalk and headed into the house, not even bothering to knock. No one would have heard or cared and besides, the place was already packed like a fraternity party, complete with a keg in the corner of the living room and beer funnels on the table next to it.

Gertie clutched my arm and asked in a reverent tone, "Is that a stripper pole?"

Sure enough, Nora had installed a clear stripper pole with flashing neon lights right in the middle of her living room.

"Hey, you match the pole," I said to Gertie as it blinked shapes of turquoise, green, and pink.

"That's because she's *dressed* for the pole," Ida Belle said.

Gertie brightened and Ida Belle shook her head.

"Don't even think about it," Ida Belle said. "You had to take off those ridiculous shoes just to make it around the block. There's no way you need to fling them up on a pole. They weigh as much as your purse, and that's no small thing to say."

Gertie was about to respond when Ronald rushed over and gave me a hug with his free arm. His other hand was clutching a champagne glass. As usual, he'd gone all out for the event—an evening gown in glittery silver, combat boots, and what could best be described as a Dolly Parton wig. Hey, at least he hadn't gone for the Dolly Parton boobs.

"I love the boots!" Gertie said.

"Of course you do," Ida Belle said.

"Everyone with taste loves the boots," Ronald said.

"They're Gucci."

He gave me a quick once-over and shook his head. "I see you're back to college dorm room chic."

I shrugged. "You can take the girl out of the dorm room..."

"But Gertie," Ronald said, "you have really outdone yourself. It's not a combination of colors or fabrics I would have chosen for myself, but I applaud your flair."

"And her self-confidence," Ida Belle said.

Ronald looked over at her. "I see you're bringing in another year with the *Farmers' Almanac/Guns & Ammo* look."

Ida Belle grinned. "You can take the girl off the farm, but you can't take the gun away from the girl."

Ronald laughed. "I just love you three."

"You're about to love me even more," Ida Belle said and pulled an envelope out of her pocket. "This is your cut of the queen winnings."

"My cut?" Ronald looked confused.

"You did the hard work of getting Fortune into the perfect dress and the hair and makeup and everything else," Ida Belle said. "And after that fiasco at the dress shop, you earned it. I've sent Daphne a very generous gift card to the Ritz spa, and if you can repair the dress, she can resell it."

Ronald took the envelope and checked his outfit for a place to put it, then smiled.

"I'll just tuck this away when I'm somewhere more private," he said and leaned in. "Ally is here with a perfectly dreamy man. I know I've seen him around but he's not from Sinful. Spill."

"That's Mannie," I said. "He's the Heberts' top guy."

Ronald sucked in a breath. "Is Ally safe?"

Ida Belle stared. "Given that she's dating the Heberts' right-hand man and best friends with Fortune, I'd say she's the safest person in Sinful."

"Good point," he said. "I think I need another drink. Nora installed a fountain in her backyard and she's running champagne through it. It's completely unsanitary but so fabulous I had to have a glass. Or two."

He waved a hand in dismissal. "We don't have to count things until midnight."

As he jaunted off, I pulled Gertie away from the stripper pole and we headed for the kitchen to load up before the food was cleaned out. It was shoulder to shoulder there. Food crowded every countertop, and a long folding table was set up spanning the length of the dining room just off the kitchen. We filled our plates and headed out the back door for a breath of fresh air and to find a place where we could lift our hands to eat without elbowing someone.

The backyard had plenty of people, but Nora had played it smart and rented outdoor furniture. There were groups of sitting areas dotted all over the patio and backyard, all with side tables to hold drinks and food. Several firepits were going with chairs circled around them, and the hot tub was at capacity. The champagne fountain was the centerpiece of the setup and I had to admit, it was pretty cool. Figuring that the alcohol would cancel out the unsanitary part that Ronald mentioned, we all grabbed a glass and headed for a cluster of vacant chairs in the back corner of the yard. That way, we could enjoy the food and watch all the partygoers.

We'd barely taken our seats before Ally spotted us and she and Mannie headed our way. They also had plates of food and took over two more of the chairs, leaving only one available in our little section.

"It's good to see the two of you here," Gertie said, grinning. "Together."

Ally blushed and Mannie returned Gertie's grin.

"I'm just glad she agreed to claim me," Mannie said. "Nora

is kinda scary."

We all laughed.

"Yeah, Carter avoids her like the plague," I said. "I'm not sure if it's more because he thinks he'll have to arrest her for having something illegal or she won't stop hitting on him."

"At least I'm in good company," he said and laughed. Then he lifted his champagne glass. "Here's to some more good company."

"And the New Year's Queen," Ally said.

We all clanked glasses and gossiped as we tackled our food.

"Aunt Celia came into the bakery this afternoon mad as a hornet," Ally said.

"Was that after she got my text?" Gertie asked.

"Probably, since she already knew about the vote," Ally said. "And I'm sure that peeved her plenty but she was mad because someone stole all the cash from her purse. She has a contractor coming on Monday and had five hundred in cash."

"When was it stolen?" Ida Belle asked.

"She got the cash out of the bank Thursday afternoon," Ally said. "But she didn't notice it was missing until lunch today when she went to pay in the café and the envelope was gone."

"Why the heck was she carrying it around with her?" Ida Belle asked. "She should have had it stuffed in a sock drawer or her freezer."

"Or up her butt," Gertie said. "No one's about to look there."

"She said with all the parade stuff, she forgot to take it out," Ally said.

"Well, who had access?" I asked.

"Exactly what I asked her," Ally said. "Her purse has a zipper top, so it's not like someone could bump against her and make off with something inside without her knowing. But as soon as I suggested it had to be someone who'd been left alone with it, she clammed up."

I looked over at Ida Belle and Gertie.

"Sounds like our friend RJ got some of that cash she needed," I said.

"What do you mean?" Ally asked.

Since I couldn't imagine it could cause trouble for Ally, I filled her in on what I'd seen transpire between RJ and Brock before the parade. Ally's eyes widened as I talked.

"And then someone killed Brock," Ally said.

"*Might* have killed him," I said.

"The ME's ruling was undetermined," Mannie said. "But he's maintaining suspicious death with a strong leaning toward homicide. Our source said he doesn't like the look of it but doesn't have concrete proof. He's hoping the cops can piece it together."

"What?" I sat up straight. "Why didn't you call me?"

"I just got the information on the way to Ally's," he said. "And since we were sure to see you here, I figured I'd just wait and give you everything in person."

"There's more?" Gertie clapped her hands. "Well, put down that plate and get to talking."

"Big made phone calls to get some background on Brock and RJ's time in Nashville," Mannie said. "One of those was to a retired beat cop who was helpful back when the Heberts had some issues with some of the shadier practices in the music industry. Anyway, this cop said Brock was known to local law enforcement—bounced checks, stiffing bars on bills, drunken brawls—the usual fare for his type, but nothing so serious it kept him in jail long enough to matter. This cop also said that rumor was Brock owed money to a local drug dealer called Payday."

"Payday?" Gertie asked.

"'Candy man' is slang for drug dealer," I said. "He's being whimsical."

"A whimsical drug dealer," Ida Belle said. "God save us."

"Well, it fits because everyone says the guy is nuts," Mannie said. "Word on the street is that for about a year now, Brock has been selling product in the clubs he and RJ were playing. And a recent delivery of product got sold but the revenue didn't make it back to the supplier."

I whistled. "That *is* a problem."

"It gets even more interesting," Mannie said. "Big also spoke to an industry person he knows. Apparently, a producer for a television series set to start filming in Nashville showed an interest in licensing that song of RJ and Brock's for the theme song of the show."

"Wow!" Ida Belle said. "That could be worth some cash."

"Then why is Brock so desperate for money if it's about to come in?" I asked. "Even a drug dealer knows dead people can't pay up. So wait for the payout and collect payment with a lot of interest."

Mannie nodded. "Except RJ is trying to cut Brock out of the deal. She's claiming she's the sole writer for the song. That Brock was just a guitar player."

"How was it licensed originally for the collaborative album it was on?" I asked.

"They were both referred to as 'contributing artists,' which is likely intentionally vague," Mannie said. "But this TV producer doesn't want to license their version of the song. He just wants the song itself and will have his own people remake it."

"So the song creator is the one in line for the cash," I said.

"Exactly," Mannie said. "RJ produced what she claims is the original sheet music and lyrics. Apparently, Brock can't read music but RJ can."

"Sawyer made her take music lessons," Ida Belle said. "She wanted her on the pageant circuit with Pansy, but RJ wasn't having any of it."

"Well, Brock was claiming RJ is trying to pull a fast one," Mannie said, "so the lawyer is going to have the ink date tested."

"To make sure she didn't fake some documents recently just to get the deal," Ida Belle said. "That's a lot of trouble for the attorney to go to."

Mannie nodded. "Which tells me there's probably a pile of cash on the line. Big said it's probably a good licensing fee up front but if the series takes off, then that's more fees with every season and even more on top of that if it goes into syndication. And no lawyer wants to get wrapped up in an intellectual property rights mess, so he's making sure he's in the clear before he moves forward with the negotiation."

"If the pot is big enough to go around, why bother trying to claim it all?" I asked. "Why not just split it to get their hands on the cash quicker? Apparently neither one is flush, so why quibble and risk the TV guy finding another song that's less problematic?"

"All good questions," Mannie said. "Big said that the lawyer hasn't conveyed to the TV producer that there's an issue, so right now, he thinks it's still a negotiation with the correct people and nothing is standing in their way except the deal-wrangling. As to why RJ is trying to take the entire haul—word is her voice is shot. She can't even handle a full set at a bar without a bunch of breaks and a constant influx of hot tea and whiskey. And apparently, Brock took up with another singer a couple months back—professionally *and* romantically."

"So the only skill set she has is gone and so is her man," I said. "I can see how that would prompt her to try to get it all."

Ida Belle nodded. "And running home gets her free board while her lawyer gets it handled."

"So she killed Brock when he followed her here?" Gertie asked.

"She's definitely got the strongest motive," I said. "With Brock dead, no more issues with the licensing. It's not like he's got an estate that's going to challenge it."

"And as you pointed out, Payday only benefits with Brock alive," Ida Belle said.

"Let me muddy the waters," Mannie said. "What if Payday heard about RJ trying to cut Brock out of the deal? In that case, he might choose to make an example of Brock. After all, he can only allow Brock to walk around so long without paying up."

"And if there's no indication that Brock can come up with the money..." I said.

Mannie nodded. "And the plot gets even thicker. Guess who strolled into town on Thursday?"

"Payday?" Gertie asked.

"Close enough," Mannie said. "His new enforcer. Our retired source said the drug task force has been trying to make a case against Payday for years, so they've been tracking the key players in his crew. Our source had drinks with one of the task force members yesterday and he told him that they tracked a recently acquired enforcer—a guy who goes by Sledgehammer—to Sinful."

"There's your guy in the shadows at the parade," Ida Belle said.

Gertie sighed. "Well, it was fun while it lasted, but this one is no great mystery. If RJ didn't kill Brock, then this enforcer did."

"It seems that way," Mannie said. "But the odd thing is Sledgehammer is still here."

CHAPTER FOURTEEN

I TRIED TO PROCESS WHAT MANNIE WAS TELLING ME, BUT NO matter how I repeated it in my mind, it didn't make sense.

"Seriously?" I asked. "He's still here?"

Mannie nodded. "In fact, he's checked into our favorite motel."

"But what for?" Gertie asked. "If his job was to kill Brock, he wouldn't check into a motel in the first place, and he definitely wouldn't stick around after he killed him."

"There's no accounting for the stupidity and ego of those in the drug business," Mannie said. "But there's no shortage of calculation, either. You can bet Sledgehammer stayed put because he was ordered to. And dealers always have a reason for their orders."

"Maybe he's planning on collecting Brock's debt from RJ," I said.

"But if RJ and Brock separated two months ago," Gertie said, "the deal Brock didn't make payment on must have been recent or he'd already be dead. Besides, who's to say RJ even knew that Brock was dealing?"

"She had to know he was using," I said. "There's really no

155

hiding that from someone you live with. And she knew how much money they made from gigs versus how much the bills were. If Brock had extra for drugs, then there was definitely another revenue stream. My guess is that as long as money was coming in, she didn't care much where it came from."

Mannie nodded. "Then her voice went to crap, they couldn't get bookings, and Brock had to find another way to get into his regular club performances."

"So he ditched RJ for another singer to keep the money train going," Gertie said.

"And so he didn't have to pay her way," Ida Belle said. "It's not like he's ever cared about his own kid. Why would he support RJ? But that doesn't leave RJ on the hook for something he did after they split."

Mannie shrugged. "If Payday figures RJ was in on things with Brock from the beginning and she's going to come into some cash, he could pressure her for payment. The easiest way would be to influence the clubs to shut her out, even if she gets her voice straight. All Payday needs is dirt on club owners or managers and he's golden. And there's a lot of dirt in the club scene."

"If she can't get work, why not just leave Nashville altogether?" Gertie said.

"She did," I pointed out. "We all assumed it was to get away from someone—probably Brock—but we also assumed it was temporary. Maybe it's not. Maybe she planned on coming back here and sticking around until she collected the TV money."

"Then she could plan her next makeover of herself and her career," Ida Belle said. "Because there's no way RJ is sticking around Sinful forever, but I could see her lying low here long enough to collect the funds to disappear."

"And getting out of Nashville lowers the potential for the

TV producer to hear any gossip about her or Brock," Mannie said. "They're not going to want any negative publicity associated with a new series."

"Well, that didn't exactly go as planned," Gertie said. "With Brock murdered, gossip about the two of them is about to become a recreational sport."

"In Sinful," Mannie pointed out. "But as long as the investigation stays down here, she's probably good. Brock wasn't important enough to matter in Nashville. And with him dead, RJ's attorney can push the deal through before anything comes out. As Fortune said, it's not like Brock has an estate to claim an interest."

"I'm confused," Gertie said. "Are we back to RJ being the prime suspect? Or was it Payday making an example of Brock?"

Mannie shrugged. "Could go either way."

"You got a description for this Sledgehammer?" I asked.

"Even better," Mannie said and pulled out his cell phone. "I have pictures. Just sent you a text."

I pulled up the images and scrolled through them. Gertie and Ida Belle leaned over and studied them along with me.

Midforties. Six foot-ish probably. Two hundred including the three gold chains around his neck. Wavy blond hair that looked like it belonged more on a surfer than a drug dealer's enforcer guy. Threat level assumed to be high given his profession but probably only medium in my world.

"He doesn't quite live up to his nickname," Gertie said. "I was expecting a guy who looked like the strong man at a circus."

"Rumor is, a hammer is his weapon of choice," Mannie said. "But there's already a convict in Nashville who goes by Hammer, so he upped the ante."

I smiled. "So no two criminals in the same area can have the same nickname?"

"It's like their own trademark system," Ida Belle said.

"Brock did have that blow on the back of his head," Gertie said. "Was that cause of death?"

"If the blow killed him, then how did he get a needle in his arm?" Ida Belle asked. "Or have an argument with another person later on? Or turn on the TV?"

Ally's eyes widened. "How do you know— You know what, never mind."

"Technically, cause of death was a heart attack due to overdose," Mannie said. "Manner of death is what's up for grabs. Could be the blow to the head caused him to miscalculate on the heroin. Could be he just made a mistake and the head injury didn't impact it at all."

"Devil's advocate," Ida Belle said. "Brock could have fallen and hit his own head, then accidentally overdosed himself."

Mannie nodded. "It's not impossible. But then there's the fighting that the guy in the next room heard, and the severity of the blow, which is why I'm guessing the ME went with suspicious."

"He thinks the head injury caused the overdose but can't prove it," I said.

"That's how I'm reading it," Mannie said. "It was a big miscalculation in dosage. One an experienced user really shouldn't make, even if they'd been drinking."

"So the ME passes it to law enforcement to sort it out," Ida Belle said. "And they won't be allowed to spend much time on it."

"Nope," Mannie agreed. "Carter will probably get a couple days to poke around and see if there's more to it, then after that, the sheriff will get pressure from the politicians about the waste of resources on an unsympathetic victim and Carter will be instructed to shelve it and move on to obvious crimes that impact taxpayers who matter."

"So if someone can cover their tracks long enough, they get away with murder," Ally said. "That's a frightening thought."

"Put it aside," I said. "It's not happening on my watch. Too many good people would have to endure a lifetime of talking behind their backs if this isn't put to rest."

Ally smiled. "You know you're the best thing that ever happened to Sinful."

"The feeling is mutual," I said.

"You need anything, you let me know," Mannie said. "I could talk to this Sledgehammer."

I shook my head. "He'd take one look at you and hightail it back to Nashville. I'd like to figure out why he's still here. First order of business tomorrow is running down some information on Mr. Hammer."

Looked like Shadow Chaser wasn't quite out of the investigation business yet.

———

We milled around outside for a couple hours, chatting with different friends and neighbors. I discovered that most of them wanted to pump me for information on Brock's death and were then disappointed when I explained that Carter didn't tell me things just because we were dating. In fact, he was more likely to confide in practically anyone in Sinful about an investigation before he'd tell me about it.

Walter had finally shown up with Jeb and Wyatt in tow, as they'd arrived at the same time. Seeing Jeb light up when he spotted Gertie and her outfit was almost as cute as Wyatt's confused and somewhat horrified expression. He'd finally shaken his head and given her a quick hug, and I figured he'd gotten somewhat used to her less-than-normal behavior.

We were all standing close to the champagne fountain when Nora approached.

"Good Lord, how long have you guys been here?" she asked.

"Several hours," I said.

"How have I missed you?" she asked.

"You've talked to us at least five times already," I said.

She waved a hand in dismissal. "Not you. You!" She gave Wyatt a sexy smile and sidled up to him.

Wyatt shot Ida Belle and me a panicked look and I struggled not to laugh.

"Why don't you come with me and tell me your life story?" Nora said, leaning up against him.

"This party isn't long enough for my life story," Wyatt said. "I'm no spring chicken."

"I don't have anything on my schedule until March," Nora said. Then she looked at the rest of us. "Now that everyone has cleaned out the buffet, I'm starting the house music. It's time to dance."

Gertie clapped her hands, then teetered on those ridiculous shoes. Jeb reached out to steady her, but with his bad back, all he did was double the problem, so Walter, Ida Belle, and I moved in to catch the two of them before they contaminated Nora's fountain.

"You should take those things off before you try to dance," I said.

"I'll take them off later," Gertie said and gave Jeb a wink. "Among other things."

"That's my girl," Nora said and tugged Wyatt away from the fountain.

A couple seconds later, house music fired up, the strong beat pumping through the speakers, and people started to bounce around. They weren't going to give MTV dancers a run for their money, but everyone appeared to be having fun. Gertie squealed again and pulled Jeb into the center of the yard. She couldn't exactly bounce in her shoes, so she settled on an odd bobbing sort of move that kinda looked like mini squats combined with trying to get out of a low car seat. She clutched a tree in order to remain upright. Jeb and his bad back didn't even try to bounce. He just bobbed one arm up and down and snapped his fingers. Ally and Mannie had joined the dancers on the patio and were smiling, their gazes locked on each other.

"That looks like it's going well," Ida Belle said, nodding toward the patio.

"Yeah," I agreed. "I just hope she doesn't get hurt. I know Mannie wouldn't do anything intentionally to hurt her, but the situation alone..."

"People will talk," Ida Belle said. "Then Ally has to decide what to do about it. My guess is that as long as it doesn't affect her business, she'll ignore them. Being Celia's niece and having Pansy for a cousin, Ally's no stranger to her name crossing people's lips."

"No, but that gossip is tangential. This would be specifically about her. Do you think people will care so much about who she's dating that they wouldn't buy from the bakery?"

"A handful, maybe. There's some serious bias in Sinful and those inflexible people crop up from time to time, but I don't think they'd amount to enough to cause problems. Still, I've seen stranger things happen here. If the wrong person gets a burr in their butt, there's enough unhappy people that can be spurred into taking up a cause because they lack anything better to do."

"You know if too many people go flapping their gums, I have money saved for my bail."

Ida Belle laughed. "You're a good friend, Fortune."

"Takes one to know one," I said and pointed at Gertie, who was headed inside, towing Jeb behind her.

Ida Belle sighed. "We better go save her from that pole."

"Or save the pole."

We heard the cheers before we got to the living room, and by the time we pushed through the crowd, it was worse than we'd imagined. Gertie had shed her tank top, and her hot-pink sequined bra was practically glowing in the flashing lights in the living room. The crowd was cheering, and Jeb was standing next to the pole, throwing one-dollar bills at Gertie as she swung around it with a heck of a lot more skill than I would have imagined.

"At least everything she could get arrested for showing is intact," I said and tilted my head to the side. "And remarkably upright."

"That's because she's upside down," Ida Belle said. "She's going to crack her head open and we're going to have to send her to the hospital barefoot because I'm not letting her go in with those shoes."

"I thought your generation only worried about getting caught out with bad underwear."

"I don't waste any worry on that one. With Gertie, I'm already assured that whatever is going on under those leggings is inappropriate in some way."

"Could be worse—she could be wearing a skirt."

Gertie squealed like a kid on the playground as she inched down the pole. She was upside down, and unlike a pro, who would have an elegant leg bent or sticking out and slide with ballerina precision, Gertie had her arms and one leg wrapped around the pole like a koala bear with the other leg straight out against the pole in what looked like a horribly awkward position. It also appeared the pole was giving every inch of bare skin pole burn. I was kinda surprised that she was managing to stay in that position without falling off, but then I noticed the strap around the ankle of the straight leg and saw it was attached to a line secured to the ceiling.

"How did she even get up there?" Ida Belle asked as the crowd cheered her on.

About that time, her head came about an inch from the floor when it reached the length of the safety strap and we got our answer. She called out and the crowd rushed forward and lifted her back up the pole while one guy turned a crank that pulled the safety strap back up for another round. When he locked it back into place, I realized that it had a mechanism that slowly released the strap until the dancer was almost at the bottom of the pole, stopping them before they hit the ground.

Which still didn't make it a good idea for Gertie. I was surprised neither Gertie nor one of the lifting crew had been injured the first go. A second round was certain to get a 911 call for a dislocated hip at minimum. But with the drunken crowd cheering her on, Gertie had apparently found the strength to go again. But this time, she got fancy and tried sticking the unsecured leg out on the way down.

It was a really bad idea.

The shoe with the fish settled just inches from the fireplace mantel where Nora's cat, a bright orange tabby, was hiding under the vines of an ivy plant. The LED lights reflected off the gel in the heel, making it look like water sparkling under sunlight. And with all the jostling, the fish did actually look like they were swimming.

So the cat made his move.

CHAPTER FIFTEEN

THE CAT LEAPED OFF THE MANTEL, KNOCKING THE IVY ON top of the safety strap wench, lodging it in place, then he wrapped himself around the shoe, digging his claws into Gertie's ankle. Gertie let out a yell and kicked her leg out and connected with the mantel, sending her spiraling around the pole like a top. But the cat was not deterred. He clung to her foot as she spun around, screeching as if someone were killing him.

The crowd scattered but not before Gertie's foot—wearing the cat—connected right in the face of someone who'd rushed toward the pole rather than away. Between the whirling Gertie, the flashing lights, and the people scrambling, I couldn't tell who it was until I heard him yell.

Carter!

I ran forward as Gertie continued rotation and the cat flew off her foot and across the living room. Mannie, who'd just entered the room with Ally, grabbed a wicker basket from the floor, caught the cat with it, and then slid the basket down the hall before the angry ball of fur could take out his failure to have a fish dinner on the nearest set of hands.

I reached out to grab Gertie's leg and right when I got a good clutch on her, the safety strap broke, and my arm went straight through her bra as she fell and yanked me to the ground with her. Before I could untangle my arm, a blanket dropped on top of me and I had a flashback to the time I was caught in a target's net. I sprang up, flinging the blanket with one arm and pulling my nine with the other. As I got in firing position, I could see Gertie's bright pink bra hanging from my wrist.

Carter, who had scratches across his forehead, stepped in front of me and raised an eyebrow.

"I'm not going to tell you to hold fire," he said. "But you have to start with either Gertie or that cat."

Ally rushed forward with the discarded blanket and Jeb yelled that he'd found Gertie's tank top. I looked down to see Gertie clutching throw pillows across her chest and laughing like a maniac, and the reason for the blanket became clear. Ally flung the blanket over Gertie again, then Jeb ran over and smuggled the tank top under there so we could avoid an R-rated event.

I was just about to ask Carter what he was doing there when Nora rushed in.

"I heard there was an accident," she said. "Is Gertie all right?"

"I think so, but she probably flashed your guests," I said.

Nora waved a hand in dismissal. "That probably won't be the last time someone gets flashed tonight."

Gertie flung the blanket off her head and looked up at Nora.

"That was fantastic fun," Gertie said. "I hope I didn't break anything."

"There was a situation with the cat," I started to explain.

"Drunken Idiot will be fine," Nora said.

"Are you talking about me?" Gertie asked.

"No. The cat," Nora said. "His name is Idiot and he's been drinking out of the fountain all afternoon. He does some odd things and has a substance abuse problem."

Finished with her declaration, Nora turned around and headed out of the room, citing a need for another drink as she left. Ida Belle, Mannie, Ally, Walter, Gertie, and I burst into laughter. Then I remembered Carter was standing behind me and looked back. He wasn't nearly as amused.

"Who died?" I asked him.

He frowned. "Why would you ask that?"

"Because you're standing in Nora's living room in the middle of her New Year's party. The party you said there wasn't enough money or beer in the world to get you to attend, even for five minutes."

"Can we talk outside?" he asked.

Ida Belle raised an eyebrow as I followed him out. There were people milling around the porch, so he kept walking until we reached the sidewalk.

"I feel like that kid whose mother walks him out of the party that the other kid threw while his parents were out of town," I said.

"At least Nora never had kids," Carter said. "One thing to be thankful for."

"So what's got you breaking hard promises to yourself?"

He glanced around to double-check that no one had walked within hearing range, then leaned toward me. "Someone took a shot at RJ."

"What?" I couldn't say I was necessarily surprised that someone might have a go at RJ after what had happened to Brock and given what I'd learned from Mannie, but it was still far down on the list of possibilities.

"She was at the Swamp Bar for a while, then said she had a

headache and headed home. When she got out of her car at her mother's house, someone put a bullet through the window. She said it would have gotten her if she hadn't dropped her phone and bent over to get it."

"So what did she do?"

"Crawled under the car and called 911. She got lucky. The shot woke up her mother, who flipped on every light in the house as she made her way downstairs. I'm guessing the shooter knew he had a very limited window to get out of there and there was no light in the driveway at all, so he wouldn't have been able to see if she was still under the car or behind it."

"Why no light?"

"The bulbs on the garage and porch had both been smashed, and the streetlight is too far away and blocked by trees to help much."

"Premeditated."

He nodded.

I frowned. "So why are you here telling me now? You never offer up information like this."

"Because I know you and know there's no way you're going to let this thing with Brock go. But this and the parade makes two attempts on RJ. Whatever the two of them were mixed up in, they probably dragged it back to Sinful, and you need to stay out of it."

"I thought Brock set the float on fire."

He shrugged. "That's what I thought as well, but he sure as heck didn't fire that shot through her car window. Maybe it was your mystery guy in the shadows. Or maybe it was someone else entirely. All I know is there are way too many variables here and I don't like it."

"What does RJ say?"

He frowned.

I sighed, frustrated by his required silence. "Well, where is she now? Can you at least tell me that?"

"She's still at her mother's house and complaining loudly about it. Deputy Breaux is sitting on the house for now, but I'm requesting some help from Mudbug if they have anyone to spare. I really don't want to have to call the state police in on this."

"Because they'll take over. So I assume RJ is wanting to get out of Dodge?"

"Oh yeah."

"Why not let her go? She doesn't have the means, or quite frankly the aptitude, to skip the country. If you really think she and Brock brought trouble here, then it should leave with her, right?"

"She doesn't have a place to go back to in Nashville. She was evicted from her apartment a week ago, which is why she turned up in Sinful to begin with. With no fixed address and no employment, she would be in the wind, working for tips in any bar across the country."

"And you couldn't have that because of Brock's death," I said, probing for more information. "Can't let a suspect leave town, right?"

He gave me a sort of nod.

I groaned. "Don't tell me she has an alibi."

"Yeah, and I'm going to share it, so the two of you don't cross paths again. The neighbor across the street was working on a motorcycle in his garage all night. He saw her come home with her mom right after the parade. Neither her mother's car nor RJ's left the house while he was outside and he was in the garage until around 2:00 a.m. Sawyer confirmed that they went straight home after the parade, had dinner, watched some television, and went to bed."

"I know there's some people with grudges," I said. "And I

can see someone taking a crack at either one of them in a bar or whatever, but knocking out light bulbs and sitting on a house is a planned event. Do you really think a local was holding on to hate that long?"

"We've both seen stranger. I can't exclude anyone in Sinful from scrutiny."

"I get it. Did you question any locals today?"

His jaw flexed but he didn't respond, which I took to mean he'd probably talked to Gina and Cecil.

"You know as soon as you question people, they'll be subject to the Sinful rumor mill and everything that comes with it," I said.

"What can I do about that?"

I shook my head. Gina's and Cecil's troubles couldn't be his focus.

But they could be mine.

SATURDAY MORNING CAME ENTIRELY TOO EARLY. I'D DRAWN my blinds so my room was nice and dark, but that didn't stop Merlin from knowing it was time for breakfast. I'd been smart enough to close the bedroom door but given the odd happenings in Sinful, I'd been hesitant to put on the noise-canceling headphones. He gave me until 8:00 a.m. before he started his siren wail in the hallway, so at least I got in a couple hours more than usual. But given that I hadn't dropped into bed until close to 3:00 a.m. I would have liked a little longer.

I needed to get those new earbuds I'd seen. I could put them on with earmuffs or a headband to keep them in while I slept. Then I'd be connected to my phone but not the cat. Of course, there was always the question of what kind of havoc he'd create if his starvation cries went unanswered, so I'd have to weigh the risks on that one. The good news was, there were no schedules on national holidays, so naps were totally on the table.

Not that I had a regular schedule anyway.

I sighed as I put on a pot of coffee. I'd just spent the entire walk downstairs thinking about sleeping. I was either tired or bored. With the coffee brewing, I fixed up Merlin's breakfast, which he scarfed down, then I let him out the back door for his morning routine. The coffee was done by then, so I sat with that first cup, savoring every hot, rich drop. The party had still been in full swing when I went back inside Nora's after talking with Carter. I'd filled Ida Belle and Gertie in on the basics, but we'd decided to leave the big discussion for today when we couldn't be overheard.

I'd give Mannie a heads-up sometime today but hadn't wanted to put a damper on his date with Ally. She was regular people and didn't handle murder attempts with the same nonchalance as the rest of us. Same with Walter, Jeb, and Wyatt. And since everyone was having a good time and none of us had any risk that I could see, there was no point in spoiling the mood. Nor was there anything actionable that we could partake in right then.

So we'd drunk and danced—Scooter had managed to get me up for a song or two, much to Gertie's and Ally's delight. And at one point during the night, Nora had shut down the music long enough to announce to the crowd that I'd won the Queen vote, and everyone had cheered and congratulated me. I'd given a shout-out to my team, including Ronald, who was so drunk at that point that he'd swapped shoes with Gertie and was wearing her bra on his head. He'd waved the cat in the air when I called his name, then tucked the animal under his arm and headed off, claiming they both needed a potty break. I was pretty sure the cat was as drunk as he was.

Drunks, stripper poles, wardrobe malfunctions, and flying cats aside, the party had been a good time, and I was a little surprised by how much I'd enjoyed it. Large, noisy crowds weren't usually my thing, but the food and the company had been good. Nora scored major points for the quality of her booze, hiring Molly to cater, and not inviting any of Celia's crew. Ida Belle said we'd pick up a gift for her and take it around next week to show our appreciation. We just had to come up with something Nora needed. I suggested liability insurance.

I'd barely finished my first cup when I heard a knock at my front door, then Carter called out from the entry. I yelled back and he came shuffling into the kitchen, looking as if he hadn't slept in days, which I was going to guess was close to accurate. He poured a cup of coffee and sank into a chair.

"I saw Merlin on the porch and decided to check in before I head home," he said. "I'm surprised you're up this early. I figured you'd be sleeping it off."

"If it wasn't for Merlin, I would be. I don't have a hangover, though. I spaced my drinking out and made sure I had plenty to eat. It would have been nice to get a couple more hours, but I'm guessing I got far more than you."

"Considering I haven't been home since very early a.m. on Friday, you'd be correct. I dropped off Tiny with my mom yesterday and given everything going on, I might just leave him there for another day or two."

I nodded. "Was the rest of the night quiet? I mean, for Sinful on New Year's Eve."

"No more attempted or successful homicides, if that's what you mean. But with Deputy Breaux keeping an eye on RJ, I didn't have a second of downtime."

"Why didn't you have the sheriff sit on her? Surely he can

still shoot a gun or call for backup if he sees anything suspicious."

"Honestly, I didn't think anyone would try to get to her again last night. Quite frankly, I seriously doubt anyone is going to try again at her mother's house."

I frowned. "Then why...oh. You were afraid she'd make a run for it."

He nodded. "And the sheriff is not known for staying awake on overnight stakeouts. RJ might not have killed Brock, but she knows something she's not telling me."

"So what are you going to do about coverage today?" I asked.

"I sent Gavin over. He jumped at the chance."

Gavin was the fairly new day dispatcher at the sheriff's department. He had big dreams of becoming a supercop, but I wasn't sure he had the ability for it. Or the maturity. But I supposed sitting in a car and calling someone if RJ left wasn't going to tax his abilities any.

"So who's running dispatch?"

"Actually, Marie showed up early this morning and volunteered to help out."

I smiled. I'd had a chat with Marie at Nora's party about the need for more manpower over at the sheriff's department.

"You've got the mayor working the phones?" I joked.

"She insisted. And I wasn't about to turn down competent help. Plus, with her being mayor, she has the town's best interest first and understands the discretion necessary."

I laughed. "Is that your roundabout way of telling me not to bother pumping her for information?"

He shrugged. "You can try."

"I wouldn't put Marie in a bad position."

"Why not? You'll do it to me."

"You're getting benefits that Marie isn't."

"Try offering them to her and see if it works."

"Nah. She's too good for me."

He grinned. "You and I might just be the only two people who could handle each other."

"I'm pretty sure that's a fact."

"So what do you have planned for today?"

"You're looking at the extent of my plans that I'm aware of. Well, I'm going to refill my coffee, but that's as far as I've gotten. I'm sure Ida Belle and Gertie will surface at some point and we'll go through all things seen and heard last night. And we probably should get Gertie's bra back from Ronald, assuming he still has it."

"That's my cue," Carter said and rose. "I'm off to bed. Try not to do anything that Marie will wake me up over. At least for three or four hours."

He leaned over and kissed me and headed out. I refilled my cup and grabbed my laptop, figuring I'd check the news and see how the world had rung in the New Year. I was on my second pot of coffee and had just heated up a cinnamon roll from Ally's bakery when the front door opened, and I heard a croak that sounded somewhat like Gertie's voice. Footsteps shuffled down the hallway and finally, Ida Belle and Gertie appeared. Ida Belle looked the way she did most every other day she appeared in my kitchen. Gertie, on the other hand, looked as if she'd been pulled out of bed and dragged out the door after a month of spring break parties.

She went straight to the counter, picked up the coffeepot, and started to drink straight from it. Ida Belle just raised an eyebrow and grabbed a soda from the refrigerator. When Gertie had finished a good eight ounces or so, she sank into a chair, still clutching the pot as though it were full of liquid gold.

"You all right?" I asked.

She looked at me, clearly confused. "All right? Good Lord, woman, that was the most fun I've had since Ida Belle's bachelorette party. I'm still basking in the New Year's glow."

Ida Belle shook her head. "You're basking in stale alcohol and cat hair."

"Well, if you drag me out of bed at the crack of dawn and then make me leave the house before I shower, you get potluck," Gertie said.

"First off," Ida Belle said, "you were lying across your entry rug. If I weighed a pound more, I wouldn't have been able to squeeze in the door. And you're the one who declared walking all the way to your bathroom was too much work. You said you'd worry about it later, much to the dismay of everyone who gets within ten feet of you today."

"Francis said I smelled great," Gertie said.

"He said he smelled *grapes*," Ida Belle said. "You were lying on top of a bag of them."

I rose from the table and grabbed my spare coffeepot from the pantry. "I'll just make another round with the strongest stuff I've got. So why were you sleeping on the entry rug? I thought Jeb and Wyatt were both staying at your house last night and driving back home today."

Since Walter and Ida Belle had arrived separately, I'd gotten a lift with Walter when he left, and as Ida Belle had stopped drinking long before the party was over, she volunteered to get Gertie and her guests home safely.

"Jeb stayed the night, but Wyatt found a better offer than my guest room," Gertie said.

I stared. "He did *not* stay at Nora's!"

Gertie grinned and nodded. "He showed up this morning at my house at the crack of dawn, insisting that he and Jeb had to get home right away because redfish were going to be biting today. But I know the walk of shame when I see it. He couldn't even look me in the eyes."

"That's not particularly easy to do when you're facedown on the doormat," Ida Belle said.

Gertie waved a hand in dismissal. "I must have fallen asleep there after they left. Locking the door took a lot out of me. But I've totally knocked that video of Fortune at the parade off the YouTube top one hundred."

"That's because everyone is concerned for the cat," I said.

"The cat came out of the entire thing better than I did," Gertie said. "Between the claw marks on my ankle and the pole burn in places I'm not going to mention, I'll be keeping Nora busy making that secret salve for a while."

Ida Belle cringed and shook her head.

"So why did you drag me out of my house unkempt and still half looped?" Gertie asked.

"Because I have news," Ida Belle said. "Cecil Tassin is missing."

CHAPTER SIXTEEN

"Missing?" I repeated. "Missing as in Gina filed a report and his car was abandoned somewhere? Or missing as in might be walking shamefully somewhere like Wyatt and didn't want his daughter to know?"

"Far as I know, the last person to see him was Walter at the store yesterday," Ida Belle said. "Cecil claimed he would be at Nora's party last night—at least long enough to sample some of Molly's food—then he was supposed to play cards with his poker group. But Whiskey's father called over to the bar looking for him when he was a no-show."

"And you know this how?" I asked.

"Because one of the card players called Walter this morning asking if Cecil had mentioned a last-minute trip when he was at the store."

"I take it he did not," I said.

Ida Belle shook her head. "But Walter did say that he bought bread, lunch meat, potato chips, soda, and a bag of cookies."

"Sounds like food for the road to me," Gertie said.

"Carter was by here earlier and didn't even mention it," I

said. "He's really taking this keeping-me-in-the-dark thing seriously."

"He might not know yet," Ida Belle said. "Cecil told Walter that Carter questioned him yesterday. So unless Carter had reason to go looking for him again, he probably doesn't know."

"Isn't Walter going to tell him?" I asked.

"Walter loves his nephew and respects his job," Ida Belle said. "But he doesn't want to get Cecil in trouble and doesn't want to add to the gossip that's already going around."

"Cecil probably just wanted to get away from all the noise," Gertie said. "He's a bit of an introvert. All this focus on him would make him itchy."

"Does Cecil have a camp?" I asked.

"He does, but it's water access only and his boat is still in his driveway," Ida Belle said.

"That's because he has a split in the hull that needs patching," Gertie said.

"How do you know that?" Ida Belle asked.

"Because I wasn't buying that aluminum weld for *my* boat," Gertie said.

"I thought you said you hit a pier and your boat was damaged," I said.

Gertie nodded. "Which is why I had to borrow Cecil's boat."

"Which you also damaged?" I asked.

"Now you see why I don't lend her anything with an engine," Ida Belle said.

"That's not the point," Gertie said. "The point is, just because someone's boat is landlocked doesn't mean they didn't skip out of here on the water. Practically everyone in Sinful has a boat, and most *nice* people will let you borrow it."

"That depends on how *nice* the boat is," Ida Belle said. "But you're not completely wrong."

"Where's Cecil's camp?" I asked.

"On Number Two," Ida Belle said.

I groaned. I'd been to the stinky island shortly after my arrival in Sinful, and to say it was appropriately named was a gross understatement. The mud there was toxic to the nose, and I'd had to sniff coffee grounds for days before it cleared my nasal passages. Unfortunately, it was also one of the best fishing spots around, so a lot of people had camps there.

"I cannot go to Number Two right now or I will be subject to a bathroom emergency," Gertie said. "In fact, I'm pretty sure the boat alone would be a problem."

"It's raining now anyway," I said. "And I'm not feeling up to a winter drenching. But we still have something landlocked to check up on."

"Sledgehammer?" Ida Belle asked.

I nodded.

———

It took a couple of hours, two showers, and four pots of coffee to get Gertie ready for travel, but she wouldn't hear of Ida Belle and me going without her.

"At least the rain stopped," Gertie said as we rode up the highway.

"Better to keep the hips intact if you have to run," Ida Belle said and looked over at me. "Did you check to see if our friend is working today?"

I shook my head. "I was afraid he might run if he knew we were coming. We'll just have to hope we get lucky."

"He still might run when he sees us," Ida Belle said.

"I can catch him," I said. "Besides, it's more about the information I need and maybe access, depending on said information. And I really don't want to train another clerk to get this done. He's a mess but at least he's sort of on board."

"Uselessly useful," Ida Belle said. "That describes a lot of people these days."

She pulled into the motel parking lot and I headed inside. Shadow Chaser had seen me coming and was already shaking his head when I walked in.

"Whatever it is, the answer is no," he said. "I cannot handle seeing another naked man. One in a lifetime was more than enough. Two in the same week would send me straight to a mental institution. Or church. Either is bad."

"I go to church," I said. "I kinda enjoy it."

He narrowed his eyes at me. "You're, like, a killer spy. How does that work?"

"I don't kill anyone at church?"

He didn't look convinced. "And I don't want you killing anyone here. We've got more bodies stacking up in this motel than the second Gulf War. The owner is starting to make noise —like it's not his fault for buying this dump and refusing to put any money into it to get a higher class of clientele. The Hilton up the highway doesn't have this problem."

"I'm not planning on killing anyone, but your current problem is already checked in. You have an enforcer for a drug dealer out of Nashville staying here. And guess who else was from Nashville?"

He groaned. "The dead dude. Crappity crap crap! Why didn't this guy clear out after he killed the other guy?"

I shrugged. "I don't know, but I'd like to find out. If I find out enough, I might be able to hasten his departure. So helping me would likely benefit you. Might even keep that body count from rising."

"I know there's a catch somewhere. It sounds good but then there's about a million ways it could go wrong."

Given that Gertie was outside, I nodded. "Probably a million and one."

He sighed. "What do you want to know?"

"I'm looking for this guy," I said and pulled out my phone to show him the image Mannie had sent me.

Shadow nodded. "Yeah, I remember him. Came in on Thursday. Never said anything. And I mean *really* never said anything. He just pointed to the vacancy sign and grunted. I gave him a price and he threw bills at me like I was a stripper in a club. Scared the heck out of me. I just handed him the key and he left."

"How many nights did he pay for?"

"One."

"But he's been here two already."

"I'm not asking him to leave. As far as I'm concerned, he can claim eminent domain on that room. They don't pay me enough to be a bouncer."

"So he's still here?"

He pushed his chair over to the window and pointed. "That's his car over near the stairs. The black Mercedes sedan with the wheels that cost more than I make in a year. Drug dealing must pay well in Nashville."

"I'm pretty sure it pays well everywhere," I said, making note of the Louisiana plate on the car. That explained why the cops didn't zero in on him when they were here before.

"So how are you going to get him out of here?" Shadow asked.

I was considering my options when I saw the object of my investigation come down the stairs, hop into his car, and drive off. I looked over at Shadow as we watched him exit the parking lot.

"No," he said, shaking his head. "I am not giving you a key to his room. For all we know, he'll be back in a minute and if he catches you there, I'll have another body on my hands."

"I can take him."

"I wasn't referring to yours. And if you kill that guy, then all the drug dealers in Nashville will show up here. I don't have enough Xanax to handle that."

"Well, I'm going in that room, so you can help make this easy and nonviolent or you can risk depleting your Xanax stash."

He eyed me suspiciously. "What do you have in mind?"

Ten minutes later, I'd swapped my T-shirt for Ida Belle's flannel. My jeans and tennis shoes were perfect for what I had in mind, so all I had to do was add a ball cap. Since we kept investigative necessities in a hidden compartment in Ida Belle's SUV, the ball cap was no problem. I just flung some water and dragged it across the parking lot to dirty it up a bit. Then I grabbed the toolbox we kept next to the medical supplies and rocket launcher, and I was ready for my undercover role.

"Are you sure I have to come with you?" Shadow asked as we made our way upstairs.

"Do you normally let a plumber into an occupied room without supervising?"

"No. But what if the guy comes back?"

"Then you tell him the story we worked out—that someone reported a leak and I'm checking on it. We'll be done in a minute. Just don't freak out and we'll be fine."

"If you say so, but I still don't think you look like a plumber. Not even with the dirty hat."

"I find it hard to believe that someone your age can be so far behind the times. Plumbers can be female, in shape, and not even have their butt crack showing when they work."

"Not in my experience."

He stopped in front of the door and looked at me. "You're sure I can't talk you out of this?"

"Positive."

He let out a huge sigh and knocked on the door. We didn't expect a response, but it was safer to go through the motions, just in case Sledgehammer had a buddy that he hadn't listed on the room. When it was all quiet inside, Shadow opened the door and poked his head in.

"Sir, we need to check the plumbing," he called out.

Still no response, so we stepped inside.

"You stay here and watch the parking lot from the window," I said. "Ida Belle and Gertie are at the highway junction, watching for the Mercedes, but if he comes in from one of the back roads or is on foot, that won't help."

"Why would he be on foot?"

"Because he ran over someone with the car?" I suggested.

"You know what, let's just not talk."

I started opening the dresser and nightstand drawers as Shadow stood next to the window, peeking out like he was the heroine in a romance movie and didn't want to get caught staring at the hot hero. Every so often, he had to let go of the mini blind slat he was holding because his hand was shaking so bad, he was making the entire set of blinds move. It was a good thing he'd already decided on a career change because hunting bad guys was something he needed to limit to those video games he was so fond of.

The dresser and nightstands were empty, so I headed to the closet. The first thing I spotted when I opened the door was a long rain slicker. The only other item was a duffel bag. Inside were some clothes and a couple boxes of rounds—nine millimeter and .45. I wasn't sure what it said about a man when he traveled with two boxes of ammo and only one change of underwear, but I was pretty sure it was nothing good.

"He's going to know you went through his stuff," Shadow said. "Then he's going to come to the front desk and kill me because there's no sign of forced entry and he'll know I let someone in."

"You've been watching too many cop shows. If he thinks anyone was here, then he'll assume it was another pro, like him, and they picked the lock. But if you want to go the forced entry route, you can go outside and kick the door in."

I put everything back in the duffel exactly as I'd found it and repositioned it in the closet.

"This is not my first time doing this," I said as I closed the closet door. "And believe me when I tell you this guy is a cake-walk compared to the people I've dealt with. Most of them were international newsworthy."

"You're a very scary person."

"You have no idea."

I checked under the bed and in between the mattresses but came up with nothing. Then I headed into the bathroom but all I found was the bare minimum of toiletries. This guy clearly hadn't planned on staying long, but then that brought up the question, why was he still here?

"Oh my God! He just pulled into the parking lot like the Indy 500!" Shadow said. "We have to get out of here!"

I quickly returned everything I'd moved into exact position and grabbed the toolbox, ready to flee.

"Good God, he's up front already," Shadow said. "We can't leave without him seeing us."

"Get over here and stand by the bathroom door. You're supposed to be supervising my work, remember."

I pulled out a pipe wrench and crawled half into the vanity. I shut off the water, so I looked like I was actually fixing something, then waited for Sledgehammer to walk in. Shadow was standing in the doorway, clutching the wall like he was about to fall over.

"Get a grip," I told him as I heard the door open.

"What the hell are you doing in here?" a low, booming voice demanded.

"A leak was reported," Shadow said. "I had to let the plumber in, but I've been here the whole time."

"I didn't report no leak," Sledgehammer said.

"The guy below you did," Shadow said, relaying our rehearsed story. "But it appeared to be coming from up here."

I heard him walk up behind me and I put my wrench on the pipe.

"First my HVAC was broken when I checked in and now the plumbing," Sledgehammer said. "This place is a pit."

"I don't own it," Shadow said. "And we got the HVAC parts delivered on emergency the same day."

"And that don't look like no plumber," Sledgehammer said.

"We come in all makes and models," I said. "I'm almost finished here."

"You're finished now. And I don't see no leak. What kind of scam are you two running?"

I cranked the pipe open a tiny bit and figured I'd turn the water back on then point out the leak, but I severely overestimated the condition of the old pipes. I'd barely put pressure on it when the joint snapped and water gushed out right into my face.

"What the hell?" Sledgehammer yelled as I jumped backward and slammed into his legs, causing him to lurch forward. His head connected with the doorframe and he dropped right on top of me.

"Turn off the valve under the sink!" Shadow yelled.

"I did!" I said, the water continuing to pummel me in the

face as I wrestled on the bathroom floor, trying to get Sledge-hammer, who was apparently out cold, off me.

"I have to turn off the main valve in the room below," Shadow said and took off.

"You've got to be kidding me," I said as I shoved on Sledge-hammer and finally managed to get him off me. Then I ran out of the room and down the stairs.

Just in time to see Round 2 of the Naked Man Chronicles.

The room below Sledgehammer's belonged to none other than our friend Jim Garmon, and he'd apparently been in the shower when I broke the plumbing. All water had diverted from his room to the burst pipe upstairs. I was halfway down the stairs when I heard Shadow scream, then he bolted out of the room, tripped on the threshold, and ran straight into a support post for the stairs. If he didn't have a concussion by the time the week was over, it was going to be a miracle.

I saw Ida Belle and Gertie pull up as I ran down the stairs, but they wisely chose to stay in the SUV. I heard shouting behind me and looked into the room and saw Jim Garmon, his head and face covered with shampoo, yelling and waving his arms around. He'd either been startled by Shadow and ripped the shower curtain off when he fled the bathroom or had decided that he required something larger than the motel's cheap towels to cover himself, because the plastic sheet was wrapped around him like a toga.

I ran past him, yelling that I was the plumber, and shut off the valve in the bathroom. Water was pouring from the ceiling and I heard the floor above creak as I twisted the main shutoff for God knew how many rooms. Then I ran out of there because the possibility of Sledgehammer dropping through that ceiling and onto me again was high, given the old and shoddy construction.

I took pity on Jim Garmon and put a towel in his hand

before running back outside, slamming the door behind me. Ida Belle and Gertie had left the SUV and were checking on Shadow, who was now sitting up but looked a bit groggy.

"He was naked," Shadow said, his voice trembling. "Again."

"Most people are when they shower," I said. "It's just bad timing."

"This isn't bad timing," he said. "It's a curse. You're a curse."

"Well, buck up because you've got a job to do, and we have to get out of here before Sledgehammer wakes up," I said.

Shadow's eyes widened and he popped up. "You're not leaving me to deal with this!"

"No choice," I said. "Garmon knows I'm a PI. If he and Sledgehammer get to talking, it could be bad for everyone concerned."

"What the heck am I supposed to do?" he asked.

"I suggest starting with giving them both new rooms on opposite ends of the motel from each other," I said. "And make sure the plumbing is working. Tell Sledgehammer you fired me on the spot and made me leave."

"And Garmon?" he asked.

"Had soap in his eyes," I said. "I don't think he got a good look at me, but I don't want to risk it. I'll be right over there in the SUV. If anyone comes at you, I'll shoot them."

We hopped into Ida Belle's SUV and left him standing there, looking as though he'd been shipwrecked. Ida Belle started the vehicle up and moved it down from the rooms but where we still had a good view in case something went sideways. Shadow went running toward the office and shot me a panicked look over his shoulder before he went inside.

"Did Sledgehammer get a look at you?" Ida Belle asked.

"Only from the back end," I said.

"Why didn't he come running out after you?" Gertie asked.

I explained what had happened and when I got to the part where Shadow fled and left me pinned underneath all that dead weight, they both started grinning. Then laughing.

"At least he wasn't naked," Gertie said.

"Did you find out anything for all that trouble?" Ida Belle asked.

"Nothing," I said. "He is traveling incredibly lean and doesn't show any signs of being here for long. I'm sure he had his wallet and phone with him, so those were out. The only other thing to identify him by—and this is loose at best—is a rain slicker in the closet."

"So Sledgehammer is the parade guy," Ida Belle said.

"Probably," I said.

"Did you plant the bug?" Gertie asked, then sighed. "Crap. I guess it doesn't matter since he's going to have to change rooms."

I'd thought while I had access that I'd plant a bug in Sledgehammer's room and see if we could catch anything with phone calls, but the little device that I'd left behind the dresser wasn't going to do us any good.

"There's always the parabolic microphone," Gertie said.

"I have a feeling Sledgehammer will be checking out after this," I said and pointed as Shadow knocked on Sledgehammer's room. A second later, the door popped open and Shadow tried to give Sledgehammer a new key, but he just shook his head and slammed the door.

"If he's still here now even though Brock's dead, that doesn't mean he's necessarily leaving the area," Ida Belle said.

"But we'd have to find him all over again," I said. "And there's no way we can tail him from the motel. A guy like that would make us before you started the engine."

"I've got an idea," Gertie said. "Meet me around back behind the tree line."

With that, she jumped out of the SUV and took off running for the breezeway that split the motel in the center and ran from the front parking lot to behind the building.

"What the heck?" Ida Belle asked and fired up her SUV.

I started to run after her, but figured it was better to get the SUV in a getaway position first. Plus, I didn't want to risk being seen by Jim Garmon or Sledgehammer. I'd just wait until Ida Belle parked, then go drag Gertie away from whatever likely bad idea she was currently working on. Ida Belle shot out of the parking lot and up the road beside the motel, then backed into a dirt opening just past the trees that ran the length of the back property line, leaving the SUV running.

I jumped out, opened the passenger door for the back seat on Ida Belle's side so it was ready for a quick dive in, then hurried through the trees. I spotted Gertie headed for the Mercedes with a screwdriver and wondered if she intended to flatten his tires. Surely not. That would only hold him here long enough to make the repair and we still wouldn't be able to follow him.

She leaned over a front wheel well, and when she straightened, I heard a man yell from the breezeway. I recognized the voice as Sledgehammer. I figured that was her cue to make a dash for the SUV, but instead, she ran to the front of the car, popped the Mercedes emblem off with the screwdriver, then took off for the tree line.

Sledgehammer was right behind her.

CHAPTER SEVENTEEN

GERTIE WASN'T GOING TO MAKE IT. THE TREE LINE WAS TOO far, and Sledgehammer was a lot faster than her. So I pulled out my nine and did the only thing I could do—I fired a shot into one of the Mercedes's back tires.

Sledgehammer slid to a stop, then ducked behind the car. Gertie didn't so much as flinch. She hit the trees at a dead run, flew right past me, and dived into the back seat of the SUV. I heard a bullet whiz by as I bolted for the passenger door, and Ida Belle floored it out of the hiding space while I was still getting in the SUV. I had one foot on the floorboard when the momentum from the takeoff sent the door slamming shut, flinging me inside.

"Why do you two insist on slamming my doors?" Ida Belle asked as she tore up the side road.

"Because people are shooting at us?" Gertie said.

Ida Belle shook her head as she headed up the narrow road and turned off into a neighborhood. "Is he coming?"

"No," I said. "And he's not going to be. I took out his tire."

Ida Belle let off the accelerator. "Well, why didn't you say so? The last thing I need is a ticket. Then there's a record of us being here."

"Which is going to be a problem," I said. "Because someone's certain to call about the gunshots."

Ida Belle exited the neighborhood onto a farm road and set off for the highway, pushing the speed limits again. "I'll go to the boat shop. It's close by."

"It's New Year's," I said. "It won't be open."

"It's Sinful," Ida Belle said. "When customers are off from work, Wade has the boat shop open."

"Mostly because he doesn't like being at home with his spouse," Gertie said and looked at Ida Belle. "Remind you of anyone?"

"The important thing is that he's open and will be our alibi," Ida Belle said.

"Unless this thing is a time machine, you can't get us there before the shooting started," I said.

"I have a plan," Ida Belle said and shot an exasperated look back at Gertie. "And speaking of plans—what the heck was that?"

"All kinds of smart," Gertie said. "I saw this special about how gangs were stealing the emblems off Mercedes."

"And what does stealing the emblem accomplish?" I asked. "Besides getting us shot at?"

"A reason for me to be close to the car," Gertie said. "I put a GPS tracker in the wheel well."

Finally, it made sense...in a convoluted Gertie-thinking kind of way.

"So now Sledgehammer thinks you were there to steal the emblem and doesn't check the rest of the car," I said.

Gertie nodded. "Those bathrooms have a window facing the rear. If he looked out, I needed him to think I was stealing something. And losing the emblem will keep him mad enough to not think too hard on what happened."

"Where did you get a GPS tracker?" I asked.

"From your stash," she said. "I figured I might as well keep one in my purse. It could come in handy."

I shook my head and pulled out my cell phone. I accessed the app and watched the dot slowly pulse next to the hotel.

Gertie leaned forward to check the phone and clapped. "Now all we have to do is wait for him to get that tire fixed and see where he goes."

"One of these days, you're going to get yourself or us killed," Ida Belle said.

"Technically speaking," I said, "as far as Gertie's ideas go, this one went well. He didn't get a good look at me because I was under the vanity and then he was out cold. He didn't get a good look at Gertie because she was running away from him. And he didn't see your SUV because it was behind the tree line."

Gertie grinned. "I'm getting good at this."

"You got shot at," Ida Belle said. "There's still some kinks to work out."

She pulled into the boat store parking lot, which was surprisingly crowded. Apparently, Wade wasn't the only person who didn't want to spend the day at home.

Ida Belle parked at the end of the building, then jumped out and headed around back. Gertie shrugged and we set out after her. She rounded the building and pulled out her wallet, slipped a credit card into the back door jamb, and popped the lock. She eased it a crack, then when she was sure it was clear inside, we slipped in and she locked the door behind us. We headed to the door connecting to the showroom and did the stealth peek again.

We had to wait for a couple of people standing nearby at a

life jacket display to move on, but as soon as their backs were turned, we slid into the store. Ida Belle grabbed some rope and Gertie picked up more aluminum weld, but I couldn't worry about that at the moment.

"Follow my lead," Ida Belle said, and we headed toward the front of the store where Wade was just finishing ringing someone up.

When the man left, Ida Belle stepped up to the counter. "Did you forget about me, Wade?" she asked.

He looked confused. "What do you mean?"

"I asked you if you had this line in a hundred feet a good half hour ago," she said. "You were going to check."

He scratched the top of his head. "You did?"

Ida Belle sighed. "Is your memory going the way of your hair? You were standing right by that motor oil display when we talked."

He scrunched his brow, then finally nodded. "Oh yeah. I'm sorry, Ida Belle. It's been crazy in here today, and drinking all that beer last night didn't help matters."

"At least business is good," Ida Belle said. "So...the line?"

"Right," he said. "Let me pull that up and see if I have some in the back."

As he started tapping on the computer, my phone rang. Carter.

"That was fast," I said and showed them the display.

"What's up?" I answered.

"Funny you should ask," he said. "I was headed to the motel to finalize some information with the clerk when I got a call from dispatch saying some guy was in the motel parking lot yelling and waving a gun. A couple minutes later, I'm questioning the guy with the gun who claims an old lady stole the emblem off his Mercedes and shot out his tire."

"Isn't emblem stealing a gang initiation thing?" I asked. "Wow. They'll take anyone these days."

"Uh-huh. Where are you right now?"

"The boat shop."

"So you were never at the motel?"

"Nothing exploded, did it?"

"The plumbing did. Oddly enough, in the gun-waver's room. He claims the plumber broke the pipe."

"Sounds like they need to find a new plumber."

"That's what the clerk said and was a bit cagey when I asked him who the old one was."

"He's barely making over minimum wage, at a motel where dead people and explosions happen on the regular. He probably doesn't know or care who the guy was."

"Yeah, but you see, the gun-waver said the plumber was a woman."

"Good for the motel. Equal rights and all. Listen, is there a point to this?"

"How long have you been at the boat shop?"

"Half hour at least. Here, you can ask Wade."

I handed Wade the phone. "Tell Carter how long we've been in the shop."

Wade looked completely confused but took the phone. "Hi, Carter. Yeah, they're here. Crap, been at least a half hour, probably more. They've been waiting on me to check inventory and I've been busier than a one-legged man in a butt-kicking contest."

He handed the phone back to me.

"Are you satisfied?" I asked.

"No."

"You think Wade is lying?"

"He wouldn't do Ida Belle that kind of favor. She always beats him at shooting competitions."

"Then I guess I'll let you go so you can get back to your emblem-stealing-gun-waving-bad-plumber problem."

I disconnected before he said anything else, and Wade dashed off for the rope Ida Belle had asked for.

"Did he buy it?" Gertie asked.

"No," I said. "But he admitted that Wade won't lie for Ida Belle and can't figure out how we were in two places at once."

"If he figures out Wade's memory is about as good as the sheriff's, we won't be able to use this excuse again," Ida Belle said. "Maybe if Carter needs some boat supplies, you could volunteer to pick them up for a while. Make sure he doesn't catch on too soon."

"You think Shadow will keep his mouth shut?" Gertie asked.

"Oh yeah," I said. "That guy is scared of becoming one of the motel's body count. No way he's admitting to being in on this."

Wade returned with the rope, and we paid up, then headed out.

"Where to now?" Ida Belle asked.

"I don't know," I said. "I want to talk to Cecil, but I don't want to go to Number Two. First, for the obvious reason, and then because I'd like to see what Sledgehammer's next move is."

"We should go get the parabolic microphone," Gertie asked. "That way if Sledgehammer lands somewhere new, we might be able to get something."

"That is one plan I can get on board with," Ida Belle said. "After all the mess, I don't want to get any closer to Sledgehammer than the reach of that microphone."

"I agree," I said. "Head to my house. We'll load up the microphone and hopefully Sledgehammer will be on the move soon."

ON THE DRIVE BACK TO SINFUL, I SAW SLEDGEHAMMER'S CAR move from the motel to a nearby service station that repaired tires. It probably wouldn't take long for the repair, so we decided to grab some lunch that was easily portable in case we had to head out in a hurry. We were having chicken salad sandwiches, chips, and chocolate chip cookies when my phone dinged and I checked the display.

"Our friend Sledgehammer has left the service station," I said and watched as the dot moved down the highway.

"Where's he going?" Gertie asked.

"He's headed toward Sinful," I said.

"After Carter questioned him?" Ida Belle asked. "That's brazen."

"Maybe he thinks everyone is hungover," Gertie said.

"More likely he thinks small-town deputies are idiots," Ida Belle said.

"Let's get the microphone ready," I said. "This doesn't feel right."

We hurried to the SUV and got the microphone ready to go, then sat there waiting for the blinking red dot to stop moving.

"He's going through downtown and into the neighborhood," I said. "Duck!"

We all lowered ourselves just as the Mercedes came into view and waited until the dot was clear of my house before we rose. I showed the blinking dot to Ida Belle and Gertie.

"That's the street Sawyer lives on," Ida Belle said.

"He's stopping!" I said, my pulse ticking up. "Go!"

"You think he's going to try again?" Gertie asked, her voice raised. "That's crazy!"

"If he killed Brock and stuck around, that's crazy too," Ida Belle said.

She turned onto Sawyer's street and I directed her to pull over when I spotted the Mercedes at the curb at the opposite end.

"Where is the house?" I asked.

"The blue one with white shutters down on the right," Ida Belle said. "The sheriff's truck is across from it."

I spotted the house a few from the end. The Mercedes was parked two houses down and across the street. I pulled binoculars out of the glove box and zeroed in on him. He studied the house for a few seconds, then pulled out his cell phone.

"Microphone," I said.

Gertie pointed the microphone at the car while I cued up the control panel. I slipped on the headphones, hit Record, and moved Gertie's arm around a bit until one side of the conversation was clear.

HER CAR'S STILL THERE.

No. Not the SUV. Brock was still driving that. This is some junker she picked up somewhere.

Yep. Tennessee plates.

I can't just walk up to the door. The cops are sitting across the street, and she's either ditched her cell or turned it off.

Look, she already knows the score and after Brock, I don't think she's going to play around. She said her lawyer was pushing the contract through now that there's no opposition and they should be ready to sign next week. She'll be back in Nashville for that for sure. I think I should get out of here before the heat catches on.

Okay, but I have to change motels. The other one got weird.

I don't know, just weird, man. Someone jacked the emblem off my

Mercedes and the cops were there a second later. Like they were parked around the corner or something.

No. I got rid of him—said I wasn't interested in pressing charges, but he ID'd me.

Yeah, I'm still using my Louisiana ID and that's where my car is registered, but if he talks to the Nashville cops, he might be able to make the connection, even though I don't have anything on the books there. I can't imagine anyone else from Nashville is in this shithole except the three of us, so if he pokes hard enough, he'll be on me again.

I get it. But if you want me to stay put, I'm going to a different motel. There's something odd about that place.

Yeah, I know what to do if she tries to run.

HE STARTED UP HIS VEHICLE, THEN BACKED OUT OF THE street and drove away. I connected the control panel to Ida Belle's radio and played back the recording.

"Sounds like Sledgehammer killed Brock," Ida Belle said.

"Which still seems strange if they wanted to collect," Gertie said.

"Maybe they figured they'd go straight to the source of the cash," I said. "All indications were that RJ was going to cut Brock out of the licensing fees. And it didn't sound like Brock had any more prospects."

"So do you think that round fired at RJ was a reminder from Sledgehammer that they could get to her at any time?" Gertie asked.

"Could be," Ida Belle said. "It's either that or someone else was mad enough to take a shot at her."

I shook my head. "Mad gets you a reflexive response. That shot was planned—remember the broken light bulbs. That's a whole different mental state."

"So Sledgehammer then," Gertie said.

I nodded because it made the most sense. And really, given the facts, it was the only thing that fit. But the whole thing stank to high heaven.

"Are you going to tell Carter anything?" Gertie asked.

"No," I said. "He'll just be mad that we've been tracking Sledgehammer and didn't tell him his background to begin with. Carter will talk to the Nashville police—if he hasn't already—and he'll eventually get the same information we got from Mannie out of them."

"But they're not going to volunteer it," Ida Belle said. "He'll have to keep poking."

"Yeah," I said. "Those task forces don't like to let details wander, so they'll play it close to the vest. But Carter has his ways of working around tight lips, just like Big."

"But he doesn't know anything yet," Gertie said.

"No," I agreed. "Or he would have hauled Sledgehammer in for questioning already."

"When he connects Sledgehammer to the Nashville dealer Brock was tied up with, he's going to know our alibi was crap," Ida Belle said.

"He already does," I said. "He just can't figure out how to disprove it. And since there was no reason to think Sledgehammer was the target of our visit, he assumes that we were there to get a look at the crime scene and created a distraction to get away."

My cell phone rang and I checked the display.

"Shadow," I answered. "What can I do for you?"

"That guy—he's gone."

"The guy with the Mercedes?"

"He's gone too, but I meant the other one—Jim Garmon."

"Well, he was there fishing. Maybe he's done."

"Except that his name isn't Jim Garmon."

"No one gives their real name, right? He said he didn't want his wife to know he was there and not working."

"But Jim Garmon is the name he gave the police. I was standing right there when he did it. And they ID'd him so that means he had to have fake ID, right?"

I frowned. It was one thing to give a fake name and pay cash to avoid your spouse. But acquiring a fake good enough to pass police inspection wasn't easy or cheap, and covert fishing didn't seem a good enough reason for the hassle or the cost.

"How did you find out the name was fake?" I asked.

"Because that deputy guy was here after Sledgehammer started shooting and then he asked to talk to Jim—or whoever he is—for some follow-up questions. But his old room is cleared out and his stuff isn't in the new one I gave him. Both keys are on the dresser in the old room. Then the deputy asked me about the dude's ID and if he paid with a credit card. I told him we didn't ask for ID and he paid cash, like everyone else. Then the deputy hurried out of here, looking mad enough to spit. I got suspicious, so I did a Google on the name and a Jim Garmon died last year in Nashville. But the dude who was staying here kinda looked like him. Enough to pass a crappy ID picture off."

"Interesting," I said.

"Interesting?" he said. "Interesting! That's all you have to say? Look, I thought when I signed up for this that you'd look at a crime scene and what happened would play out in your head and then you'd tell the cops, and they'd arrest people. But I've got dead guys checking in and out and naked people and gunfire and exploding plumbing, and I can't handle all this pressure."

"I don't think you have to," I said. "Naked guy and Mercedes guy both left, remember?"

"That's true," he said, sounding hopeful.

"Yep, so all you have left to deal with is the plumbing."

"Thank God! Listen, I don't suppose you guys could stay away from here for like a year. Or at least six months. My therapist charges two bills an hour and I don't have insurance."

"Unless you collect another murder victim or a suspect that I'm tracking, you have my word."

He sighed. "So no chance is what you're saying. But I'm officially out of the investigative business—even just providing cover. If you need something here, I'll give you information and a key, but I'm not leaving this office and I've never seen you before in my life."

"It's a deal."

I hung up and relayed the conversation to Ida Belle and Gertie.

"I did *not* see that one coming," Ida Belle said.

"So who the heck was the guy posing as Jim Garmon?" Gertie asked. "You think the drug dealer sent two people?"

I shook my head. "I don't think so. If he had employees following up on each other, they wouldn't have been staying at the same motel."

"Maybe Garmon was here to pop Brock and Sledgehammer is here to make sure collection happens," Ida Belle said. "We only have Garmon's word that a woman and man both argued with Brock that night. What if Garmon was the one arguing with Brock and he called Shadow to complain for his alibi?"

I sighed. We were missing something. And I had a feeling it was right in front of us.

"So what now?" Gertie asked.

"Let's go talk to Gina," I said. "I want to see if she knows where her father is and get some more background on RJ and Brock."

"If her dad is hiding out, she's not going to admit it," Gertie said.

I nodded. "I know. But maybe I'll know if she's lying."

CHAPTER EIGHTEEN

THERE WAS A TRUCK PARKED IN FRONT OF THE HOUSE WHERE Gina lived with her father. Neither Ida Belle nor Gertie recognized it but as we headed up the steps, I could hear arguing inside.

"Give me one good reason," a man's voice boomed. "One good reason why you keep telling me no. He's gone, Gina. Permanently this time. Your reason for pushing me away is over and done with."

I looked over at Ida Belle, who mouthed *Cooper*.

"Well, I have a whole new set of reasons now," Gina said. "Brock dying didn't solve anything. It made everything worse. My dad and I are both suspects and now he's disappeared. The cops have been here questioning me every day. And the gossipmongers are already at it. The stink of Brock Benoit is going to follow me around the rest of my life. You don't want that on you."

"I want *you*."

"Not this way. I couldn't live with it."

"Then leave Sinful with me. I make enough for me, you, and Billy to get by."

"You have no idea how expensive a child is, and I want more for Billy than just getting by."

"You can get some more day care babies in another town if you want. People are always looking for good childcare."

"You think the gossip won't follow us somewhere else? All of my day care parents have already canceled with me. All with lame excuses, but I know the real reason. With no references, how do you expect me to get people to leave babies with a stranger? I wouldn't."

"All the more reason to leave. And we could manage until people got to know you in a new town."

"Even if all that were true, I can't leave my dad here to deal with this alone. If it weren't for me hooking up with Brock, he wouldn't even be in this position. All of this is my fault, and I can't just skip away, leaving him holding the bag."

"So he can come with us."

"He won't leave Sinful. I've already tried. His friends are here. His camp. It's the only place he's ever known. This house is paid for and he can retire with full pension next year. The only way he's leaving is in a coffin."

"Or handcuffs."

"What are you saying—are you accusing my dad? Get the hell out of my house!"

I jumped back and we all hurried off the porch and across the lawn to the sidewalk, then started leisurely strolling toward the house. We'd barely started to stroll when the front door flew open and Cooper stomped out.

He barely gave us a nod as he went past. Then he hopped in the truck and peeled out as he pulled away. Gina stood in the doorway, staring at him as he drove off, her expression a mixture of angry and sad. We were almost on top of her before she realized we were there.

"Oh!" she said, and her eyes widened. "I'm sorry. I didn't realize... What are you doing here?"

"We'd like to speak to you for a minute, if you have the time," Ida Belle said. "Sorry if we interrupted something."

She blew out a breath. "Only another man thinking he knows everything."

"That's pretty much the definition of men, though," Gertie said.

Gina stared at her for a second, then let out a single laugh.

"You might as well come inside," Gina said. "I've already given my neighbors enough to talk about. No use having you three standing out in my yard like vacuum cleaner salesmen."

"You're not even old enough to know about vacuum cleaner salesmen," Gertie said as we headed inside.

"No," Gina agreed. "But my grandma used to complain about them from 'back in the day.' I suppose now it's something different but if I don't know someone, I just don't answer the door. You can't be too careful when you're watching other people's kids. Even in Sinful."

"Is Billy here?" Ida Belle asked.

She shook her head. "He's at a friend's house. At least he still has one for the time being."

We followed her into her kitchen, and she sank into a chair. Apparently, her distress outweighed Southern protocol because she didn't even bother offering us anything. We were probably lucky she let us in.

"Are you all right?" Gertie asked. "Cooper seemed a bit angry when he left."

"Well, then that makes two of us," Gina said. "Except mine is more than a bit."

"You want to talk about it?" Gertie asked.

She put her hands up. "What's there to talk about? Cooper wants me to marry him and live happily ever after. But when you have a kid with a man who's been murdered, and you and your father are prime suspects, what kind of future is there? Even if I left town, my dad never would, and I can't leave him to deal with this alone. Besides, I care too much about Cooper to drag him down with my mess."

"But shouldn't that be his decision?" Gertie asked gently. "If you love each other, you can work it out."

She shook her head. "I *do* love him. But I don't know that I trust him, which is why I said no to his proposal even before all this mess happened. Cooper always thought I was still hung up on Brock and that's why I wouldn't commit, and I couldn't tell him the truth, so I just let him think it. It was lazy and unfair, but it gave me the out I needed."

"Has Cooper given you any reason not to trust him?" Ida Belle asked.

"He's a man." She shrugged. "Call it unresolved emotional issues or whatever but Brock really messed me up. Made me question my ability to know a good man from a liar, and my worth as a romantic partner. Made me question a lot of things."

"You can't let choices you made as a teenager ruin the rest of your life," Gertie said. "We'd all be in trouble if we spent a lifetime paying for things we did as teens."

"You'd be in trouble if you spent a lifetime paying for the things you did this week," Ida Belle said to Gertie.

Gina rewarded her joke with a small smile. "I know I should leave it in the past, move on, forgive and forget...all that. But knowing it and being able to do it are two different things. I was young and stupid when I got involved with Brock. Looking back, I should have known better. All the signs were there."

"What signs were those?" I asked.

"For starters, that he and RJ were more than just friends,"

she said. "I think he used me just like they both did Marigold, just in a different way."

"I heard Marigold had a crush on him," I said.

She shrugged. "Probably. She told me once that I should be careful what I believed—that the three of them were leaving Sinful as soon as we graduated, and I wasn't on their list of traveling companions. Whatever."

"You didn't believe her?" I asked.

"That Brock and RJ planned to leave town, sure, but Brock and I had already talked about them leaving Sinful with me when I went off to college. That they were bringing Marigold, no way. They kept Marigold around because she had a car, and she'd do most anything they asked her to do. Like a servant or a pet. It was gross the way they treated her—all nice to her face then mocking her as soon as she was gone. But Marigold's mother didn't like Brock at all. If Marigold had taken off with them, the car and her allowance would have disappeared."

"Along with their interest in keeping Marigold around," Ida Belle concluded.

"If Brock and RJ were more than friends back then, wouldn't him having a relationship with you be a problem for her?" I asked.

"If she thought it was real, maybe," Gina said. "But RJ is cold. Calculating. Between my allowance and babysitting money, I kept Brock pretty much funded, and I'm guessing a lot of it went to RJ. She always ran the show. Brock put on this big-man act, but behind the scenes, it was RJ calling all the shots."

"But what about when you got pregnant?" I asked.

"That's the first time I saw a crack in her veneer," Gina said. "I think Brock lied to her about the extent of our relationship and she was beyond mad. Not that Brock sleeping with me meant anything to him, mind you. He was just getting what he could out of the deal. I can see it all clearly now, but back then, I stuck my head in the sand. I wanted to believe I was special. That I mattered to someone who was larger than life by Sinful standards. So stupid."

"We all want to matter," Gertie said. "And I think you do to Cooper. You need to resolve this not trusting men thing. You have a son. And a father. You trust them, don't you?"

She frowned. "I trust my son about as much as I trust any child that age. I've caught him lying to get out of trouble. And if you use my dad as an example, I'm not sure they grow out of it."

"What do you mean?" I asked.

"My dad is gone," she said. "Disappeared sometime yesterday. Never showed up to play poker last night with his buddies and his cell phone is turned off. I've been trying half the night and all morning to track him down, but no one's seen him since he left the General Store yesterday."

"Did Carter question him before he disappeared?" I asked.

"He questioned both of us," she said. "Not together, of course, but he was here over an hour the first time and then again with me today. I think Carter thought if he didn't have us come down to the sheriff's department that it might spare us the gossip, but you know how neighbors are. And it's not like everyone doesn't know Carter's truck. When I opened the door to let him in, I saw blind slats lifting all over the block."

"Do you think something happened to your father?" I asked.

"No," she said. "At least, I don't think so."

"Then why would he leave?" I asked.

"Because he lied?" she suggested.

"To Carter?" I asked.

"Maybe," she said. "I think so."

"Do you think he killed Brock?" I asked.

She stared out the window for a bit, then shook her head. "I just don't know. I don't want to believe that, but I think he might have gone to the motel that night to confront him."

"Did you ask him about it?" Ida Belle asked.

"Of course," she said. "But he said when he lost all his chips at poker, he came home. He said I was already asleep and that he went straight to bed."

"But?" I prompted.

"He was lying," she said. "I've gotten good at reading people. And when you've lived with someone your entire life, you learn their tells."

"How would he even know Brock was at the motel?" Ida Belle asked.

She shook her head. "I have no idea. A rumor, maybe?"

"So what if he did go to the motel and confront Brock," I said. "That doesn't mean he killed him."

Gina nodded. "That's what I thought. Until he disappeared. And you know what else—Cooper isn't telling me the truth about that night either."

———

I LET OUT A LONG SIGH WHEN IDA BELLE PULLED INTO MY driveway. I knew what we had to do, but I still didn't like it. Unfortunately, now that the situation with Gina and Cecil had moved from possible gossip issue to definite gossip issue, I couldn't come up with a good reason to delay the next interview.

Ida Belle looked over at me and let out a responding sigh. "We have to find Cecil, right?"

"I'm afraid so," I said. "Gertie, how's your constitution?"

"I've had two rounds of Alka-Seltzer and a handful of Tylenol," she said. "I'm golden."

"One of these days, your liver is going to crawl out of your body and walk away," Ida Belle said.

"Unless it happens today, I'm good for a boat ride," Gertie said. "But should we start with Cooper? Gina said he was lying about that night too, and he had just as much reason to want Brock gone as Cecil did."

"Yeah, but he didn't disappear," I said. "And assuming he doesn't plan to, he'll be right here in Sinful when we get back. Let's address the more difficult of the two first."

"And while it's still daylight," Ida Belle said.

I nodded. "Let's all change into something we don't mind burning when we get back. Meet here in thirty and we'll head out."

So half an hour later, we were loaded up in my airboat, Ida Belle in the driver's seat, and pulling away from my backyard. Ida Belle was just preparing to launch when my cell phone rang.

Carter.

"Hang on," I said and answered.

"What's that noise?" he asked.

"We're in my boat."

"What for?"

"We didn't have anything better to do so figured we'd go check on Gertie's camp. No one's been there since that last storm. Why? What's wrong?"

Carter's voice had an edge to it. The kind that meant he was required to do something he didn't want to do.

"I've got a warrant out on Cecil Tassin."

My heart sank. "Oh no! Why?"

"You remember that guy whose Mercedes tire you shot out?"

"I have no idea what you're talking about."

"Uh-huh. Anyway, he saw Cecil in his truck in the back

parking lot at the motel that night. Shortly after the guy in the room next door to Brock reported hearing arguing."

"This is the yelling-gun-waving guy, right? Is he reliable?"

"He gave a description of Cecil and his truck, right down to the muffler leak."

Crap. Worst fears confirmed.

"That sucks hard for Gina," I said.

"Trust me, I'm not happy about it, but what choice do I have. It's not like some random at the motel would know that Cecil had a grudge against Brock and use him as a convenient frame."

"No. That doesn't seem likely."

"Anyway, I just wanted to let you know because maybe you guys can help Gina out and—you never heard me say this—see about getting Cecil a good attorney."

"So you know where to find him? Because rumor is he's done a disappearing act."

"I'm running down some leads. His boat's out of commission, but on the off chance you see him out in the bayous, call me. Do *not* tip him off. Cecil knows these bayous as well as Ida Belle. He could hide out there until he died as long as someone kept him in beer."

"I get Cecil going after Brock, but would he take a shot at RJ?"

"I don't know. I've been talking to people all morning. Plenty don't like her but all agree on a single important point —she's not worth it."

"And yet..." I said. "Is she staying put at her mother's?"

"She called earlier, demanding protective custody so she could leave. Said her mother's on her nerves."

"She probably wants to stay at your house," I said.

I could practically feel him cringing.

"Yeah, well, you can file that under things that aren't

ever going to happen," he said. "I tried explaining that protective custody is only on the table when people have criminal information on a big fish, but apparently, she thinks law enforcement should function as her personal bodyguards."

"To save her from her own poor decisions, most likely," I said.

He sighed. "I was sure that Brock set that float on fire, but unless a dead man can shoot a gun, it wasn't him that went after her last night."

"Which leaves you with the disappearing Cecil."

"I'm afraid so. Oh, and I need you to steer clear of the motel. That Mercedes guy is bad news. Has a long and creative rap sheet but has managed to skirt the worst punishments Louisiana can deal out. He's slippery and dangerous, and hopefully on his way out of town."

"And you still trust him on the Cecil description?"

"Unfortunately, I can't see any reason not to. Be careful and let me know if you see or hear anything."

"Will do," I said.

I slipped the phone back in my pocket and filled Gertie and Ida Belle in.

"This is horrible news," Gertie said. "But what about the argument with the woman after that? If it was Cecil he was arguing with, then Brock was still alive after Cecil left."

"But we still don't know for sure how Brock died," Ida Belle said. "Or if Jim Garmon made everything up to throw the cops off track."

"My head hurts," Gertie said. "So do we still think Sledgehammer killed Brock or not?"

"He remains my first pick," I said. "And he's my first pick for taking a shot at RJ. The fact that whoever shot at her missed tells me he was either a bad shot, which doesn't describe most people in Sinful, or he never intended to kill her."

"Just scare her," Ida Belle said. "That fits."

I shrugged. "As much as anything does. The truth is, at this point, everyone could be lying and there are several people who have a motive to kill Brock. But the thing I can't figure out is how Sledgehammer would have a perfect description of Cecil and his truck unless Cecil was really at the motel."

"True," Ida Belle agreed. "It's not like Sledgehammer would be privy to old Sinful gossip and know who the logical person to frame would be."

"Not to mention knowing that Cecil didn't have an alibi for that time frame so would be a good person to cast suspicion on," I said.

Gertie clutched her head. "So we think Cecil *was* at the motel?"

"I think we have to assume so," I said.

"And he argued with Brock?" Gertie asked.

"I can't think of any other reason he'd go except to see Brock," I said.

Gertie sighed. "Me either. But I don't want it to be Cecil."

"Neither do I," Ida Belle said. "For Gina and Billy's sake."

"We still don't know for sure that Cecil caused the head injury," I said. "Maybe they argued, and Cecil left and someone else caused the head injury. Maybe the woman did."

"But what if the woman was Gina?" Ida Belle suggested.

Gertie sighed. "I don't suppose RJ's neighbor could be lying about her car being there all night and we can pin everything on her."

"Then who took a shot at her?" Ida Belle asked.

"Crap," Gertie said and waved at Ida Belle to get going.

I couldn't help feeling just as helpless as Gertie. Every indication was that Cecil had been at the motel the night Brock died, and since no one could think of any reason for him to be there other than to confront Brock, I had to assume that was the case. And even if Cecil wasn't the one who'd put that knot on Brock's head, his name was going to be on everyone's lips unless Carter could prove it was someone else.

Or unless we could.

CHAPTER NINETEEN

IDA BELLE GOT US TO NUMBER TWO IN RECORD TIME. I could have had my eyes closed and known when we were within a hundred yards of the stinky island. Ida Belle had explained that the mud here was different from everywhere else and that was the source of the stink, but I was still skeptical. I had a feeling that a geological search would find a portal into hell somewhere nearby and that was the real source of the stomach-turning odor.

But the fish loved it. So the fisherman loved it.

Where there were fish, there were alligators, but since it had rained this morning, the water was still cloudy, and I didn't spot any of our dangerous friends on the slope we used to dock the boat. There weren't any other boats, either, but Cecil could have easily pulled his boat into the weeds and waded up the bank in a multitude of places around the island.

Ida Belle guided the boat up the slope and I tied it to a tree in case the tide came in before we got back. Ida Belle pointed to the trail to Cecil's camp and we headed out. It wasn't a very long hike, but it did present some challenges in the form of our reptilian friends. Alligators could be lurking in any of the tall grass, and sometimes you were on top of them before you knew it. If they felt threatened, they might charge rather than retreat. Normally, we'd talk a lot while walking through swamp grass because usually the gators would head off if they heard people. But we didn't want to alert Cecil that we were coming, so we walked silently and very carefully, which made passage slower than usual.

We were a good ten minutes into the walk when Ida Belle drew up short and pointed to the roof of a structure peeking up over a clump of trees. I nodded and took point and we crept down the trail, keeping our eyes and ears open for any sign of Cecil. But so far, only the sound of the water hitting a bank off to my right and our own footsteps broke into the silence.

The marsh grass grew shorter the closer we drew to the camp, and eventually, we couldn't squat anymore or we'd have been crawling. We made a dash for the trees behind the camp and ducked behind the brambles surrounding them. I inched to the side and peered around. There was one window on the back of the structure, and it was only a short twenty-foot sprint from where I was standing.

I signaled to Ida Belle and Gertie that I was going to make a run for it, then took off. I slid to a stop in the loose dirt behind the camp, then flattened myself against the wall under the window. At first, I couldn't hear anything, then I made out movement inside. Feet shuffling across the wooden floor, a cup being placed on a counter. I gave Ida Belle and Gertie a thumbs-up and headed around the corner to the front door to confront Sinful's latest disappearing citizen.

Cecil was standing on a screened front porch when I walked around the corner. He took one look at me and his eyes widened, then he glanced around, obviously looking for a way to flee. There were windows on the side of the camp and the one on the back, but things had a tendency to rust and fail out in the salt air and those windows were definitely the old kind. The odds that they even opened anymore were low. And even if they did, he had a good fifteen-foot drop to the ground, and I doubted he was in good enough shape to make that unscathed.

I must have been right with my speculation, because his shoulders slumped and he sighed.

"What do you want?" he asked as Ida Belle and Gertie emerged to stand beside me.

"Gina's worried about you," Ida Belle said.

"Gina needs to tend to her own life and stop wasting time on me," he said.

"The police are looking for you," I said.

"So let them look," he said. "I'll tell you the same thing I would tell them—I don't know anything about Benoit's death."

"Someone saw you at the motel the night he died," I said. "A stranger, who positively ID'd you and your vehicle."

His cheek twitched and his eyes shifted slightly.

"Then that stranger is lying," he said. "I played cards and went home when I lost my money. Didn't go anywhere else."

"Cecil, there are other suspects," I said. "Maybe you confronted Brock, but he was alive after you left. If you saw someone else, you might be able to clear your name."

"How the heck would I see someone when I wasn't there?" he asked. "Now leave me alone."

He stomped inside the camp, slamming the door behind him.

"Should we call Carter?" Ida Belle asked. "It was one thing to talk to him before, but now that there's a warrant..."

I sighed. "I know."

I stared at the camp for a bit, weighing my options, which

were pretty much slim and none. Finally, I pulled my phone out.

"He's lying," I said. "He was at the motel."

"But that doesn't mean he's the one who hit Brock," Gertie said. "We need to find out who the woman was that was fighting with Brock later on."

"If there really was a woman," Ida Belle said.

"If there wasn't, that will leave Cecil out to dry," Gertie said. "I know Carter won't quit there, but that doesn't mean the DA won't take it and run."

"She's not wrong," Ida Belle said to me. "But I still don't see that you have a choice."

I nodded. "After he takes Cecil in, I'll tell him about Sledgehammer. At least that way there's another good suspect in the mix. Maybe the DA will prefer focusing on a known criminal with a much better motive for killing Brock than a local with no criminal record."

And that's when we heard a boat engine fire up. We whirled around just in time to see Cecil shoot out of a clump of marsh grass in a small bass boat.

"He did not crawl out of a window and jump from that height," Gertie said.

Ida Belle pulled some grass to the side and looked under the camp. "Trap door in the middle. I can see the ladder on a piling."

I shoved the phone in my pocket and started running. "My boat!"

Cecil may have given us the slip and gotten out of the camp, but there was no way he could outrun us in that small boat and he knew it. The only way for him to get away clean was to leave us stranded.

I could hear Ida Belle and Gertie pounding behind me. Unfortunately, I heard Cecil's boat engine cut off, then back on just seconds later. He'd reached the landing. I burst out of the grass and onto the shoreline, but I was too late. He'd untied the boat and pulled it far enough from the shore that I couldn't risk swimming to get it.

Then I saw him lift his gun. He was going to shoot my boat!

I pulled my nine from my waistband and heard Gertie gasp as I aimed and fired.

Right into his boat motor.

"Put that gun down or the next one goes into you," I yelled.

He looked at me and apparently believed everything I'd just said because he put his arm down. Then he slumped down on the back bench, and I saw his shoulders heave. I pulled out my cell phone and called Carter.

"I found Cecil," I said.

"You what? Where?"

"He's currently floating in a boat off the west side of Number Two."

"Is he alive?"

"He is right now, but if he tries to shoot my boat again, he won't be. You better get out here before he gets stupid or I change my mind."

"I'm on my way."

Gertie shook her head as I shoved my phone back in my pocket.

"For a second there, I thought you were going to shoot him when you first pulled your weapon," Gertie said.

"For a second there, I was going to cheer her on if she did," Ida Belle said. "You don't shoot a boat. Good Lord, what's happened to decency in this town?"

"Who does that boat Cecil's in belong to?" I asked.

"Cooper," Ida Belle said.

I sighed.

"Well, this puts a damper on everything, doesn't it?" Gertie said. "Now he has to do all his talking with the DA and he's dragged Cooper into his tomfoolery."

"I think Cooper was already in the thick of it," I said.

"You think they partnered up?" Gertie asked.

I shrugged. "In this particular case, either Cooper lent his boat to Cecil or Cecil stole it."

"It doesn't look good either way," Ida Belle said. "And now you have to tell Carter about Sledgehammer."

I pulled my phone out and accessed the tracker. Relief coursed through me when I saw the flashing dot at a diner up the highway.

"How mad do you think Carter's going to be?" Gertie asked.

"On a scale of one to ten?" I asked. "Fifteen."

Ida Belle walked over to a log and sat down. "If we hadn't put our nose into this mess, we wouldn't have found out about Sledgehammer, and you wouldn't have that recorded conversation with his boss. Without that information, the DA would just move for charges right away on Cecil, and RJ would be freed up to leave. She'd skip right back to Nashville to sign that contract with Sledgehammer hot on her tail."

"And Cecil would be left holding the bag," Gertie said.

"For all we know, the bag might be Cecil's to hold," I said.

Ida Belle shook her head. "This whole thing has turned out to be a way bigger mess than even I anticipated. And I anticipated quite a bit."

I plopped down on the log next to her. I had to agree.

———

CARTER MUST HAVE BEEN AT THE SHERIFF'S DEPARTMENT AND the boat must have already been gassed up and ready to go, because it was only thirty minutes before I saw him headed toward us. Both boats were drifting away from Number Two with the outgoing tide, but with the alligators starting to cruise around for their evening meal, I hadn't worried about Cecil making a swim for my boat. It was too far away from him to risk it.

Carter must have decided that since Cecil obviously wasn't going anywhere, he'd acquire my boat first and then have an opportunity to chew us out without Cecil overhearing. Because that's exactly what he did.

"What the heck were you thinking?" he asked. "You knew I had a warrant out for Cecil before you ever came here. And since Gertie's camp is in the other direction and Ida Belle's fishing camp is on the other side of this island from Cecil's, I'm sure you didn't stop by here to check on it."

"Yes, we were looking for Cecil," I said. "We stopped by to check on Gina earlier and she was worried about him. We thought it was a crap thing to do to her, so we came out here to see if we could find him and convince him to go in."

"Obviously that didn't work out," he said.

"Obviously."

"You weren't afraid he'd make a swim for your boat?"

"If he had, I would have put a hole in it out of principle."

Ida Belle gave me an approving nod. "It's like you were born here."

"Did he say anything?" Carter asked.

"Only that he was never at the motel," I said.

"And you believe him?"

"Not necessarily, but there's something else you need to know. You know that gun-waving-Mercedes guy?"

Carter narrowed his eyes. "The one you claim not to know."

"Oh, I don't know him, but I know about him. He might have been a Louisiana native, but he's not anymore. He's an enforcer for a drug dealer in Nashville called Payday. Word is Brock sold product in the clubs he and RJ played and didn't pass the profits back up the line."

Carter stared at me for a moment, then cursed and stomped around for a bit.

"And you spied on this guy?" he said finally, staring at the three of us as if we'd lost our minds. "And you." He looked at Gertie. "You stole an emblem off a drug enforcer's Mercedes? All three of you have a death wish."

"I was just trying to get some evidence that he killed Brock so we could clear things up for Cecil and Gina," I said.

"You know how it's going to be for them," Ida Belle said.

Carter threw his hands up. "Of course I know, but Cecil isn't helping matters running away. And unfortunately, drug enforcer or not, the Mercedes guy was telling the truth."

"You have another witness?" I asked.

He nodded. "Cecil took the back way out through the neighborhood and passed by probably the only convenience store in the area with a working security camera. Lucky for me, it's not aimed properly on the pumps and was instead pointing at the street. It was him. No doubt about that."

"But that doesn't mean he killed Brock," I said. "Maybe he confronted him, but he's not the guy who put the knot on his head. That could have been Sledgehammer."

Carter's eyes narrowed at me when I mentioned the blow to Brock's head and then I remembered I wasn't supposed to know what the ME had said.

"Who told you—" he began, then cut himself off. "Sledgehammer?"

"I have an audio file you're going to want," I said. "He's watching RJ. I think Payday expects her to settle Brock's debt."

"With what?" he asked. "RJ's broke."

"She is now, but there's a TV producer interested in licensing that song of theirs for a series."

Carter put his hands on top of his head and squeezed. "You know what—I'm going to get Cecil back to Sinful and book him. When I'm done, I'll come by your place and you're going to tell me everything. In the meantime, I need the three of you to go home and stay there."

"Our own homes or Fortune's?" Gertie asked.

Carter whirled around without answering and headed back to his boat. He didn't even glance at us as he pulled away.

"That went well," Ida Belle said.

"About as well as I figured it would," I said.

"Don't worry about it," Ida Belle said. "Carter is just frustrated because you have a way of getting information before he does. And given his ambivalence concerning the Heberts, he's going to try on mad for a while."

"Looks like it fit him pretty good," Gertie said.

"Well, there's no point in worrying about it now," Ida Belle said. "Let's get home and into the shower and then we'll see what we see."

We headed over to my boat and climbed inside. I watched as Carter started back toward Sinful with Cecil in his boat and pulling Cooper's boat behind him. I was sure Ida Belle would give them a wide berth when she passed, but I was equally sure I'd feel his disapproval, regardless of the distance.

CHAPTER TWENTY

IT WAS CLOSE TO 10:00 P.M. WHEN I HEARD A KNOCK ON MY front door ,and then the key turned and Carter poked his head in. I looked up from my recliner but didn't bother to sit up. It had been a long day and I saw no point in reducing my comfort level for another butt-chewing. I could hear his diatribe just as well reclined.

I'd sent Carter the audio file I'd recorded of Sledgehammer when I got home and had relayed what I knew about the potential song licensing deal when he called afterward. But I'd left out my chat with Jim Garmon, or whoever he was. Based on my conversation with Shadow, Carter already knew something was off with Garmon, but it wasn't as if he could put an interview with a dead man up as evidence.

I also left off the part about the tracker on Sledgehammer's car because it hadn't moved from the diner. Since it was highly unlikely he'd been eating for hours, I had to assume it had fallen off or he'd found it and removed it. Either way, it was another tidbit that would only contribute to more arguing but wouldn't help the case.

Carter went into the kitchen and came back with a beer,

then flopped down on my couch. I remained silent. It was, after all, my house. If he had something to say, he could say it.

"Cecil Tassin will be transferred to New Orleans Monday morning and charged with manslaughter," he said.

I popped up in the chair without using the lift button. "What? The evidence is all circumstantial. And there's another suspect. A really, really *good* suspect."

"Cecil confessed."

My jaw dropped and I stared at him. Surely he was joking. But the slumped shoulders and the haggard expression told me everything I needed to know.

"But you don't believe him," I said.

"Not completely. I think he went to the motel because I have video proof that he was in the area at the same time your buddy Sledgehammer described Cecil and his vehicle. And although Sledgehammer is an excellent suspect, I have a hard time believing he would have known enough about Brock's past to frame Cecil and throw the scent off him."

"What does Cecil say happened?"

"That he went to the motel to confront Brock about the child support he's never paid and they got into a fight. Cecil punched him and Brock hit the dresser and never got back up. Cecil figured he'd killed him, so he bolted."

I frowned. "Did Brock have any marks on his face?"

"Since you seem to know about the ME's findings, you already know he didn't."

"And since it was a knot, not a gash, there's no blood to trace on the dresser. So why would Cecil say he punched Brock when he didn't?"

"One guess."

And then it hit me. "He's covering for someone. That's why he was hiding out. But how did he find out where Brock was staying in the first place? Or that he was even in town?"

"He refuses to answer that."

"But if the guy who told Cecil where to find Brock is the perp, then why would he tell Cecil at all? He wouldn't want anyone to know that he knew, especially if he planned on having a run-in with Brock himself."

"I agree. It makes no sense. And if Cecil won't give me a name, I can't sort it out. I've subpoenaed his phone records, but that will take a while and it doesn't cover everyone he could have spoken to in person."

"And the information could have come around second- or thirdhand." I blew out a breath. "Is it possible that Cecil hit Brock and he passed out because he was drunk or high or both, but he didn't actually hit him hard enough to bruise?"

"I asked the ME that and he said it's not completely outside the realm of possibility, but that it was more likely someone shoved Brock and he hit a corner of the wall or bedpost. Or someone took a crack at him from behind."

"And that injury caused him to overdose," I said. "I assume there were no other prints on the syringe."

"Only Brock's."

"Of course. But does that make his death manslaughter? Brock died from doing an illegal drug. What if the head injury didn't affect him at all? He was drinking as well, right?"

Carter shrugged. "Yeah, but not enough that someone with his experience couldn't handle it. By the letter of the law, the DA can make a case for manslaughter. I wouldn't go there, but you know the DA is looking for a political run. He's taking on anything he thinks he can get a violent offender conviction on to get his stats up."

"But we don't know that he'd get a conviction. I can't imagine a jury would side against Cecil once they heard Brock's background, especially when you throw Sledgehammer in the mix. And what about the shot at RJ? Cecil has no reason to go after RJ."

"I agree and I told Cecil as much. But he's sticking to his confession. That makes him an easy mark to add to the DA's count. The DA will work out a plea deal and Cecil will go down for this."

"That's crap."

"Sure, but what can I do about it?"

"Try to make a case against Sledgehammer," I said.

"How?"

"Sledgehammer had a room at the same motel and was on site to see Cecil, so there's opportunity. Motive was Brock owing his boss money."

"Which he can't collect if Brock's dead."

"But if Sledgehammer is the one who pushed Brock and caused him to hit his head, then there's your manslaughter perp. Not Cecil. He probably just meant to rough him up and scare him a little, not kill him."

Carter looked hopeful for a second, then shook his head. "Cecil's not covering for Sledgehammer."

Crap! The flaw in my logic.

"Then what *is* Cecil doing?" I asked. "If someone told him that Brock was staying at the motel, that's not a crime. It doesn't even make them an accessory unless Cecil told them he planned to go there with the intent to commit a crime. And since you don't think Cecil was the one who actually assaulted Brock, then why lie about it at all? He didn't do it, so therefore, the person who gave him the info isn't on the hook any more than Cecil is."

Carter frowned. "Maybe Cecil saw the real perp at the motel."

Suddenly, I remembered Sledgehammer's conversation with Shadow.

"The HVAC repair," I said.

"What?"

"When I absolutely was *not* at the motel pretending to be a plumber, Sledgehammer complained to the clerk about all the repair issues and cited his HVAC, which was apparently broken the day he arrived. Shadow said something about having the parts brought in on a rush and getting it fixed the same day."

Carter looked confused. "Where are you going with this?"

"Who hated Brock as much as Cecil did and drives a hotshot truck locally?"

His eyes widened. "Cooper. And Cecil had Cooper's boat."

I nodded. "If Cooper saw Brock at the motel when he delivered those parts, he would have told Cecil. The poker players said Cecil was distracted and lost his money early and went home. And I'm sure he *was* distracted, but maybe he lost on purpose because he'd decided to confront Brock."

"And Cooper was already there. But why leave? If Cooper was the one who fought with Brock and Cecil saw it, then he would have known Brock wasn't punched."

"Maybe he saw Cooper after the fight and Cooper told him to clear out but didn't give details on what transpired."

"It's possible. But would Cecil go to jail for Cooper?"

"Not necessarily. But he'd go to jail for Gina. Cooper wants to marry her. And if he was willing to settle up with Brock for her, then Cecil might be willing to sacrifice a few years of his life to make sure Gina and Billy are taken care of."

Carter's shoulders slumped. "Assuming Cooper *is* the source of Brock's location, you know who else he was likely to have told."

I sighed. "Gina."

———

I WAS UP EARLY SUNDAY MORNING. SLEEP HAD TAKEN HOURS to happen and once it did, it wasn't restful. I dreamed all night about drug dealers, country music, and people shooting boats. And I woke up feeling just as guilty as I had the night before. If I hadn't gone to find Cecil, maybe he could have stayed hidden long enough for Carter to build a case against someone else.

I sat down with my coffee and sighed.

But who was that someone else?

Cecil was protecting someone, and that was either Cooper or Gina. I didn't want to see either one of them go down for Brock's death any more than I wanted Cecil to. So ultimately, it was going to suck no matter what.

It was barely 7:00 a.m. when my phone rang. I picked it up, expecting to see Ida Belle's or Gertie's number on the display, and felt a moment of panic when I saw Ally's.

"Ally? Is everything all right?"

"Please tell me you were awake. I need to talk. Can I swing by?"

"Of course."

The bakery wasn't officially open on Sunday, but Ally went in before daylight to bake goods for Francine's, so it wasn't a surprise that she was already up and around. But the panic in her voice wasn't normal. Nor was phoning me first thing in the morning. Something was wrong.

A couple minutes later, she pulled up and I was standing at the door, ready to let her in. I ushered her to the kitchen where she refused coffee but accepted water, and then she dropped into a chair at the kitchen table.

"Oh, Fortune, it's awful. I saw Gina coming out of the sheriff's department this morning and waved her into the bakery. She said she'd been trying to get her dad to tell her what happened but he's not talking. They told her that he's being sent to New Orleans tomorrow to meet with the DA. He confessed to assaulting Brock."

I nodded. "Carter told me last night."

"It can't be true. Not Cecil. He's a good man and he loves Gina."

"Being a good man and loving Gina are also reasons for him to try to settle up with Brock."

"You think he did it?"

"Honestly? I have my doubts, but as long as Cecil insists on copping to it, there's nothing Carter can do."

"Carter's hands might be tied, but yours aren't."

I sighed. "Ally, if Cecil didn't do it but is claiming he did, then he's covering for someone."

Ally's eyes widened. "No! There's no way Gina did it. She was drunk that night, remember?"

"I remember what she told us," I said. "But there's no proof. And aside from Gina or maybe Cooper, who else would Cecil cover for?"

Ally looked as miserable as I felt.

"And there's that shot at RJ," I said. "Gina's the one who hates her. Do you really think Cecil would take things that far?"

She was clearly conflicted and I didn't blame her. So was I.

"Then there's nothing you can do?" she asked. "There's no other angle to explore? Surely this is all a mistake. It has to be. Promise me you won't quit looking. Remember how guilty I looked when I was accused?"

"I remember."

It had been a horrible time for me, knowing Ally was innocent but watching the evidence stack up against her.

"There's a couple of things I can follow up on," I said. "But if it comes down to Cecil covering for Gina, I have to tell you

I'm inclined to keep anything that points her way to myself. That's Cecil's choice to make."

Ally nodded. "If that's what really happened, then I'll accept what he's doing. But I want to make sure he isn't making a mistake. That it wasn't someone else."

She rose from the chair and leaned over to hug me.

"Thank you," she said before hurrying out.

I grabbed my laptop and went to work. First on my list was locating Brock's new girlfriend. She was probably the only person who could tell me what went down between Brock and the drug dealer besides RJ. And there was no way RJ was going to talk to me.

It took me an hour of poking around blogs and Instagram before I found recent pics of Brock playing guitar in a bar with a singer other than RJ. Then I went on the trail to find a post where the singer was tagged and get a name—Mandy Miller. Another search produced a cell phone number to use for bookings, so I gave it a ring. It was early, but if Mandy didn't answer, I'd leave a message, pretending to be looking to hire a band.

I was just preparing to leave a message when a sleepy voice answered.

"Mandy Miller?"

"Yeah, who's this?"

"I'm an investigator from Sinful, Louisiana," I said. I didn't bother to specify the private part. Let her think I was the police.

"Is this about Brock?" she asked. "Because the local cops already came and told me what happened. And I'll tell you like I told them—I never left Nashville and I don't know what happened. I was on stage singing the night he was killed."

"You're not a suspect, Ms. Miller. I was just hoping you could help me with some information so that I can catch the person who did this. I understand Mr. Benoit was in trouble with a drug dealer called Payday—something about missing payment for product?"

"I don't know anything about that," she said, but I could tell by the sudden tension in her voice that she was lying.

"Ms. Miller, you're not on the hook for anything Mr. Benoit was involved in. His involvement with the dealer predates your involvement with him."

"Ha! Got that right. Because his *involvement* with that bitch predates me. God, she called here every day, harping about Brock ditching her, harping about that stupid SUV they bought—like they hadn't been dodging the repo people when Brock left with it—harping about Brock and me taking her gigs."

"Are you referring to RJ Rogers?"

"Of course."

"But Mr. Benoit was the one dealing drugs in the clubs."

"Look, I don't know what Brock was doing for sure, because he never told me. And the night he came home with his right wrist broken, he said I was better off not knowing. But if you think for one minute that all of it doesn't track back to RJ, you're wrong. RJ ran everything, including Brock. Why do you think he left her?"

"They broke his wrist? When was that?"

"Two weeks ago. The doctor said it was a small fracture and would heal quickly, but he had nerve damage. He couldn't even hold a pick, much less play the guitar. The doctor didn't know if it would come back or not."

"That's a bad situation."

"You think? And then that bitch tried to cut him out of that TV deal."

"Is that why he followed her to Louisiana?"

"He said he was going to fix it."

"How was he going to do that?"

"I don't know. I think he had something on her. Something to use to get his share. But since he's dead, I guess she gets what she wanted."

She let out a choked cry. "Look, I've got to go. I've got to find a new guitarist and a cheaper place or a roommate. I cared about Brock. Might have even loved him if we'd lasted. But he's gone and I've still got to get by."

She disconnected before I could thank her, and I leaned back in my chair.

So my friend Sledgehammer had apparently paid Brock a visit back in Nashville and given him a warning break. Then when Brock took off for Sinful, Sledgehammer had followed and what—given him a shove that resulted in a knot on his head that led to an overdose?

It was the logical explanation for everything until you factored in Cecil's confession.

Were there two confrontations with men at the motel that night? Jim Garmon was no longer a reliable witness. Jim Garmon wasn't even Jim Garmon.

A thought hit me and I straightened in my chair.

What if Brock had a confrontation with someone else before he even got back to the motel? He could have had one at the parade or at a gas station or at the liquor store up the highway. There was no way to determine whether the knot was derived an hour before Brock died or ten minutes before. Sledgehammer could have easily had a bout with Brock before anyone else confronted him at the motel.

I pulled out my phone and checked the tracking app, but the signal was completely gone. The last location was still the diner up the highway, but at least it was a starting point. I pulled up Google maps and located the nearest hotel in relation to the diner, then grabbed my phone. We needed to see if we could pin down Sledgehammer's location again. And then I wanted to pitch my idea to Carter, because he was the only one who could form a case for reasonable doubt to deliver to the DA.

I grabbed my phone and sent a text to Ida Belle and Gertie.

Operation Save Cecil in the works. Meeting at my house ASAP.

It only took seconds for them to both respond. I put on a new pot of coffee. We had some planning to do.

CHAPTER TWENTY-ONE

TWENTY MINUTES LATER, THEY WERE BOTH UP-TO-DATE ON everything I'd learned from Carter the night before and what I'd gleaned from Ally and Mandy Miller that morning. First up was another visit to Gina. I wanted to ask her again about what she did on parade night. And this time, I'd be watching her closely. I hadn't questioned her story the first time but then, I hadn't really considered her a suspect either. This time was different, and I'd be looking for those telltale signs that normal people had when they were lying.

Not that I caught every lie. Some people were so good they even got by me.

Gina answered the door right away but didn't invite us in. Instead, she gave us a dirty look.

"Go away!" she said. "This is all your fault. You should have left him on the island. Then he wouldn't be sitting in a jail cell."

"We went looking for your father because you were worried about him," Gertie said. "We didn't expect him to run and attempt to strand us out there."

Gina's lower lip quivered. Then she burst into tears and

flung the door open before whirling around and hurrying down the hallway. I wasn't sure whether that was our indication to follow or if she was off to load a weapon, but I took it as the first and followed her.

We found her in the kitchen, standing at the counter, her hands shaking as she drank from a bottle of water. I figured we'd be less threatening if we sat so I slid into a chair at her kitchen table and Ida Belle and Gertie followed suit. Then I waited. I wanted her to start the conversation because I wanted to know where her mind was. What she was focused on.

"My father didn't do this," she said.

"How can you be sure?" I asked. "Brock did you wrong and your father loves you. A witness places him at the motel and a security camera shows him driving nearby shortly after another witness overheard a man arguing with Brock. Then he ran and hid, tried to strand us on Number Two, and ultimately confessed."

"He's lying," Gina said. "You think I can't tell when my own father is lying? He doesn't lie about much, which means he's not very good at it. And I've become very adept at knowing when people are lying, especially those close to me. He didn't fight with Brock."

"But the last time we talked, you said it was possible your father confronted Brock," I said.

"Confronted maybe, but not killed," Gina said. "There's just no way..."

"I believe you," I said. "So why is he lying?"

Gina's jaw dropped and she stared at me a moment, then blew out a breath.

"I...I don't know," she said, clearly surprised that I'd accepted her assessment so easily but not expecting the question I'd asked. "I guess I hadn't thought that far."

"That's understandable," Gertie said. "You've been focused on getting him out of this. You haven't made it around to wondering why he was doing it in the first place."

She slumped into a chair and shook her head. "I don't know why he would lie. It doesn't make sense. He loses everything for claiming he hurt Brock and gains nothing. My father is a good man, but he's no martyr and doesn't have the kind of ego that needs to be fed."

I nodded. "So the logical assumption is that if he didn't fight with Brock, he knows who did and is protecting them. So who would he protect, even if it meant his own suffering?"

"Me and Billy, of course," she said, then her eyes widened. "You don't think *I* did it?"

I held up my hands. "*You* just said that your father would protect you even if it cost him. We have to ask."

"But I was here—and drunk. I barely made it from the back porch to my bed, and not even that far without getting sick first. I woke up the next morning fully clothed down to the shoes I was wearing the night before. Even if I blacked out, there's no way I could have driven to the motel, gotten in a fight with Brock, and driven back here. I didn't even know that Brock was here until I overheard you guys talking with Ally."

I watched her closely as she delivered that statement. She was overwrought and agitated but I didn't think she was lying. I couldn't be positive, as the situation was so emotionally charged that the behavioral lines could blur, but I was willing to give her the benefit of the doubt for the time being.

"So if it wasn't you, then who else would your father make this kind of sacrifice for?" I asked.

"I don't know," she said. "It's prison...I can't imagine..."

"What about Cooper?" I asked.

She started to shake her head but then the idea caught

hold and I could see the uncertainty in her eyes. "He wouldn't," she said.

"Who wouldn't?" I asked, not sure if she was referring to her father or Cooper.

"Either...both," she said.

"Cooper thinks Brock was the reason you wouldn't marry him," Ida Belle said. "Are you sure he wouldn't take an opportunity to confront him, especially if he knew Brock was back in town?"

"But he didn't know," she said. "None of us knew...but then, that's not true, is it? My father had to have known or he wouldn't have gone to the motel. But how did he know?"

"Cooper makes deliveries to the motel, doesn't he?" I asked.

"He makes deliveries anywhere that needs parts," she said, then gasped. "He said he had to make a last-minute run to New Orleans last week for HVAC parts for the motel. He wanted to know if we needed anything from the city. Oh my God. What am I supposed to do? My father can't go to prison for something Cooper did, but I don't want Cooper to go either. It was just a fight. No one intended to kill Brock, or they would have shot him. Sorry it sounds so cold, but that's the truth."

I nodded.

Maybe it was the truth. Maybe not.

We left Gina with a whole new set of worries and climbed back into Ida Belle's SUV. Everyone sat silently for a bit, then finally, Gertie looked over at me.

"It's like RJ and Brock came back to town and ruined Gina's life all over again," she said.

Because there was so much truth in that statement, I only nodded.

"Was she lying?" Ida Belle asked me.

"I don't think so," I said. "But I'm not a hundred percent. Or maybe I just don't *want* to think so."

"I don't either," Gertie said.

I sighed. "Sometimes this whole becoming a normal person thing really gets in the way of how I used to do my job."

"You're not losing your edge," Ida Belle said. "You're just seeing more of the gray. It was always there, but you didn't have the proper life experience to take it into account. And in your defense, you didn't have to. You didn't pick or investigate your targets. You carried out orders. Someone else made the determination."

I nodded. She was right, but somehow, it didn't make me feel any better.

"Gina seems certain that her father didn't do it," Gertie said. "But she's floundering on Cooper."

Ida Belle nodded. "Hence the disclaimer that if one of them did it, they didn't intend to kill him."

"Which might be the case," I said. "Could be whoever shoved Brock left him still standing and making excuses. But it could also be that if someone shoved him and he passed out for a bit, they thought they'd killed him and fled."

"It's definitely not the best look," Gertie said. "But I can hardly blame them for not sticking around and calling 911."

"The DA can't prove that's the way it happened," Ida Belle said. "So at least there's that."

"Sledgehammer still could have done it," Gertie said. "Even if Cooper confronted Brock, Sledgehammer could have gone in after and done the shoving."

"Sledgehammer is definitely not off the hook," I said. "If you make the assumption that whoever pushed Brock and took a shot at RJ are the same person, that leaves Sledge-hammer and Gina as the two who make the most sense."

"Any movement on the tracker?" Ida Belle asked.

"It's gone silent," I said.

"Could it have hit a dead spot?" Gertie asked.

"It's possible," I said. "But it's more likely it fell off and was destroyed. Still, I have an idea on how to find him again."

"You think he's still here?" Ida Belle asked.

"As long as RJ is here, I'm going to operate on the assumption that his boss has told him to stay put. So far, Sledge-hammer thinks he's skated under radar, and Cecil confessing helps him even more."

"Is Carter looking for him?" Gertie asked.

"I don't know," I said. "I think he's got to focus on Cooper first, and he would have to do things by the book anyway."

"Sledgehammer's not going to talk to Carter anyway," Ida Belle said.

"No," I agreed. "But if we can run him down, we might be able to overhear another conversation. Carter can't use it as evidence, but we might be able to figure out a way around that."

"Like what?" Gertie asked.

"Like one of us saying we personally overheard the conversation," Ida Belle said.

"So lying under oath," I pointed out.

Gertie waved a hand in dismissal. "As long as there's not court on Sunday, I'm good. And it's not exactly lying. If we hear something with the microphone, then that *is* personal. Just the location and circumstances are a little hedged. If it puts the right person in jail, I'm good with it."

I nodded. So was I.

"So where do you want to start looking?" Ida Belle asked.

"The hotel nearest to the diner where the tracker last signaled," I said.

Ida Belle started up the SUV and we headed off. The hotel was a couple exits farther up the highway than Shadow's domain, and we drove most of it in silence. I assumed we were all processing the potential outcomes—both positive and negative—and then attempting to come up with how to handle collateral damage if the negative outcome was the one that prevailed. By the time we reached the hotel parking lot, I still didn't have any answers.

"I don't see the Mercedes anywhere," Ida Belle said as she cruised the parking lot.

"Let's head inside and I'll ask at the front desk," I said.

"You think they'll tell you?" Gertie asked.

"If I tell them he works for a known drug dealer and is dangerous, I'm guessing they will," I said.

"Good point," Gertie agreed.

Ida Belle parked and we headed inside. I showed the photo of Sledgehammer to the clerk working the front desk, but he didn't recognize him. Still, this was a much bigger facility and probably had several front desk employees.

"Let's head to the dining room and see if any of the waitstaff recognizes him," I said.

We walked down a hallway to the small restaurant that served the hotel and I drew up short.

"Table in the corner," I said. "Reading the newspaper."

Ida Belle sucked in a breath. "It's our friend Mr. Garmon."

"Let's go have a chat with him," I said.

CHAPTER TWENTY-TWO

"ARE YOU SURE IT'S SAFE?" GERTIE ASKED, STUDYING THE disappearing man. "I mean, not in a potential death sort of way—I'm good there—but if he's a suspect, then do you want to let him know we're onto him?"

"I have an idea about Mr. Garmon," I said. "And I don't think it's what everyone else has in mind."

I strode across the dining room and as I drew close to his table, he looked up from the paper. His eyes widened as he caught sight of me, and he placed the paper on the table as I took a seat.

"Looks like I'm not the only one tracking Sledgehammer, Mr. Garmon," I said. "Or should I call you Officer or Detective..."

He leaned back in his chair and smiled. "Detective Price will work. I should have figured you'd make me."

"You ran me," I said.

"A PI shows up, asking questions about a potential homicide that my target might have been involved in, and I have to," he said. "I was surprised to find a former CIA agent in a place like this, though. How'd you end up here?"

"That's a long story and not one I have time for at the moment. Remember when I told you I had a friend I didn't want railroaded over Brock's death?"

He nodded.

"Well, that fear of mine has come to pass, and our DA isn't so much interested in the truth as he is keeping score for his future political run."

"I'm sorry to hear that," he said. "But there's nothing I can do. I told you what I knew."

"So everything you said was aboveboard?"

"Every bit of it...even the part about the chili."

"And you didn't leave anything out—like that Sledgehammer was the man who argued with Brock?"

"I didn't hedge anything...I never heard the other guy's voice. It was just a low rumble."

"But you saw him leaving—wouldn't you have recognized Sledgehammer?"

"I saw a guy with a hat and a long coat flapping in the wind, in dim light and from behind. It could have been anyone. When I ran to put on pants, the chili hit."

"Was Sledgehammer's car in the parking lot when you got to the motel?"

"No, but I was there for a while before the arguments started."

I shook my head. "I have to say, Detective Price, you're not doing a great job following your target."

A flush ran up his face. "You don't know anything. I got the call to come after Sledgehammer the day another detective saw him leaving the state that morning. My team leader said Brock Benoit disappeared the same day and thought maybe he'd head home to hide. So he sent me here, seeing if Sledgehammer followed since he's got Louisiana ties and would know the area. I flew in and checked into the motel before either of them arrived, figuring if Brock didn't have someone local to stay with, he'd go as cheap as possible. Having the room next door was pure luck."

"When did you locate Sledgehammer?"

"Not until the parade. I spotted his Mercedes leaving downtown but couldn't get to my car in time to follow. I didn't even know he was staying at the motel until the next morning when I saw him driving out of the motel parking lot."

"Why didn't you have a tracker on his car?"

"No warrant."

I raised one eyebrow.

"Fine. No clear opportunity. If I blow my cover, we could lose three years of work. Sledgehammer had never laid eyes on me before now and I couldn't do anything to draw suspicion."

"And after Brock was killed? You didn't think you should fill the local cops in on exactly who Sledgehammer was and what you think he's doing here?"

"I called that clerk about the trouble in Brock's room," he said, clearly frustrated. "But I couldn't afford to stick my neck out any further. I was only here to collect evidence, not take anyone down."

"A man died, and Sledgehammer might have been the one who made that happen."

"Brock Benoit didn't matter to my superiors. Neither does Sledgehammer, for that matter. It's Payday they're after. But the fact that Sledgehammer stuck around after Brock died makes my superiors think there's more to find and I agree. If I'd filled in the locals, they would have brought Sledgehammer in for questioning. And when he walked over lack of evidence, Payday would have called him right back to Nashville and any opportunity to learn what he was doing here would be gone."

I shook my head. I didn't like it, but I couldn't blame him for following orders. Lord knows, I'd spent plenty of years with a set of operating parameters concerning my work. Sometimes, I'd even managed to stay within them.

"A good man is going to go down for this," I said.

"From what I hear, he confessed," Price said.

"He's covering for someone," I said. "Definitely not Sledgehammer, but someone he thinks did this. I think he's got it all wrong."

Price blew out a breath. "Look, if I hand Sledgehammer over to the locals right now, it will only make things worse. Sledgehammer's new to the crew and Payday owes him no particular loyalty. Without enough evidence, Sledgehammer would drive away from questioning and right back to Nashville, where Payday would have him popped. These dealers recruit guys like Sledgehammer for a reason—they're expendable. Why do you think he wasn't pulled after Brock died?"

"So you're just going to let him run loose...maybe kill someone else?"

"I didn't *let* him do anything. I didn't even know he was staying at the motel until the day after the parade. Look, if Sledgehammer caused Benoit's head injury, then why is your guy taking responsibility?"

"I wish I knew. But you definitely heard a woman arguing with Brock after the man left?"

"Absolutely."

"Was it RJ Rogers?"

He shrugged. "RJ Rogers was never on our radar, so I wouldn't know her voice. Hell, I didn't know Brock's voice before I came here. *He* never hit our radar until he didn't settle up with Payday. My focus is Sledgehammer. Brock was incidental."

"So is Sledgehammer at this hotel now?"

He didn't answer for a minute, then he finally shook his head. "Not that I've been able to determine."

"You lost him?"

His jaw flexed. "I'll find him again."

"I suppose it wouldn't do any good to ask for a courtesy call when you do."

"I suppose it wouldn't. I'm sorry about your guy, but there's a lot more at stake here than one man."

———

IT WAS A SOMBER GROUP WHO MADE THEIR WAY BACK TO Sinful. No one spoke for the first ten minutes into the drive. In fact, Ida Belle didn't even ask me where to go. She just started up the SUV and directed it down the highway toward home. I'd briefly considered driving up the highway to scout the other hotels between here and New Orleans, but then I figured Price had already done that. If he'd located Sledgehammer somewhere else, he wouldn't be staying at a different hotel. It was far more likely that Sledgehammer had relocated to New Orleans. He knew the city and it was a lot easier to get lost there than out in the sticks.

Finally, Gertie broke the silence.

"So Sledgehammer is in the wind," Gertie said.

"Yeah," I said.

"Are you going to tell Carter about Detective Price?" Ida Belle asked.

"Why? So four of us can be angry over a situation that won't change? Price's superiors aren't going to give him permission to cooperate and Carter can't make him. And as much as we all hate it, he's right. At this point, blowing his cover serves nothing. Brock is already dead and Price can't positively identify either person who was in Brock's room that night."

"I think it was Sledgehammer," Gertie said. "Giving Brock a reminder."

"Then why is Cecil lying?" Ida Belle said. "It all comes back to the same round and round. Either he saw Cooper there or Gina. If we think Gina is telling the truth, then it was Cooper."

"Do you know where Cooper lives?" I asked.

Ida Belle nodded.

"Go there," I said. "I think it's past time we talk to him."

Cooper rented a small house on what used to be a large ranch. The land had been broken up some years ago when the patriarch retired. He'd remained in the main house and kept another lot with what used to be the ranch hand's house and used it as a rental. It was a one-story cabin. Nothing fancy, but it was neat and maintained well. There were even two pots of winter flowers on the porch. Cooper's hotshot truck was parked in front.

"Gina could do a lot worse than this," I said.

"She could," Gertie agreed. "Cooper is a nice young man."

I blew out a breath. "Then let's go see if our nice young man is a killer."

I saw the blinds move as we approached and as we were climbing the steps, the door opened.

"I thought you were the cops," he said.

"They've been here?" I asked.

"Carter was," he said. "Put me through it pretty hard but I'll tell you like I told him—I ain't putting Cecil on blast."

"We're not here to bury Cecil," I said. "We're here to break him out."

He stared at us for a bit, and I saw a tiny flicker of hope flash through his somber expression.

"Then I guess you best come in," he said.

We followed him inside to a cozy living room with old leather furniture and a thick navy blue rug. Soft white walls made the small room look bigger and the lack of clutter helped make the space feel open. The only sign that a young single man lived here was the obscenely large television on the wall.

"You saw Brock when you delivered HVAC parts to the motel," I said.

His eyes widened and I could tell I'd surprised him with my direct approach. He looked down at the floor, then back up at me and ran one hand over his hair.

"How'd you know?" he asked.

"It tracks," I said, but I didn't mention that Gina had offered up his route that day. "And I'm really good at my job."

"You were CIA, right?" he asked. "I heard talk about you down at the Swamp Bar. Whiskey says you're the smartest person he's ever met. A lot of people don't put much stock in what he says, but I know better. Whiskey ain't no slouch in the smarts department."

"No, he's not," I agreed. "So are you going to tell me the truth about what happened parade night?"

"I can't," he said, looking miserable. "You're hooked up with Carter. You'll have to tell him."

"The way you told Gina that Brock was at the motel?" I asked.

He straightened in his chair. "No! I never told her. I wouldn't. That piece of—he already hurt her enough. No way I'd let her know he was back around. Especially with her already struggling with RJ being back and flitting around town like she owned it again."

"But you did tell Cecil," I said. "And he went to the motel to confront Brock. We know that for sure. There was a witness, and his truck was caught on a nearby security camera. The question is, when your phone records come in—and I'm sure Carter's already subpoenaed them—is your cell going to ping off a tower up the highway?"

The panic immediately set in his expression and I knew I'd hit a bull's-eye once more.

"Tell me what happened," I said. "I won't repeat anything to Carter unless it gets Cecil off the hook for this. You have my word."

"What if that DA puts you on the stand?" he asked. "You'd have to lie under oath."

"The DA will never know we talked," I said. "Unless you tell him."

He shook his head. "I ain't telling that guy nothing. Far as I'm concerned, I never saw Brock Benoit and if I was driving up the highway after the parade, it was because I was hungry or needed some Copenhagen."

"That's a solid plan," I said. "No one can place you at the motel, but someone did place Cecil there. I need to know what happened. I can't help Cecil if I don't have all the facts."

"What if I ain't got them either?"

"Tell me what you do have."

He nodded. "I told Cecil about seeing Brock at the motel when I delivered the parts. I didn't recognize him when he walked by my truck, but then he asked the clerk something and I knew the voice."

"Did he recognize you?" I asked.

He shook his head. "He didn't even glance my direction and even if he had, he probably wouldn't have known me. I was invisible to guys like Brock Benoit. After I heard him talk, I took another look, and I could see it then. Just rough, you know? So I pulled my hat down, just in case, and watched until he went into a room."

"Then you called Cecil."

"No. You don't tell a man that sort of thing over the phone, and I had to make sure Gina didn't overhear. I asked him to come by here before he went to his poker game. Said I had something super important. I'm sort of surprised he showed, but I must have sounded spooked."

"And how did he take the news?"

"About as good as you'd expect. How would you take that news if it was your daughter Brock had screwed over? Your grandson that he abandoned and never sent so much as a dollar to support?"

"I'd be mad as hell," I said.

"Yeah, well, multiply that times about a hundred and you got it right."

"So you made a plan with Cecil to confront Brock? Were you planning on asking for money or just taking some blood equity out of him?"

"No! Nothing like that. We just wanted him to leave before Gina saw him. He really messed her up and we were both afraid of what that might do. If he had any inclinations of sticking around, we were going to change his mind."

"And how were you planning on doing that?" I asked.

"Cecil was going to sic the cops on him for not paying child support. If he didn't have the money for the support and a fine, he would have gotten jail time."

I sat back in my chair, a bit surprised. That was an angle I hadn't considered, and it was a smart one.

"So what happened? Did Brock refuse to leave?"

"I don't know what happened. I was supposed to meet Cecil in the parking lot, and we were going to give Brock a warning. But while I was driving over, Cecil called me and said to go home. That Brock wasn't there. I said we could wait until he got back, but Cecil said we'd just see about it in the morning before he got up."

Cooper frowned, his expression shifting to worried.

"He sounded weird," Cooper said. "I asked him what was going on, but he just said he had a headache and he'd call me the next day. Then he hung up and when I tried to call back, it went straight to voice mail."

"So did you go to the motel?" I asked.

"No. I thought it was strange, but I couldn't think of any reason he'd be lying to me about Brock not being there. And me confronting Brock about child support wouldn't carry any weight. I was just going in case Brock got squirrely with Cecil."

"What about Gina?" I asked.

He looked confused. "What about her?"

"Do you think she could have gone to the motel?"

"No! She didn't even know Brock was there."

"Are you sure Cecil didn't tell her?"

"Positive," he said, but I could see the flicker of doubt.

"Did you talk to Gina that night?"

"No. I asked her to go to the parade with me earlier that day, but she said she wasn't about to give RJ attention along with the rest of Sinful. Said she was staying home and watching TV."

"You didn't go by the house?"

"She didn't sound much like she wanted company. So I went to the Swamp Bar and didn't leave until it was time to go meet Cecil."

"Did you call?"

"She didn't answer. But that doesn't mean anything," he said, his voice shooting up a bit. "She refuses my calls all the time. I keep pushing for more with us and sometimes she doesn't want to hear it."

I nodded. "Anything else you can tell me?"

"Just that I know Cecil didn't do anything," he said.

"Then why did he confess?"

Cooper shook his head, and I could tell he was worried.

"I don't know."

CHAPTER TWENTY-THREE

SUNDAY EVENING DRAGGED INTO SUNDAY NIGHT. THE ONLY positive was that the DA didn't work weekends, so at least Cecil was still sitting in a jail cell and hadn't yet followed through on a bad decision to sign away his life on trumped-up charges and an inaccurate confession. Carter had called me that afternoon, but only to say he'd be headed home after work to try to get some sleep. I didn't bother to ask him if he'd made any progress on proving Cecil innocent. The tone of his voice told me everything I needed to know.

Ida Belle, Gertie, and I had driven by RJ's house when we'd gotten back to Sinful. Her car was still there, and a Mudbug deputy was parked out front. Apparently, Cecil's being in custody hadn't eliminated the threat to RJ either in her mind or Carter's or both. It was a good thing, since I had serious doubts that the man sitting in that jail cell had done anything wrong.

The problem was, I also believed Cooper.

Which only left us with Gina as the one Cecil was covering for.

We'd spent the rest of the afternoon at my house, going

over and over the facts as we understood them, but we couldn't make a case for anyone except Sledgehammer and Gina. When we added Cecil's confession into the mix, Gina was the only one left standing. And with Sledgehammer in the wind, there was no opportunity to get some evidence by listening in. In between bouts of mulling and complaining about no answers, we'd take a drive around Sinful, but there was no sign of the black Mercedes. And my phone remained silent. No calls from our friend Detective Price. Not that I was expecting any.

I'd given Price a day to find Sledgehammer but come tomorrow morning, I was telling Carter exactly who Jim Garmon really was and what he was doing in Sinful. No way I was letting Cecil sign a confession when the perfect reasonable doubt suspect was right in our midst.

I tossed and turned most of the night and didn't manage to truly drop off until early morning. Of course, that meant I slept later than usual and woke up feeling groggy and exhausted. But as soon as my eyes opened, my mind started whirling again, so there was no use to try to sleep anymore. I headed downstairs and put on coffee. I wasn't surprised to see I'd already received a text from Ida Belle asking if I was up. I texted back and she indicated she and Gertie would be over shortly.

Misery loves company.

I was on my third cup and had already broken out my backup pot when they shuffled in. Gertie saw me drinking from one of my oversize hot chocolate mugs and took out two more of them before bringing both coffeepots to the table. We all drank in silence for a couple minutes, then finally Ida Belle leaned back and sighed.

"I wish I could say I dreamed the answer last night," she said. "But mostly, I just had frantic nightmares."

"I had heartburn," Gertie said. "All that talk about chili from Price, and I got a craving around midnight and made up a batch."

I stared at her. "Price complained about the chili making him sick. And that made you want to eat some?"

She shrugged. "He said 'chili.' That's really all it took."

I understood. Eating chili was no worse a decision than the four beers and eight cookies I'd consumed in one sitting last night.

"I wish we could get in to talk to Cecil," Ida Belle said.

"I don't think it would do any good," I said. "Look, I lost a night's sleep over this, but I don't see any way around it. We all believe Cooper was telling the truth and we all believe Cecil is lying. That only leaves Gina. And unfortunately, it all fits. Gina hated Brock and RJ and has no alibi for either night. Cecil might have told her about Brock being at the motel or she could have overheard him talking to Brock. She could have driven over there, fought with Brock, and left."

"You think Cecil saw her at the motel?" Ida Belle asked.

I nodded. "Maybe driving away. Then when he got there all hell was breaking loose, so he left and called Cooper to warn him off. Sledgehammer was in the parking lot which is when he spotted Cecil leaving and heard his muffler."

"So we don't think Sledgehammer saw the woman who argued with Brock, right?"

"Doubt it, or he would have ID'd her as well to keep the cops looking anywhere but at him," I said. "If I had to guess, Sledgehammer had his confrontation with Brock, then headed to his car. Maybe he went for some smokes or called his boss or was retrieving something from the trunk. What we know for certain is that he was in that parking lot after Brock died and so was Cecil."

Gertie let out a long-suffering sigh. "You really think it was Gina, don't you?"

"That was at the motel? Yeah. That caused Brock's head injury? No. I'm still betting on Sledgehammer for that one."

"But we can't prove it," Ida Belle said. "And the reality is, both Cecil and Gina being on site wouldn't be a good look. No smoke without a fire is what the DA will think. So even if Cecil knows Brock argued with a man before Gina showed up, he's still not going to come clean. Doing so would send the police right back out to find that woman as soon as our friend Detective Price has to come out of the shadows and tell everyone his witness statement as Jim Garmon was accurate. Cecil confessing stops the investigation."

Gertie threw up her hands. "We have to do something!"

The knock on my back door surprised us all. Carter usually came in the front and I wasn't really sure how Mannie got in, but it was rarely by knocking or in broad daylight. I opened the door and found Ronald standing there holding my Queen dress encased in plastic and looking a bit annoyed. He hung the dress on a hook next to the back door then sat at the table with Ida Belle and Gertie.

"Coffee?" I asked.

"God no," he said. "It's horrible for the skin. I want you to know it has taken me days to get that dress clean but I did it, one sequin at a time. Went through four boxes of Q-tips."

"Is that why you look aggravated?" Gertie asked. "You know, all that frowning doesn't help the skin either."

"Oh no!" He tried to blank his expression but didn't quite manage it. "That woman is a nightmare! I've had a harder time controlling frown lines the past week than I have in the last year."

"What woman?" Ida Belle asked.

"That loser RJ," he said. "She was at the bank this morning, complaining and being rude to everyone. And since employees can't say anything because of all that 'customer is always right' nonsense, I told her exactly what a crap person she was."

"And what did she have to say to that?" I asked.

"She called me a ridiculous queen," he said. "Like being ridiculous or a queen is an insult. So I said, 'at least one of us is a queen,' and everyone laughed, so she went huffing out of there. Thank God she's leaving."

I sat up straight. "She's leaving?"

He nodded. "She said she was running an errand for her mother, then was headed back to Nashville. I saw luggage in her car."

"Carter must have had to cut her loose," Ida Belle said.

"Well, she'll never make it through New Orleans without being pulled over for that plastic taped on her window," Ronald said. "Assuming the car can even get her to New Orleans. It sounded like the engine was falling out when she left the bank."

"It's supposed to rain today," Gertie said. "That's probably why she left the plastic on."

"So then stick around a day longer and get the window fixed," Ronald said. "She cashed a check for five thousand dollars. I'm sure Sawyer could afford to loan her a couple hundred."

"Guess her line of credit funded," Ida Belle said.

Gertie nodded. "And contractors love their cash. But RJ loves her creature comforts. I'm surprised she'd risk leaving with the weather looking like it does."

"Her protection disappears along with the order to keep her in town," I said.

Ronald rolled his eyes. "I would ask who would want to hurt her but that's most everyone. So the question is who would make the effort?"

"She and Brock ran afoul of a drug dealer back in Nashville," I said.

"Good God!" Ronald said. "Then why on earth would Carter keep her around? Let her leave and take her trouble with her. There's already enough damage in the wake of those two. The next bullet meant for her might go through a car window and into a neighbor."

My cell phone rang and I checked the display.

Shadow Chaser.

"Who'd you rent a room to this time?" I asked when I answered.

"There's a woman here," he said, his voice low. "She asked me for a jump and I'm not sure, but I think it's on that car the dead guy was driving. The cops told me the bank was sending a repo guy to pick it up. She has keys and waved a paper. If it had started, she would already be gone, so it's not really my business, right?"

"Dark hair, green eyes, curvy, and rude?"

"That's her."

I started to tell him to call the cops but given that Mandy said it was the SUV 'they' had purchased, her name was probably on the title. That meant she wasn't stealing it and a repo was the bank's problem, not law enforcement's.

"Where are you now?" I asked.

"In the office. I told her I'd drive around back and help her out once I found the jumper cables, but then I looked out the back window and saw her standing by the car smoking a cigarette and I had this flash...like I'd seen her before."

I felt my pulse quicken. "When?"

"That night. The night the dude died."

She cashed a check for five thousand dollars.

Her voice is shot.

She knew I could see her.

I went straight from my car to the back patio.
RJ ran everything, including Brock.
I think he had something on her.
She always insisted on being in the front seat.
He couldn't even hold a pick.

I jumped up from my chair and ran for the door. "We have to get to the motel!"

CHAPTER TWENTY-FOUR

IDA BELLE AND GERTIE WERE RUNNING BEHIND ME WHEN I jumped in the SUV. Ida Belle started up the engine and tore out of the driveway, not even bothering to ask why.

"Shadow, what arm was the needle in on the dead guy?" I asked.

"What? I don't know. Jesus. What does this have to do with the car?"

"Think!"

"Uh, well, he was sitting in the chair facing the door and the needle was on the side next to the closet door, so left. It was in his left arm."

"Okay. Listen to me. I'm on my way, but I need you to take as long as possible getting that car started."

"Oh my God! She's a bad guy, isn't she? Can't I just get in my car and leave?"

"No. Because she'll know why you left and she'll run. You're going to be a real-life action hero. Don't let me down."

"What if she tries to kill me? I don't even have a weapon."

"I'll be there in a matter of minutes."

"There is no way you're getting to this motel from Sinful in minutes."

"You don't know my driver. Look, tell her you can't find the cable. That will buy you some time. Then tell her you have to lock up the office and forward the phone. Put the cables on wrong, then say you need to look up how to do it on your phone. Whatever it takes to keep her from leaving. Are you wearing a hoodie?"

"Yeah, but why—"

"Don't disconnect this call. Put the phone in your hoodie and I'll be able to hear everything."

"Oh my God, she's coming back to the office!"

"Then pretend you can't find those cables."

I put my phone on mute and turned on the speaker.

"I'm sorry, ma'am," Shadow said. "I know we have a set of jumper cables somewhere, but I've never actually used them. Worse case, there's a station not far from here. It would only take me a couple minutes to pop over and buy some. But I know we have a set somewhere. Just give me a minute."

I could hear the sound of drawers opening and rustling.

"Yeah, okay," RJ said. "Just as fast as you can, right? I have another car to get on a transport today and I'd really like to get out of here before the weather gets bad."

"Sure, I'm looking as fast as I can."

"I'm going out to smoke."

"Thank God," Shadow whispered. "She's standing right outside. I hope you can hear me. I hope you're almost here. I wish I could pick up the phone but she's looking at me. Crap! Now I really can't remember where the jumper cables are."

"He's losing it," Gertie said.

"What is going on?" Ida Belle asked.

I filled them in on Shadow's situation and then hit them with my big announcement.

"RJ killed Brock."

"What?"

"How?"

They both exploded at once.

"Remember Gina told us how she could see RJ in her room, flaunting her life to rub it in? Well, that works both ways. Gina said that parade night she went straight from her car to the back patio and then got drunk and passed out in a lawn chair. I think RJ saw her passed out with her purse right there on the patio with her and used Gina's car to go to the motel."

"Which is why RJ's neighbor working in his garage didn't see her leave," Gertie said.

"And more importantly, why Cecil is lying," Ida Belle said.

I nodded. "Cecil must have seen Gina's car leaving the motel, like I thought, but it wasn't Gina driving. It was RJ."

"But why kill Brock?" Gertie asked.

"Because she wanted all the money from the licensing rights," I said. "But Brock wasn't going to let her get away with it. Remember, Mandy told me she thought Brock had something on RJ. I think I know what it is."

"What?" Ida Belle asked.

"I think RJ was driving the car back in high school when they wrecked. I think after they wrecked, they moved Marigold into the driver's seat because they were both drunk and she wasn't. Then they were going to call for help. But the car caught fire and those people stopped to help, which accomplished the same thing as far as their story, but severely injured Marigold."

"That's the reason Marigold won't ride in the back seat," Gertie said. "She was in the back when they wrecked."

"And you told me Marigold didn't like to drive at night

because of her vision," I said. "So the odds of her driving on unfamiliar roads that late at night are low."

"So you think Brock was going to tell Christina the truth if RJ cut him out of the deal?" Ida Belle asked. "But if the truth came out, the deal would probably go away because of the negative publicity. Then they'd both lose out."

"I think Brock was willing to lose as long as RJ didn't win," I said. "He was done letting her call the shots."

"But why is RJ on the hook for Brock's debt?" Gertie asked.

"I'm not positive," I said. "But I think it was RJ who made the original deal with Payday. When she could no longer perform, she lost her access to the clubs."

"So Brock bounced, hooked up with a new singer, and took over the drug dealing business," Ida Belle said. "But he wasn't as sharp as RJ and tried to steal from Payday."

"I still don't get how RJ is on the hook if Brock cut his own deal."

"Maybe Payday considers them partners," Ida Belle said. "And he's not willing to change his stance because he thinks he can collect from RJ since she's got the licensing money coming."

"So it was RJ who put the knot on Brock's head?" Gertie asked.

"No. I think that was Sledgehammer," I said.

"But you said RJ killed him," Gertie said.

I nodded. "She overdosed him. Remember, Brock couldn't even hold a pick, so there's no way he got a needle in his left arm using his right hand. I'd bet money he has recent track marks on his *right* arm. But RJ probably didn't know about the nerve damage, so she put the drugs in the wrong arm."

"So Sledgehammer fought with Brock, then left," Ida Belle said. "Then RJ came and what?"

"My guess is that between the alcohol and the head injury, he started getting dizzy and sat down. Maybe he lost consciousness or maybe she offered him a fix and he was jonesing too hard to turn it down. The TV remote was in the chair, so as he died, he slumped and pressed against it, shooting the volume into the stratosphere."

"So RJ gave him a lethal dose," Gertie said.

"Then drove home and went to bed like nothing happened. I knew she was cold, but that's something else entirely."

"So it was Sledgehammer who took that shot at her?" Ida Belle said. "A warning?"

"Actually, I think she shot her car window out herself," I said. "It made her the target. The victim. And distracted even more from making her a suspect."

Ida Belle pressed harder on the accelerator. "And now she's got five thousand in cash and is about to acquire a better car—one that will take her far away to hide until she can collect that licensing money and a vehicle that Sledgehammer isn't looking for."

"Found them!" Shadow's voice came over the phone.

We heard a door open and close and then Shadow again.

"Ma'am, I found them. I'm just going to forward the phones and lock up the office, then I'll grab my car and meet you in the back."

"Yeah, all right," RJ said.

We heard more shuffling and then a car door open and close and Shadow's voice came full force on the line.

"Are you still there?" he asked.

"Yes. And we're maybe eight minutes out."

"Really? Okay. I can make eight. Eight is good. There's not going to be a gunfight, is there? Does she have a gun?"

"Probably," I said. "If she pulls it out, then dive under the nearest car and let me handle it."

He groaned. "I really, really hate you."

"I'll cover your next month of therapy."

"Like that will put a dent in it. Okay, have to put you back into my pocket before she sees me on the phone."

"Should we call Carter?" Gertie asked when I put my phone back on mute.

"We don't have any proof," I said. "I'm hoping when we confront her that she'll mess up, so be ready to record when we get there—both of you."

They nodded.

"Is it going to reach?" I heard RJ asked.

"I don't think so," Shadow said. "Let me back up and move closer."

I clenched my hands as I looked out the windshield. I'd stopped looking at the speedometer when it broke 100 mph, and our speed had increased since. She was pushing it as hard as she could, and I prayed we got there before RJ disappeared. With 5K in cash, who knew how long it would take her to surface.

"Will you get on with it?" RJ asked, and I could hear the frustration in her voice.

"Look, this isn't my skill set," Shadow said. "I need to look up where they go. Unless you know—you're the repo person. Shouldn't you know cars?"

"What are you insinuating?" RJ asked.

"Nothing. I just thought you'd know and I wouldn't have to look it up."

"Jesus. Here's a picture."

"Shadow's doing a good job of faking to stall," Gertie said.

"I don't think he's faking," I said.

"Going somewhere?" a man's voice boomed over Shadow's phone.

My heart dropped.

Sledgehammer.

I clenched my phone and we all listened to the horror story playing out that we couldn't do anything to stop.

"Send Carter a text and tell him to get over to the motel before Sledgehammer kills RJ and Shadow," I said to Gertie.

"Oh my God!" Shadow said. "He's got a gun. I didn't do anything, I swear. She needed a jump."

"Open the trunk," Sledgehammer said.

"I can make this right," RJ said. "I have money—five grand."

"And you were just headed my way with it, right?" Sledgehammer asked. "Do you think I'm stupid? And five grand isn't half of what's owed."

I heard keys rattling and the sound of metal squeaking.

"It's not even my debt," RJ said, sounding frantic. "Brock went solo after he left me. You know that."

"But you brought him in," Sledgehammer said. "That means you're on the hook for him, whether you're sharing sheets or not. You should have picked better. I'll be taking that five thousand, though, and I'll be taking you—back to Nashville to see Payday. He can decide whether he wants to wait on you to settle the rest or make an example of you."

Ida Belle took the exit for the motel going so fast, I was pretty sure the SUV was airborne for just a second.

"Now keep your hands up and sit next to the car," Sledgehammer continued.

I heard shuffling and a scream that I was certain had come from Shadow, then the sound of a trunk slamming shut.

"I'm in the trunk," Shadow said, his voice a combination of abject fear and disbelief.

Ida Belle looked over at me. "How do you want to approach this?"

"I'll jump out at the front of the motel and access the back lot through the breezeway," I said. "You continue around. This glass should protect you from whatever weapon Sledgehammer is holding. Use your SUV to block them from driving out. Do *not* get out of the SUV for any reason!"

I looked back at Gertie. "Any word from Carter?"

She shook her head. "But he read the message."

"Then he's on his way, but he knows not to risk contact."

Suddenly, muffled gunshots came through my phone.

"They're shooting," Shadow said. "I'm going to die."

"Just stay down and cover your head," I said.

"I'm locked in a trunk! I can't get more *down* than that!"

"We're almost there," I said. "I've got to disconnect."

"No—"

CHAPTER TWENTY-FIVE

He was yelling when I disconnected but I couldn't help it. Stealth was the operative word right now. Ida Belle slowed down as she approached the motel so that they couldn't hear her engine racing, then eased across the parking lot. Just before she reached the breezeway, I jumped out of the SUV and ran to the motel as she continued to the rear parking access at the end of the building. I didn't see the Mercedes anywhere, so I assumed Sledgehammer had parked nearby and sneaked up on them.

No more shots rang out, and I wondered if it was over and Sledgehammer had put an end to RJ right there in the parking lot. I prayed that Shadow hadn't been caught in the cross fire. If he had, it was all on me. I should have let him drive away when he had the chance, but I really hadn't thought he was in any danger. And from RJ, he wouldn't have been. But Sledgehammer had completely changed the game.

I crept up to the breezeway access and someone opened a room door nearby.

"Police are on the way," I whispered. "Stay inside and stay down."

He nodded and immediately closed the door. I prayed anyone else in the rooms had locked their doors and hit the deck when the shooting started. I also prayed that none of them would try to 'help.'

I peered into the breezeway and found it clear. Ida Belle's SUV had just made the corner around the motel, so I slipped into the breezeway and hurried to the back of the motel. At the edge of the back opening, I paused and listened, but the only thing I could hear was the low rumble of Ida Belle's SUV in the distance.

I didn't have any protection in my current position, so I got down on all fours and crawled over to the bumper of a big truck parked near the breezeway exit. Then I pressed my head on the ground and scanned the area for feet. I spotted the black combat boots I'd seen Sledgehammer wearing behind the SUV I'd seen with the hood up. The car next to it must be Shadow's. There was no sign of RJ, but Sledgehammer was crouched low and moving toward the front of the SUV, clearly scouting for her.

"You might as well give up!" he shouted.

RJ's response was a shot fired through the windshield of the SUV.

That put RJ somewhere behind a truck just a few down from the one I was ducked behind. I moved around to the side so if she shifted to the back, she wouldn't see me. I checked under the cars again and couldn't see Sledgehammer's boots. Then I saw movement at the corner of a dumpster behind the SUV. He'd changed positions to put a better barrier between him and RJ. Unfortunately, that put a better barrier between him and me.

I heard Ida Belle's SUV round the corner, and she honked the horn, then revved the engine.

"What the hell is that?" Sledgehammer yelled. "You th[ink] your getaway driver is going to save you?"

He fired off two rounds at Ida Belle's SUV and they ri[co]cheted off the bulletproof glass and to the side.

I took the opportunity to take a shot at Sledgehammer, [but] all I had sight of was a bit of his shoulder. I heard him yell a[nd] figured I'd grazed him at least. I peered around the fro[nt] bumper of the truck and saw RJ go through a hole in the hur[ri]cane fence that ran down one side of the back lot. I could[n't] pursue her without exposing myself to Sledgehammer, but [I] couldn't afford to let her get away either.

I waved at Ida Belle and pointed at the fence. She put th[e] SUV in reverse and was backing up when Sledgehamm[er] whirled around the dumpster and opened fire on the SUV. Id[a] Belle floored it in reverse, but as she was about to whip aroun[d] the side of the motel, Sledgehammer landed a direct hit righ[t] through her front grille. The engine died and steam starte[d] coming out. I was pretty sure I could hear Ida Belle cussing all the way across the parking lot.

"Whoever's out there, show yourself and put down your weapon!" Sledgehammer shouted. "The broads in that SUV are sitting ducks. You've got three seconds to step out or I'll light up the trunk of that car and the guy in it dies."

If it had just been me and Sledgehammer in the parking lot, I would have taken the chance on a Western showdown. I had no doubt I could pull faster, and I always had a spare. And I wasn't worried about Ida Belle and Gertie because God only knows what kind of firepower they could put in Sledgehammer before he got anywhere near them. But it was his threat to fire into the trunk of Shadow's car that concerned me. He was shooting the .45, and a round would have no trouble penetrating the truck lid.

"Three...two...one!"

I stepped out from behind the truck, my weapon in the air, and prayed he'd give me even one second to pull off a miracle. He peered out quickly from behind the dumpster, then tucked back in. From where he was standing, he had a clear shot at the trunk of the car. But I didn't have a clear shot at him and there was no way to get one without transferring a good twenty feet over in plain sight. I could draw and fire my backup weapon in no time at all, but I couldn't run faster than a bullet.

I heard something behind me, then a whiz overhead, and jumped back behind the truck just as the dumpster exploded. I looked back and saw Gertie hanging out of the top of Ida Belle's SUV, clutching a grenade launcher and cheering.

Sledgehammer staggered out of the smoke and flames, his clothes shredded and hanging on him like smoldering rags. He tried to lift his arm but he was spent. He collapsed in a heap right behind Shadow's car. I ran over and gave his gun a healthy kick, then checked the car for the keys.

"Shadow?" I called out. "Are you all right? Where are the keys?"

"He threw them in here with me," Shadow said.

Ida Belle and Gertie ran up and Gertie pulled a small crowbar out of her purse. I didn't even stop to question it. I just shoved it in the crease and popped the trunk open.

Shadow was curled up in the trunk in the fetal position. He lifted his head and blinked several times and I scanned him for blood.

"Are you injured?" I asked.

"My shoulder hurts," he said, sounding dazed as I helped him out of the trunk. "But I didn't get shot, so I guess that's good."

He looked down at Sledgehammer and laughed.

"Oh good, a half naked man. It's been at least a day."

Then he promptly passed out.

"Where is RJ?" Gertie asked.

"She went through the fence," I said.

About that time, an engine fired up behind the tree line and a second later, we stared as Sledgehammer's black Mercedes roared by.

"Crap!" Ida Belle said. "My SUV is completely blocking the side. You can't get a car through there."

"These cars wouldn't catch that Mercedes anyway," Gertie said. "Especially with the head start she has."

I reached into my pocket for my cell, ready to call Carter, and felt it vibrate as I pulled it out.

I started laughing as I showed them the blinking red dot.

CHAPTER TWENTY-SIX

THE NEXT AFTERNOON, IDA BELLE, GERTIE, RONALD, AND I were enjoying a nice dip in my hot tub when Carter came around the corner. When he saw all of us sitting in the bubbling water holding plastic champagne glasses, I thought he was going to turn around. But instead, he headed our direction and took a seat on the end of the porch.

"I see you're celebrating," he said.

"You should be too," Ronald said. "Sinful is free from the scourge once more."

"It's only the first week of the year," Gertie pointed out. "We've got time to import some more scourge."

"We've got enough homegrown, thank you," Ida Belle said. "No need to import more."

"Amen," Carter said. "Fortune's relocation here increased my workweek by at least fifteen percent on average. My job is going to cut into my sleeping time soon. Or worse, my beer drinking time."

"You worked enough last week for two people," Ronald said. "Toss off your clothes and climb in here with us."

Carter stared. "You're not all naked in there, right?"

We all laughed, and his expression shifted from fearful to slightly horrified.

"Of course not," I said and rose up enough to show my bathing suit strap. "We're all legally clad, even though this is private property."

"Within clear view of the bayou," Carter said.

"They can't see us in here," Gertie said.

"But you have to get out at some point," Carter said.

"Details," Ronald said. "You're overly concerned with details."

"So am I," I said. "And I assume you're stopping by to give us an update on everything."

He nodded. "First up, Sledgehammer has some burns and a concussion, but he's going to make it. I'm having a hard time convincing people that the grenade belonged to Sledgehammer and he set it off accidentally, but the alternative is a couple of old ladies doing it, so they're willing to shove it under the rug."

"If they only knew," Gertie grumbled.

"Be glad they don't, or you'd be sitting in a jail cell," Carter said. "But since Sledgehammer can't remember a thing about the blast, you're good."

"What about RJ?" I asked.

"RJ has been transferred to Nashville where she will work with the DA to build a case against Payday."

"Don't tell me she gets away with everything!" Gertie said.

"She doesn't," Carter said. "The DA here is working with the DA there to coordinate a punishment for the crimes here in conjunction with leniency for her cooperation there."

"Did it go down like I said?" I asked.

"I think so," he said. "But unfortunately, we can't prove it all."

"What about Brock's death?" Ida Belle said. "That's the big one."

"Brock's recent track marks were in his right arm, and given the wrist injury, the ME agrees that everything could have gone down exactly as Fortune posited. But RJ either wiped everything down or wore gloves, because her prints weren't in Gina's car or Brock's motel room."

"Don't tell me Gina and Cecil are still on the hook," I said.

He smiled. "Not even a little. RJ forgot one place—Gina's car keys. With that and Shadow's testimony that he saw RJ at the motel that night, added to Cecil's testimony that he saw Gina's car leaving the motel, the DA has a strong case. Then you add that the gun she fired at Sledgehammer is the same one used to shoot out her own car window, and you have enough to paint a picture of just who Riley-James Rogers is."

"So what's on the table?" Ida Belle asked.

"The DA's offering her manslaughter in exchange for her cooperation with the Nashville DA. It's a far better option than a murder one trial because given the evidence and the character witnesses they could pull, I don't think she'd fare very well."

"What about the check she cashed off her mother's account?" Ronald asked. "Was it forged?"

"Yes," Carter said. "RJ did a credible job at her mother's signature and Sawyer is lying and saying she signed it. The experts say different but if Sawyer doesn't want to press charges, they'll probably let the whole thing go."

"Sawyer is never going to admit what that girl is," Ida Belle said.

"What about the car wreck?" I asked.

"She claims Brock was driving," Carter said.

"Maybe he was," I said. "When Marigold had that panic attack at the parade, we all assumed it was because of the fire, but maybe that wasn't the only reason. Brock was standing right next to the float just before the fire broke out. What if Marigold saw him? She didn't panic when she saw RJ."

Gertie nodded. "I have to wonder why RJ risked inviting Marigold to be on the float. She had to know Brock would come after her. Marigold seeing him could have gone in a different direction. What if she remembered what happened and figured out a way to communicate it?"

"I think RJ wanted to make sure Marigold was still incapable of ratting them out," I said. "But given that she'd dumped the girl and fled town after she was injured, and the fact that she had probably gotten wind that Christina suspected Brock had been driving, she didn't figure it would be smart to show up to her house."

"So she invited her to be on the float and that way it looked like she was doing something nice, but she got to see what Marigold was like," Gertie said. "That sounds just like the coward."

"Plus trying to garner the sympathy vote by having Marigold on her float," Ida Belle said. "But if Brock was driving, what was he going to blackmail RJ with?"

"With those two, who knows," Ronald said.

"That's true enough," Ida Belle said.

"At least Christina finally gets to know that the accident wasn't Marigold's fault," Carter said. "And RJ *will* serve time, so even if she's lying about who was driving, she's still paying for something."

"Hopefully, knowing that will give Christina some peace of mind," Gertie said.

I nodded but another idea was forming—another picture was evolving from the chaos. And if I was right, I might be able to give Christina even more.

"And something else eventful happened and I got permission to share," Carter said. "When I was at Cecil's house earlier giving them the good news, Cooper showed up and asked Gina to marry him again. Right there in the middle of the living room."

Gertie sucked in a breath. "And?"

Carter grinned. "And she said yes."

We all started cheering and clinking our champagne glasses.

"I also have some more good news," Carter said when we finally quieted down. "But not case related."

"Me too," Gertie said. "I'm getting a stripper pole put in my living room just like the one Nora has."

Carter paled a little.

"I'm researching hip replacements," Ida Belle said.

"Well, my announcement isn't that, uh...colorful," Carter said. "But I wanted you to know that I'm finally getting some help down at the sheriff's department."

"That's great!"

"About time!"

"Thank God!"

"I hope he's sexy!"

We all responded at once and Carter gave Ronald a nervous glance.

"Anyway," he continued. "Sinful, Mudbug, and a couple other towns in our area of coverage have been struggling with the same shortages of staff and money. The accountants couldn't come up with a way to fund everyone, but they came up with something to bridge the gap—a flexible deputy."

"What the heck is a flexible deputy?" Ida Belle asked.

"Sounds interesting to me," Gertie said and winked.

Ronald nodded. "Sign me up for flexible men who know how to handle their weapons."

"Anyway," Carter said, "I figured I'd bring him by so I could let him know where all the real trouble originates in this town."

He whistled and we all looked at the corner of the house.

And then Harrison walked around it, grinning.

I vaulted out of the hot tub and did a complicated high-five-shooting-guns thing that we always did and then gave him a wet hug.

"I can't believe it," I said. "You're going to be a cop?"

"Better a cop than a PI."

"Remind me of that when you're stuck following the rules."

He grinned. "I see nothing's changed."

"Seriously, I can't believe you're leaving DC."

"It was time," he said. "The city is too crowded, too busy. When you first came down here, I thought you'd die of boredom in a week, but all those YouTube videos have changed my mind about the excitement small towns can offer."

"I am Legend," Gertie said, and we all grinned.

"What about Cassidy?" I asked.

"She can't wait to have land and a horse and is ditching pediatrics for the ER at the hospital up the highway. She's looking to get back into the action when I retreat."

"Tell her to expect Gertie soon," Ida Belle said.

I nodded. "And I'd put a hold on that 'retreat' idea until you've been here a while."

Ronald sighed. "The best ones are always taken. I bet he's flexible, too."

We all laughed.

CHAPTER TWENTY-SEVEN

A WEEK LATER, IDA BELLE, GERTIE, AND I STOOD AT Christina's front door with a box of cookies from Ally's bakery. Ida Belle and Gertie thought we were there to check on Marigold and see how she was doing with her new therapist, but I had a surprise for all of them.

Christina beamed when she saw us and waved us inside. "I'm so happy to see you all. I just finished up a fresh batch of lemonade. Does anyone want that or sweet tea?"

We all opted for lemonade and took a seat in the kitchen. I saw Marigold sitting at the end of the porch with her notebook.

"How's Marigold doing?" I asked.

Christina put the glasses on the table and sat with us. "It's been incredible. The therapist your friend recommended has taken her on for free, like you said they do sometimes, and is thinking she will be able to create a way of communicating that Marigold can learn."

I couldn't hold in my smile any longer. "What if I told you that Marigold has already created her own form of communication?"

"Sure," Christina said. "The pictures are great but limited."

I shook my head. "I had this thought about Marigold's notebook and asked my friend to send some of the pages to a code-breaker I know at the CIA."

Christina's eyes widened. "A code-breaker?"

"Yes," I said. "You know those stick figures that Marigold draws? If you translate them to letters, they spell complete sentences."

Christina sucked in a breath and Ida Belle's and Gertie's jaws dropped.

"You're kidding me!" Christina said.

"Not even a little," I said. "I sent the findings to her new therapist yesterday and she was able to translate Marigold's most recent notebook. With some training, you'll be able to do the same."

Christina started to cry, and Gertie put her arm around her and squeezed.

"That's incredible," Ida Belle said.

"That's not all," I said. "You remember the pages with emojis?"

"Is that words too?" Christina asked.

"Even better," I said. "It's music. And one of those pages of music was the song that RJ and Brock recorded when they first got to Nashville—you know, the one that TV producer was interested in licensing. I knew Brock had something on RJ and when the stick figures turned out to be words, I was sure the emojis had to be something as well."

"So she didn't give up music," Christina said.

"When the song turned up in Marigold's musical note code, I got in touch with the attorney who was having the original score ink dated and asked him to test it against handwriting as well."

"That's why you asked me for a handwriting sample?" Christina asked.

"Are you saying that Marigold wrote that song?" Ida Belle asked.

I nodded and Gertie jumped out of her chair, yelling like she'd won the lottery.

"I don't understand," Christina said.

"Unless Marigold's memory is completely intact, we may never know all the details," I said. "But what I know for sure is that Marigold wrote that original score. When I explained the situation, the attorney agreed to take Marigold on as a client and continue to broker the deal with the TV producer."

"And he still wants the song?" Ida Belle asked. "Even after the bad publicity surrounding RJ and Brock?"

"Yes," I said. "He was even more blown away over Marigold's story and wants to be part of making her song famous."

I gave Christina a big smile. "It's going to mean a lot of money for you guys."

Christina launched out of her chair and threw her arms around me. "I don't know how I'll ever thank you. You've saved my life and my daughter's. Everything that was bad, you've made good. You're an angel."

I felt my chest tighten as I hugged her back.

"Maybe just today."

More investigations with Swamp Team 3 coming later this year!

To check out other books by Jana DeLeon, visit her website janadeleon.com.